Treasure Hunt

Volume Two
Raptis Trilogy

Tracee Raptis

VOLUME TWO: RAPTIS TRILOGY

****

Treasure Hunt

Volume Two
Raptis Trilogy

Tracee Raptis

Metaterra® Publications

Metaterra® Publications
TREASURE HUNT
VOLUME TWO: RAPTIS TRILOGY
Tracee Raptis

Copyright © 2017, 2016, Tracee Raptis and Angela Browne-Miller.
Copyright © 2017, 2016, Metaterra® Publications.
www.Metaterra.com
Library of Congress Cataloging-in-Publication Data.
Raptis, Tracee
TREASURE HUNT
VOLUME TWO: RAPTIS TRILOGY
/ Tracee Raptis, Author / Angela Browne-Miller, Afterword /
1. Thriller. 2. Mystery. 3. Crime. 4. Drug Smuggling. 5. Treasure Hunting.
6. Scuba Diving. 7. Romance. 8. Psychological. 9. Heroines. 10. Adventure.
Title:
TREASURE HUNT
VOLUME TWO: RAPTIS TRILOGY
ISBN-13: 978-1-937951-37-5 (paperback)
See Amazon.com for Paperback and Kindle Ebook formats of this book.

ISBN information for the other volumes in this Raptis Trilogy
(also on Amazon as paperback and Ebook):
DIVE TOUR • VOLUME ONE: RAPTIS TRILOGY
ISBN-13: 978-1-937951-36-8
REDEMPTION • VOLUME THREE: RAPTIS TRILOGY
ISBN-13: 978-1-937951-38-2

Published in the United States of America for U.S. and worldwide distribution.
Metaterra® Publications, www.Metaterra.com
Book interior design by Metaterra® Publications & Angela Browne-Miller.
Afterword and Editing by Angela Browne-Miller.
Book Cover Concept and Design by Alicia Beulow with Tracee Raptis & Angela Browne-Miller. Interior art – Basic Scuba Diver Gear Diagram by Tracee Raptis.
Book Cover Illustration by Alicia Beulow.
AUTHOR, PUBLISHER, RIGHTS, & PRESS, CONTACT: DoctorAngela@mac.com
Ordering information and bulk ordering information available through:
Amazon Paperback and Amazon Kindle. Also contact Info@Metaterra.com.
****

In loving memory of
Marvin
who was a mentor, buddy,
and patient boss.

VOLUME TWO: RAPTIS TRILOGY

****

Table of Contents

VOLUME TWO: RAPTIS TRILOGY

****

Prologue

Early 1700s

It was the middle of the night. A large wooden vessel listed lifelessly on the last legs of its important journey across the Atlantic. The ship was helpless against the relentless hurricane force winds lashing violently at the masts, ripping away any remains of the sails. Each time a huge wave heaved the vessel up then down with trembling force, the large square copper nails holding the ship together were torqued to the breaking point under the extreme pressure. The long, thick wooden planks sculpting the hull creaked as the tar between them stretched, contorted, then loosened.

The ship's crew were true men of the sea. Yet, despite their traveling under the guidance of compasses and constellations, the ship had blown far off course. Riding the storm out was their only option. Tossed back and forth with the sea's undeniable force, even the strongest of sea legs couldn't compete. The ship's priest sat quietly in the corner, crossing himself and rubbing his rosary beads as he hailed Mary and prayed.

The captain of this ship and his officers were on an important mission for the King. As they huddled battened down below in the ship's office, they still were patriotically guarding their precious cargo. Indeed, still secured in the bottom of the ship, serving as ballast, were the loads of platinum and gold they would not leave. This ship was to deliver this cargo as well as a valuable golden medallion.

This medallion was the second of three created for the young King, all of which had been gifts from his father when he was born. Now the King was delivering these medallions, one per ship, as rare special gifts with meaning. These were being delivered to secure new land, three islands. This new land was a strategic acquisition for the King, as it supported his expansion into new territories.

Some months earlier, the first ship sent to the New World had been lost at sea, with no word. Everyone and everything on that first ship had sunk, along with the first of the three most precious medallions. The captain of that first ship had been close to his destination, close to capturing the glory of maneuvering across the open sea to the New World. But then he had been overtaken and enveloped by a monster hurricane. Alone at sea, the crew of the first ship had lost sight days earlier of all support ships, all land, all hope.

Now this second ship faced mounting danger as a large reef rushed up from the depths without warning. It was too late to turn away; they were heading right into this uncharted barrier reef. The bow of the wooden ship was first hit as it was tossed up and onto the large reef. The next big wave tossed the large vessel further up like a toy, then pushed it forward and slammed it back down again. Then, crashing further into the reef, those copper nails twisted and buckled, then released under the pressure. The ship's large planks creaked and shrieked. A huge jagged crack ripped through the hull.

Then that huge crack in the hull opened like a raw egg, dumping its rich yolk of golden coin into the turmoil of the waters below. The ballast of treasures immediately dropped to the bottom, finding a nest as the ocean pushed and devoured the remains of the large wooden ship.

Soon there were only skeletal remains of the grand vessel that had been split by the reef and shredded by the storm into absolute flotsam. The grand wooden vessel with all its crew and cargo was soon lost. This ship was never found, though her treasures were never forgotten.

VOLUME TWO: RAPTIS TRILOGY

****

TREASURE HUNT

****

PART ONE

THE HUNT

1950s

VOLUME TWO: RAPTIS TRILOGY

****

1

"It's here! I'll be damned. It's here!" Robert screamed out to the others as he surfaced with a splash. The three other men were also surfacing, each one turning and looking toward Robert with great curiosity and excitement.

The calm ocean was a picturesque turquoise blue, the slightest ocean breeze barely enough to stir the hair on the head but not enough to ripple the water. In the distance there was a distinct line across the ocean for as far as they could see, a line dividing it into two different blues. The edge of the darker blue was like a fine line on a map, signaling where the sea dropped off to much deeper depths. This was where large wooden ships of the past had sailed by in their creaky wooden hulls filled with tired malnourished sailors praying for land to be near while carrying cargos of untold fortunes to the New World.

Now a tall and muscular young black man was standing at the back of the divers' small fishing vessel, standing guard as the men splashed up to the water's surface. This young guard was dressed only in a pair of shorts two sizes too large and held up with a U.S. Navy issued belt, its insignia proudly displayed on the buckle. He stood there silently looking out, scanning the horizon, deep in thought.

Out on the water, Robert raised one arm over his head and waved to the young man. Acknowledging Robert's signal with the slowest of nods, he grabbed the line wrapped around a cleat on the side. This line was attached to a homemade anchor constructed of melted lead and formed into the shape of a mushroom, now buried deep in the white sand below. The young man pulled up on the anchor rope with quick hand-over-hand movements. Soon the rope was coiled on the floor of the boat at his bare feet. Weathered beyond his young years, his hands were calloused yet extremely gentle. They had strength and exactness that appeared almost mechanical. He relied on his powerful hands for many things in his life.

With the anchor in place he moved back to his usual station on the boat, at the stern looking out, scanning the horizon. He grabbed the cord to the motor and with one strong tug the tired old outboard sputtered to life. He turned the bow of the boat toward Robert and slowly inched forward.

A frenzy of fins splashed through the water as the rest of the men raced toward Robert who had just lifted an old china plate out of the water. Robert's strong legs kicked so hard that they lifted his upper body high out of the water. The men swam toward him from all different angles; they each wanted to be the first to touch the treasure, this old plate. The boat slowly glided over to the windward side of the circle of men, putting the engine in neutral, hovering in the darker blue water to protect them from the elements as Robert spoke.

"There's a stack of them down there! Right below us, I'm guessing about forty-five feet!"

Butts and splashing fins gave way as the other men took deep breaths and dove down, swimming for the bottom. Holding their breath, the men frantically fanned at the sand with their hands. Some returned to the surface with treasures of their own; others bolted to the surface for air before they could reach out and take hold of the treasures they had found. Back down they went until, one by one, each had grabbed for the first souvenir he spotted before bolting back to the surface.

"It must be the galley!" One of the men shouted as he ripped the mask off his face to get a closer look at the treasure in his hand. It was a small, broken cup; it appeared to be china teacup.

"I found a silver fork!" Russell shouted.

The excitement over the china plates turned to the two forks Russell held in his hand. Robert instinctively grabbed at the forks as Russell held his hand up high over his head, laughing as he foiled Robert's attempt to grab the forks away.

"Easy boy, ask and you shall see...." Russell teased.

The other treasure hunting divers laughed, their joyful sounds amplifying and distorting through their snorkels. Even Robert had to laugh at himself. They were all giddy with excitement. Russell held the forks out for all to see. The men knew the significance of finding the china, but the real excitement of actual silver, actual precious metal of some kind ... it was also there!

The small boat was idling in neutral with the young man in earshot. The deadpan look on his face revealed zero emotion. He looked down as he could sense Robert looking toward him. He did not want to make eye contact with any of the men in the water.

"There's more! Lots more! About fifty feet east of here!" Robert was signaling with his raised hand, as he was trying to grab his snorkel with his other hand to shove back into his mouth. Again there were butts and fins diving, swimming, splashing to the bottom. Everyone wanted his fair share.

Each man surfaced again, each this time with both hands full. They followed Robert's lead, all swimming toward the boat. The young man leaned over the edge of the boat, being careful not to tip it and taking the first items from Robert.

****

"Thanks, Moses. There is much more down there. Put it over there toward the bow." Robert pointed to the bow of the boat where his clothes were neatly folded and stacked with the precision of a submarine officer. Moses complied without changing expression or saying a word. He was completely deadpan, refusing to make eye contact with anyone. Moses was in another world, a world of his own.

The other men swam up behind Robert with the same request. As soon as Moses took their treasures, each turned around and dove back down to the bottom, grabbing for more.

Robert and Russell were the first to reach the bottom. Each holding his breath, neither wanted to be the first to surface, always in a perpetual competition of skills. The sand floated away as the men fanned at it, revealing curves and edges of new, different, shiny objects.

Robert noticed a flash of silver and started to fan harder.

Russell saw it too and raced to it, getting over to the flash of silver first—where he found a skull wearing an old, deteriorating handmade mask with metal edges. Robert got there just as Russell was pointing to the eye sockets which in that eerie light were seeming to still be looking out through the mask, staring out from the skull. Fragments of something were shining up through the eye sockets. Oddly, those eye sockets appeared in that light to be weirdly alive eyes, truly haunting. From the looks of what appeared to remain of the rest of the skeleton, the now dead man had been attempting to protect something. What was left of his arm and leg bones appeared to have been reaching out in all directions over the area of the reef where he had landed.

For a moment the eyes looked right into Russell. A sharp chill raced up his spine. Startled at this sensation as well as at his own reaction to all this, Russell gasped hard, so hard that he inhaled saltwater through the sides of his mouth. He rapidly bolted for the surface as he began to gag underwater.

Robert raced to swim upward next to Russell. The other two men, who had been swimming downward, stopped and quickly followed the others back up to the surface, sensing something was up. Perhaps a shark was near. Russell surfaced, gagging through his snorkel with Robert surfacing next him. Russell and Robert looked at each other in shock, as if they had just seen a ghost, then raced back down under the water to see this again. After another quick look, during which they signaled each other not to touch or disturb in any way the skull and skeleton, they were both still unnerved and raced back up to the surface where the other men were still trying to figure out what was going on.

"Dammit, there's a dead man's face looking at us down there! It's like he's alive!" Russell was still coughing, trying to hack out the saltwater that was burning his throat and windpipe.

Robert put his face mask back in the water to peer downward. Yes, they had both just seen the same thing. And that dead man had been protecting something, was it the treasure? What had gone on down there?

"What is it? A body? A dead body?" Brent asked them, ready to dive back down. But he didn't want to swim down there alone. He and the others looked at Robert for guidance.

Robert shook his head no, meaning both no not a body, and no don't go down there stay here, do *not* go down there yet. ... Then Robert's attention turned to Moses who was suddenly gunning the engine.

With the engine in neutral, Moses had suddenly twisted the throttle handle. He was gunning the engine which now whined and sputtered loudly, emitting puffs of white gray smoke.

Then, having all the men's direct attention, Moses used a quick flip of his thumb on the gear shift. The boat burst forward, abruptly stopping within feet of the men. Then Moses flipped the throttle switch again to put the engine in reverse. Moses's command of the small vessel was one of exact precision. He hadn't wanted to hurt the men, he had simply wanted to spook them.

The men drifted toward each other, moving into a huddle as they watched Moses. He was clearly upset about something. He'd been showing some kind of non-verbal protest when he lurched the boat forward at them, bringing it to a standstill just before hitting them. He knew what he was doing. So now again Moses put the boat in neutral and gunned the throttle, a deep frown on his face. Moses seemed to be seriously disturbed about the new undersea find. He was motioning for the men to get into the boat.

"What the hell? What do you think Moses knows?" Brent said under his breath to Robert.

"Like you think he's gonna tell us?" Russell never trusted anyone.

"Damn it, shut up!" Robert shouted.

With the engine back in neutral, Moses once again gunned the throttle and motioned for them all to climb in, growing more agitated when the men did not comply immediately. Moses didn't need to say a word, the look on his face said it all. Again he put the boat in forward and gunned it, this time continuing the boat in forward motion, steering around the men in a large circle as the small wake bobbed the men up and down. Stopping the boat as quickly as he had started it, again Moses put the boat in neutral. He glided up to them, motioning for the men to get in.

"What? The party's over? Because he said so? Shit, that stupid ol' boy ain't even saying anything...." Brent put his mask back on his face in a defiant way.

Brent's younger brother, Eugene, always following his brother's lead, decided to put his two cents in. "I don't care about some dead man down there. I've seen lots of those, so I'm going back down. That stupid boy can jump in and help. I want some of that silver down there."

"Just a minute you two," Robert lashed out. "Show some respect here." Robert wanted the men to stay cool because Robert had finally found what he was looking for, the shipwreck. He had known the wreck was out there somewhere, and finally now here it was. There was a delicate balance here, because this strange young man, Moses, was the one who had revealed this destination. And it had taken Robert two years to get Moses to trust him, to show him this spot. Robert didn't want to lose his trust now.

Robert swam over to the boat where Moses stood. "What's up, buddy?"

"Yeah, right. You talk to that guy like he's going to talk back to you...." Brent moaned at Robert.

"Shut up, Brent." Russell glared at Brent, making it clear that Brent had to back off.

Moses just kept shaking his head no as he motioned for everyone to get in.

"He wants us to get in," Russell added.

"No shit, Sherlock. Why?" The brothers were being belligerent.

Russell scowled as he treaded water between his old friend Robert and the two bothersome brothers. Russell was the toughest and by far the largest of the four men at six feet five inches tall. The others were quite small in comparison and didn't really want conflict with Russell.

Robert, the apparent leader of the group, had been a lieutenant on a submarine and the two brothers had served under him. Russell had also served in the Navy, and as an officer on a support ship for submarines. His expertise was mechanical repair of machinery.

With a growing impatience on the verge of erupting into panic, Moses again put the engine in neutral and revved the engine. Small puffs of gray smoke shot out the back end.

Robert knew he had to do whatever it took to save his delicate friendship with Moses.

<u>2</u>

"Get in guys," Robert ordered. He grabbed the side rails of the boat and hoisted himself in first, immediately reaching for his compass. He took as many settings as he could remember and started looking for something to write these down on. He rummaged a bit and found paper and pen.

Brent and his brother Eugene were still resisting getting back onto the boat, and still complaining about having to leave when they'd just found what they were looking for.

Robert frowned at them, then went on with his readings. He pointed his compass toward the peak of the mountain on the island to the north. He took another reading and then another, writing each one down and then double checking. He felt eyes watching him and looked up.

Moses was looking sadly at Robert and the other men.

Russell sat next to Robert after he finished coaxing Brent and Eugene into the boat. "I don't understand what's up with this. Is this some kind of gravesite?"

The moment everyone was finally back on board, Moses put the boat in gear and roared off in the direction of the northwesterly swells. Moses did this even before Brent and Eugene had a chance to sit down. Brent and Eugene were surprised as their feet give way to the racing tilt of the boat. They each slammed down into their respective seats.

"I don't know. I get the feeling we weren't supposed to take anything." Robert said under his breath to Russell, who was trying to put two and two together.

"Do you think he knows that dead man down there?" Russell asked Robert as quietly as he could, given the roar of the boat.

The tiny boat sped, dancing across the small wakes, spraying saltwater in the men's faces. Robert inched his way to the back of the boat where Moses was in control.

"You know that man down there, don't you?" Robert asked Moses.

The expression on Moses's face did not change as he just kept looking forward. The young man's face was so drenched and dripping with saltwater spray that Robert couldn't tell if Moses was trying to keep from crying. But it sure looked like it. Moses was very upset about something.

"Moses, I'm sorry man, I don't know what's going on with you." Robert tried to get Moses to talk to him, to explain.

Moses kept his focus on the water as he sped the boat away. He was clearly on a mission to get home and not look back.

Robert glanced back at Russell who had been watching.

Russell just gave a shrug.

Brent had been watching, too.

"Dammit Robert, I'm sorry but I thought you said this was a sure bet." Young Brent started in again, his somewhat underdeveloped voice grinding on Robert like a gluttonous whiny kid in the sun asking for more ice cream.

Robert was no longer the lieutenant in charge, but he was still the leader of this group. Robert knew that just one look from him, one frown at the men, was enough to stop anything he didn't like. He frowned.

The submissive side of Brent instantly prevailed; he sat back and looked down quietly as his younger brother looked over at him, shaking his head. One year younger in age—Irish twins, as they were called—Eugene was bigger in size. He was two inches taller and more muscular, with thick dark hair growing out of every inch of his skin. Eugene was for sure a stark contrast to skinny, white skinned, bleach blonde-haired Brent. All their lives they'd had to prove to everyone they were even brothers. Only their own father, a short and robust Italian man, never demanded proof. He loved them both.

Robert looked over at their pilot, Moses, feeling uneasy talking about Moses right in front of him. "Look you guys...this is Moses' boat, and this is his dive site."

"Like he told you all that before we got going with him...." Brent impulsively interjected.

Russell was on the brink of popping Brent with one swift blow and oh, how he wanted to.

Eugene sat there looking down at his feet, hating any confrontation and not saying a word.

"I thought I told you to fuckin' shut up!" Russell's voice was on the brink of rage as he stared Brent right in the eyes. Russell was just as frustrated as Robert because it had taken years to gain Moses's trust. Even after they thought they had earned Moses' trust, they'd had to put in more time—months and months of living here, using hand signs and having countless one-sided conversations to get Moses to show them this place, this wreckage site. Now they all wondered if they would ever see it again.

Robert grew silent and focused, as he scanned and memorized the landscape. He would find his way back to the wreckage site without Moses if need be. Using his own Navy-issue compass, Robert looked at the coordinates again and again, writing everything down. The seascape would certainly change but the mountain peaks and points would endure. He was confident he would be able to find the spot again without any help from his old friend Moses.

But sitting back and trying to relax, Robert couldn't help wonder what Moses was thinking. Robert had known him for four years now. They'd met when Moses was still a kid a little under eleven years old. Robert's submarine would pull into the base on the island where Moses lived, and Moses' mother had a little store just a short walk away. All the men from the submarine would make that little store their first stop when they came into port. They would go there to cool off with some alcoholic libations along with some of Miss Hattie's jonny cakes and jerk chicken.

****

Robert had taken a liking to Miss Hattie's shy kid, the boy who never talked. This boy had always been there watching, standing on the outskirts, never asking for anything. Always sweeping or helping his mother with one chore or another, he stuck close to her side. Whenever the submarine had pulled into port, Robert had brought Moses a treat from somewhere else. Even giving him a postcard from another destination was enough to make Moses smile and drift off into some kind of dreamland. Even the Navy-issue belt that Moses still to this day used to hold up his pants had been a gift from Robert when Moses was little.

No one really knew why Moses didn't speak. Some said Moses couldn't speak and some said he just didn't, that it was a self-selected kind of mutism. When Robert once asked Moses' mother about his lack of speech, she herself answered, "He just chooses not to talk." What else was there to say about it?

The youngest of fourteen kids, Moses had come as somewhat of a surprise. The youngest of his siblings was ten years old when Moses was born. His father thought of Moses as a miracle, another son after so many years, after thirteen other children, eight of them sisters. His father had taken Moses everywhere with him, even before the child could walk. He told Moses he was special and that God had a plan just for him. Moses had had a very special bond with his father.

****

All of these thoughts of his youth were buzzing through Moses's head as he now sped the small bouncing boat back toward the solace of home. He could not deal with the feelings rushing through his body. He was overwhelmed and couldn't stop the visuals from playing out in his head. Going further and further into himself, he tried to pull up fun memories he had in his head, memories of some times with his father, walking, fishing, skin diving.... But right now, Moses just couldn't find those fun memories.

The final memory of his father flashed in Moses' head. Moses' body responded by gunning the engine, and the boat sped faster, bouncing without a rhythm over the small, choppy swell. The men clung onto the sides while they glanced at each other. Once out of the rhythm of the ocean swells, the boat began to ricochet off the small white caps that mounted in the deeper channel. Moses hung on to the port rail, with one hand steadying himself, the other on the throttle as he charged forward. It was as if he had seen a ghost.

VOLUME TWO: RAPTIS TRILOGY

****

<u>3</u>

Moses couldn't stop the last memory of his father from flooding his brain. Once again, the smell of his drunken uncle's breath behind those half rotten teeth began to permeate Moses' senses. He rammed hard into the backside of a swell with the bow of the boat, hoping to push the rest of the memory away, far out of his thoughts.

The men held on tighter, each one now holding on for his life.

A splash of saltwater hit Moses in the face. The boat nearly careened out of control. The visual of that horrible memory was so vivid now, so real, it was taking him over as much as he was trying to escape it. Moses could see his uncle stabbing his father to death as he sat there in the background watching helplessly. Blood had been pouring everywhere on that boat.

As he slammed the men forward through the water, Moses looked down, seeing the red blood of his father pooling around his own feet. Moses' eyes grew wider in stark terror. The men clinging to the boat watched Moses in confusion and fear. Now Moses saw the blood mixing with the saltwater, sloshing back and forth at his drunken uncle's shins. The ranting raves of his uncle were audible now, they filled Moses' young ears. The little Moses was paralyzed with fear, unable to help. He could remember to this day that through that horrible scene, Moses never heard or saw any fear in his father. His father had never cried out or even asked for help, he had just dropped.

Suddenly the boat slowed down as Moses' hand inadvertently let go of the tension on the throttle. The men thought Moses was in some kind of trance; they could see his face contorting

VOLUME TWO: RAPTIS TRILOGY

****

into the series of feelings he was experiencing. From what the men could gather, it was fear, real fear they were seeing. Like a movie running inside his head, Moses was helpless to the memory that had him in its grasp.

When Moses physically leapt back as the memory overtook him, it was because Moses was seeing his uncle taking a swipe at him with his long, bloody knife. His uncle was about to kill him too.

****

"Aww, you not wort it, you not wort anyting," his uncle had slurred at him. "Dis bastad not wort it, he happy, he satisfied.... Me? I wan to be rich! Dis ganna make me rich...not like you, don't say no ting...." Moses' uncle had lurched toward him several times, pointing the bloody knife over and over, pretending he was going to stab little Moses. Now this uncle's stupid drunken laugh filled the boy's ears. Moses let go of the throttle as he reached up and clamped his hands over his ears.

The boat lurched fiercely to the left. Robert reached over, grabbing the long arm of the throttle, steadying the boat forward.

Instinctively, Moses reached back for control of the throttle, pushing Robert away with his elbow. Without looking at him or saying a word, Robert sat back and let Moses have control of the boat again.

Robert and Russell looked at each other, talking to each other with their eyes, seeing together this horrible surprise ending to this amazing day, imagining what was going through that young man's head.

Again Moses turned the throttle with his firm grip. The engine revved, and the boat sped away, pushing into the backside of the swells as the bow cut through. Saltwater splashed across the bow and soaked them all like wet, dripping dogs. Moses shut his eyes, still hearing his uncle's voice like it was next to him….

****

"Your stupid fadder, he so simple. He tinks dis wealth be for ever one. Me? I'm not gonna share." Moses had seen his uncle's sweaty face drain the whiskey bottle through his lips down his throat, his second bottle that day. His uncle had tossed the empty overboard and wiped at his big lips with the back of his sweaty hand, grunting under the mass of his own weight as he stood up, balancing himself.

His uncle had positioned an old dive mask back onto Moses' father's now stiffening face. His uncle had run his fingers around the edge of the mask, grunting as he wedged his fat fingers to get the mask firmly onto his nearly dead brother.

Then Moses' father's face was looking out through the mask. Moses could see the wide open eyes of his father through the glass, looking right at him as the uncle rolled his father over the side rail. Young Moses held his father's gaze, or what he thought was his father's gaze as he thought maybe his father was still alive, as his father splashed into the water and began to sink. That gaze would never leave Moses' heart and mind, never. Those eyes would look at Moses through time, they would always be there. Those eyes knew and would always know, and so would Moses.

After his uncle had watched the body spiral down to the bottom of the sea, he had turned to young Moses, again pointing his knife. "Clean dis boat up!" The uncle had slurred as he rocked the boat. In his drunken rage, Moses' uncle had been trying to steady himself as he put his own mask and fins on. He tossed a can without a lid toward Moses and motioned for him to bail out the bloody water floating around their feet.

Reaching over, this drunken uncle had smacked at Moses when he didn't respond.

"I said, you clean dis mess up now! Dey say you dumb ... I tink you dumb ... you dumb fadder tink you smart, how smart is he now?" The little boat rocked as the uncle spoke, again sending the bloody water splashing up one side of the boat over the arches of their feet then to the other side. Moses looked down, expressionless, trying to avoid eye contact with his uncle for fear the evil spirits his mom talked about would suck him in, or worse, jump into him.

Frustrated with the lack of response from the young boy, his uncle had leaned down and slapped him upside the head with an open hand, making a hissing sound of disgust. Then he had stepped over the side and into the water.

The uncle was overboard and trying to push his overweight body underwater to inspect the treasure. Moses picked up the salt-rusted can and slowly started to fill it with the red water, pouring it overboard into the turquoise water, watching the two colors blend. The dark red color of dead poured into the bright turquoise water, turned it into an unrecognizable color. Moses reached over and swirled it together with his hands, hoping that this was a game his father was playing. Young Moses had told himself that if he watched hard enough, his father would rise up from the sea and laugh, that maybe this was another one of his father's games.

With a splash of water, Moses' uncle suddenly rose up from the depths screaming with laughter, too drunk to tread water. Moses watched him awkwardly struggle toward the boat, trying to hold both hands, full of gold coin, up out of the water. Moses saw the man begin to sink with the weight of his treasure, his head going under then popping back up through the surface, coughing out saltwater from his lungs. He lunged and grabbed the side of the boat, dropped the coins into the boat, and dove back down for more. After only three trips down to the bottom, Moses' uncle was exhausted and out of breath.

"I tink I make you work for your worth ... you ain't worth nothing else, you know." Moses' uncle picked him up by the scruff of his neck and drew him close to his face, ordering him, "You dive down, you do the work." Before he realized what was happening, Moses was shoved backward, overboard, into the water. Treading water, young Moses looked up at his uncle, afraid of what was next.

"You need dis, and you better bring me someting.... Get to work." The uncle tossed the skin diving mask down to Moses. Moses held it in his hand. Before this day, Moses had always been proud to put on the mask his father had made him. Now Moses shuddered as he tread water with his bare feet, there were no fins for him to wear. Moses put his mask on. Then he put his face down into the water. Directly below he saw his father's body, lying on the bottom, face down. Small fish were swarming around the body, pecking at green liquid that was escaping from the wounds. Moses dove down, swimming as hard as he could to reach his father.

It was completely silent there under the water. Moses liked the silence. Once down to the bottom, he reached out and grabbed at one of his father's arms, trying to lift him. He pulled and struggled to get his father's body off the sea floor, trying as hard as he could with his small frame and no fins. Finally, Moses had to leave his father behind and shoot up to the surface for a breath. The sounds of his drunken uncle's voice filled his ears the moment he surfaced. Moses took another deep breath and dove right back down to be in the silence. He wanted to stay with his dad.

Holding his breath, he could not stay down long. Every dive he made he wanted to make his dad more comfortable, resting his head on a plate he found to keep his head out of the sand. Moses folded his father's hands on top of his chest to make it look like he was sleeping.

Each time Moses surfaced without a handful of gold his uncle yelled at him. "I said you better bring me someting if you wanna get back in dis boat. Me'son, you tink dis a joke?"

Young Moses dove again. This time he surfaced with a plate.

"You good for nuttin, I told you! Nuttin!" The uncle grabbed his arm with the plate in it and yanked him out of the water, lifting the boy into the boat. "I should leave you here with your no good fadder...."

Moses clutched the plate as his body was tossed toward the bow of the small boat.

"I can find this place without your fadder." Barely able to focus, the man held Moses' father's handmade compass up to his eyes as he was talking to himself, and Moses watched him scrawling numbers and words and drawing pictures that made sense only to his uncle, as he was illiterate. He was doing all this writing on the inside of his father's Bible. It was the very old, worn leather-bound Bible his father carried around with him at all times, despite his own illiteracy. He said the word of God was enough to protect him. Every night his father would recite passages from the Bible that he had memorized in his youth.

Now his father was dead and his book was being scribbled in and torn at. Moses listened to his uncle mumble words as he attempted to write down things about how to get back to this place with these treasures.

Young Moses scanned the horizon. They were miles out at sea.

"I know you can get back here, I know dat," his uncle said hatefully as he sat down next to Moses. Moses could smell his uncle's breath, as its unbearable stench filtered out through his half-rotted teeth. Then his uncle smiled and put his arm around Moses, as if he were Moses' new best friend.

Moses sat motionless.

"I know you'll bring me back here, you will if you want to see you fadder...." The uncle stood up with a grunt. He reached over across the rocking boat and grabbed the cord hanging off the outboard motor. With one pull, the motor started up with a sputtering roar.

Moses watched his uncle sit down and gun the engine into gear. The boy looked back as they sped away in the direction of Bantica, the town where they lived on the island of San Pedro.

The waves splashed and soaked them as the man recklessly maneuvered the boat through the chop in the deep-water channel between the reef and the islands. The open water was dangerous in the channel. Large swells formed where reefs shot up to the surface from the depths. This was why there were many stories of ships and boats alike sinking out here. It was very dangerous.

Moses had been coming out to this spot since he was barely able to walk. His mother had always trusted Moses' dad with his life. Even at the boy's young age, Moses could find that dive spot. His father knew Moses had a special brilliance, that he could remember things, unusual things, numbers or pictures or anything his father showed him. Once his father showed him something, Moses could retain it and bring it back like a flashcard in his head. His father had never seen anything like it.

Moses could see the shoreline now as his uncle started up again.

"Oh no me'son, you not goin home, you coming wit me, you mom will never miss you."

Moses looked toward the shore, silent. His uncle turned the boat and passed the channel that they'd been supposed to turn into. Young Moses knew he had to jump to get home. He saw his dad's Bible on the other side of the boat, tucked out of the way to keep dry. At his feet below were Moses' mask and his father's compass. He was still clutching the plate he had brought up from below.

Before the uncle could put it together, Moses swept up the mask and compass. He leaped to the other side of the boat to retrieve his father's Bible. The uncle let go of the steering column and reached out for Moses. The uncle grabbed at Moses' arm, his long dirty fingernails almost piercing through Moses' skin. The boat went into a hundred-and-eighty degree spin and the drunken uncle fell, landing on his back with a loud grunt, followed by a moan.

Moses leapt off the boat, leaving the Bible behind. He swam for a reef that jutted up to the surface, knowing his uncle would not bring the boat any closer or swim after him.

"You not wort it! A shark gonna get you!" The uncle taunted him.

Moses' hand was scraped and bleeding from holding on. He was doing everything he could to keep from breaking the plate or letting the compass slip away with his other hand. His long calloused feet clung to the reef as he wrapped his legs around it, ignoring the stabbing, cutting pain of the live coral.

"I'm leaving you here to die. You not gonna make it. If you did, what you gonna say?"

4

Moses winced. All these years later, Moses could hear his uncle's drunken laughter and smell his terrible breath. The smoke and stench of the small engine gunning in neutral still haunted him. This trip out to this treasure had brought it all right back, loud and clear.

Moses was in a trance, reliving those bad memories, as the boat splashed its way across the deep channel. Moses' hand was still on the throttle turned up full force, wide open. The weight of all five men aboard was the only stabilizing factor on the boat in this wild ride through the wind chop.

Suddenly Moses went from full speed ahead to a complete standstill. The men had already been holding on tight but now they couldn't keep from lunging forward and into each other. The wake from behind caught up and lapped into the back of the boat, filling it with salt water.

Moses stood in a trance, water around his ankles, looking out.

"Great, what the fuck is he up to now? He almost had us home." Brent was soaked with salt spray and now everything else was wet. He wasn't very happy with the way his day was going.

"Uh yeah, Robert, now what?" Eugene always had to put his two cents in.

"I said relax, guys, we're almost home and we'll talk about it later." Russell tossed the men open empty cans so they could start bailing the water around their ankles. Russell was beginning to feel like a baby sitter for these two young men, the brothers. He glared at them. Robert kept his eyes on Moses, and didn't comment as Russell continued, "Didn't your mama ever teach you boys manners?"

The brothers looked at each other and started to chuckle with laughter.

"Oh yeah, she taught us good," Eugene started laughing at his brother, and then they jokingly punched and slapped at each other, sharing an inside joke.

"At least she taught us not to marry no Bangkok Betty!" The two young men were laughing again.

"Why you—" Russell stood up with his fists clenched, ready to power both of them right down Brent's mouth. At that moment, the boat lurched forward and Russell lost his balance and clutched the edge of the boat, his butt slamming down in his seat.

Moses had just turned into the channel to head toward the dock.

"She's not from Bangkok! And her name is not Betty!" Russell was red in the face as he spoke. "Her name is Imelda and she's from the Philippines! Got that?"

"Yeah, well she still don't speak much English...."

"You call that English you're speaking, Brent?"

Robert couldn't take the bantering anymore. "You guys shape up or you're out of here tomorrow."

The two young men looked at Robert and blinked their eyes. They knew the lieutenant meant business.

Moses slowly maneuvered the boat up to his private, somewhat makeshift dock. His mother's large frame and smile to match filled the doorway to their home. In back of their home they had their own private world. Beautifully groomed and thought-out paths curved around papaya and banana trees. A large mango tree shaded a great deal of the house.

Oil fumes sputtered out of the old outboard as Moses put it in neutral to drift up alongside the dock. With perfect timing, he turned the engine off as it glided up. Just as he had done hundreds of times before, he hopped off the boat at just the right time and secured it to the dock. All the while, Moses was ignoring the other men and their offers to help him, as if they didn't exist.

Moses reached down and picked up his mask. It was carefully wrapped in an old towel tucked in the corner for safekeeping. He treated it like china and guarded it like gold. It was the one his father fashioned for him. Robert had once given Moses a Navy-issue dive mask. Robert had been proud to present it to Moses in a fatherly way. Moses had smiled and tried it on but still insisted on wearing the old mask with its many repairs.

Moses walked up the path to his house quickly, turning slightly sideways to get past his mother, first stopping for a quick kiss on the cheek, a ritual everyone who met his mother had to participate in. Her large frame jiggled in her colorful muumuu as she moved to let him by. The dress' material was worn thin from repeated washing, the bright colors faded to a muted tropical pattern.

When she turned, the sun shone through the thin material and left little to the imagination of those who choose to look. With her body in constant motion, she smiled and moved her broom back and forth, humming to herself. Dust and dirt gave way, revealing an immaculate rock path underneath. Always sweeping, keeping hands and mind busy, was important, she said. She was known on the island as Miss Hattie.

Back at the boat, the other men quietly gathered their goods. No one argued over what belonged to which of them. Each was too busy wondering if there was going to be another chance to retrieve more. Russell was busy examining the two silver forks he had found for any markings, and once satisfied, he stuck them in his back pocket.

"You men go home. We'll meet at my place at..." Robert looked at his watch and tapped the crystal as if he didn't believe it, "... seven o'clock, can you do that?"

The men glanced at each other and then back at Robert without saying a word.

Russell looked at Robert, trying to catch his eyes. Robert looked away, knowing what was coming next. "Sorry, Russell, you know you have to leave Imelda at home tonight. We have to stick to the rules and that includes wives as well."

"It's getting way hard to leave the house without her in the evenings, Robert. She doesn't understand, she thinks I'm having an affair."

"Hmm, any kind of suspicion is not good. This is for her own good though, it's not that we don't trust her. It's just that if she doesn't know anything that she can't tell anything."

"Do you really think it could be that big a deal? I mean, pirates and all? This is the 1950s now you know, not the 1700s or 1600s."

"Pirates, assholes, anyone—they're all suspicious as far as I'm concerned. How many people, men in particular, do you think have seen that plate hanging on Miss Hattie's wall? Miss Hattie's already said everyone asks and wonders about the plate. I don't think we're the only ones to have done our homework."

"Hmm, but hopefully the only ones who've gained Miss Hattie's—"

"—and Moses'—"

"—trust."

The other two men were silent; they both knew that somehow they had crossed Moses' line.

"I thought he understood we wanted a plate of our own."

"I think Moses understands a lot more than we give him credit for. Did you notice how he found that dive spot without even picking up his compass?"

"Hmm, have you taken a good look at that compass? It's homemade!"

"Yes, like his old mask he won't let go of."

"It's that skeleton, or what was left of that skeleton, that man down there. He was upset about this discovery, about this dead man, not the fact that we were bringing items up, can't you see that?"

"How much do you think Moses really knows about that shipwreck?"

"Hard to say. But after today, I think he knows a lot more than I ever guessed."

Eugene and Brent were standing to the side without saying anything, wanting to be a part of it, but knowing that it was better at this point to just be silent.

"You men go on home," Robert commanded. "I'll go in and try to communicate with Moses I don't know what, if anything. Anyway, I now have the coordinates." Robert pulled a crumpled piece of paper from his pocket. It had some barbaric drawings and numbers on it. "If worse comes to worse, I'm positive I can find that place again on my own." He looked down at the paper in his hands, resisting the temptation to nervously twist at it.

"That's great, but where are we going to come up with a boat?"

"Yeah, we need a boat." Eugene quickly mimicked his brother's words.

"We'll cross that bridge when we come to it. You men move on and we'll meet up in a couple hours." Robert said. Then he looked back toward the house. Miss Hattie was sweeping away in the same rhythm she was sweeping five minutes ago, never losing her pace as she sang to herself. She looked up and waved at them. All the men politely smiled and waved back. There was something about her that made you want to go up to her and collect a hug, like she was everyone's mother.

"Go on now...." Robert walked away from the men, heading toward Miss Hattie's home.

The men followed his orders and walked away.

5

"And how was your diving today, Mr. Robert?" Miss Hattie greeted him with a wide grin. "I don't see no lobsters, no lobsters for me today?"

"Oh there are plenty of lobsters out there for you, Miss Hattie." Robert gave her a quick peck on the cheek. She let out a little girl giggle. "We just didn't get any today."

"What did you get today then? You bring me some conch?" Robert wasn't sure how to respond. He didn't have anything, he hadn't had a chance to look. He didn't want to lose Miss Hattie's trust, just like he didn't want to lose Moses' trust, but he felt the need to be honest. She was a fine woman and he respected her.

"Moses took us to find a plate of our own."

Miss Hattie was silent upon hearing this. She looked Robert back straight in the eye. That seemingly permanent smile had now disappeared. Instead was a look of great concern. "Moses took you out to find a plate?"

"Yes."

"You know, I told him, never go back out to see plates, dese plates. Dey trouble, big trouble."

"Well, we only got a couple of plates and then Moses wanted to come home, in a hurry."

"Yes, he knows that's evil out there. I told him, he has to stay away from dat evil place."

"Evil?"

"Yes, dere is no good to become of anything found dere." Miss Hattie's usually smiling face had taken on a strange deadpan stare that gazed way into and beyond Robert eyes.

Robert wasn't sure how to respond. He had to keep Miss Hattie's trust, so should he tell her what he'd found? "We found something else beside plates out there. Something strange was out there, yes. It was like a ghost chasing Moses."

Miss Hattie looked down and started up her sweeping again, doing the same step she had just swept clean.

"I know he dere. Someweere...." Miss Hattie started to sweep faster.

"Who's out there?"

"De husband you know ... he never came home. Yes, dey all went divin for dese plates.... Moses, the only one who came home—he was only eight years old, ya know!"

"Who else was with them?"

"The brother, me husband's brother. I never seen either of dem again."

"I'm sorry, I never knew or thought to ask where your husband was."

"I knew dey mus be dead dat day, othawise my husban be home. Dee look on little Moses' face tol me dat day my husban not comin back." Miss Hattie's perpetual carefree smile was still gone.

"I'm sorry. I didn't know. I'm sorry."

"I tol Moses dese plates arrrr eeeevil, stay away, ya know." She went on again, "Everybody ask me about deee plate. I say I don know. Dat's de truth, I don know. Oh, me husban, he had big dreams. Big, big dreams." Miss Hattie started to wave her arms all around to show that his dreams were bigger than she was. "Now? Now I have nutting. I have all deeeeese mouths to feed and no husban, dose dreams de jus dreams. Stay way from dose plates and dose dreams. Ya hear me?"

Robert was silent as he listened. He must've found her husband or her brother under the water. "Yes ma'am," he said submissively, although his intentions were quite different.

"Can I go in and see Moses?"

She let out a short chuckle.

"You can try, go see. I tink he be in his room for days now. I seen it before you know, but I never know what's in dat boy's head."

Robert gave her another kiss on the cheek. With this little ritual completed, she moved aside for him to pass. She started up humming to herself again as she continued her sweeping. It was as if the conversation they'd just had never happened.

****

Robert walked inside and through the maze of small rooms which made up the house. Each room had been added as needed, added when they could afford it or could find materials to use to expand it. Finding his way to a back room where Moses stayed, he saw that his door was shut. Robert knocked on the door only to be met with silence. He reached for the door knob and turned it slowly to the right. The door opened slightly but then it with met with resistance. Moses had pushed objects up against it to keep people out.

"Moses, Moses, I didn't know. No one knows.... Are you OK?" Robert was met with more silence. He tried peeking through the cracked-open door to see if Moses was even really in there. There he was, sitting down on a small bed with his back to the door, just staring out a small window.

"Moses, you can trust me...." Robert looked though the crack in the door and saw the young man shaking his head no. Robert shook his head too, he was too tired to plead with the boy. So he turned and slowly walked away, feeling horribly badly for never realizing what had happened to Moses and his mother.

<u>6</u>

Dusk set in, muted orange and pink colors washing across the sky. The humidity in the air equaled its temperature, both ninety-eight, stiflingly hot and heavy. The long fronds of coconut trees dotting the street lay motionless, without even a slight breeze to ruffle their feathers. Brent and Eugene were still perched on the stools they had claimed at the bar right after leaving Robert and Russell at the dock. They were eagerly discussing the day's finds. The fan above just swirled the heat around the bar, didn't cool anything, but helped keep the mosquitoes at bay.

"What'll you 'ave, mate?" Peggy the bartender shouted out to Robert as he walked in.

"Oh Peggy, I'd like to have it all." Robert walked up to her. Taking her hand slowly, he brought it to his mouth and gave it a light kiss.

Peggy blushed bright red and let out a slight girlish giggle, covering her mouth. Then she smiled a large smile, revealing her characteristically British crooked teeth.

"Oh, go on you!" She teased back.

"But right now I'd settle for a cold beer. A very cold beer!"

"Well, I can arrange that one." She turned and opened the refrigerator. Its old motor let out a whine and then kicked in after a moment's hesitation, cooling her shins. The noise made the small homemade radio behind the bar impossible to hear.

Peggy reached over and turned the music up before handing Robert his beer.

The usual crowd of about seven was well into its routine of drink after drink. A chess game between two old friends that had already been going three days was continued in a corner.

A new stranger sat down at the end of the bar. Dressed in crisp Bermuda shorts and a light linen shirt, his gold watch glistened as it caught the reflection of the glaring overhead light. Mysterious, clean-shaven, and quite dapper, he looked to be someone important (or someone who thought he was important) and somewhere in his late forties. He looked around the room, nodding with a smile at those who acknowledged him as he sipped on a beer.

"New guy in town." Peggy tilted her head toward the stranger as if Robert needed a clue.

"Yes, I see. Thank you, dear." Robert picked up his beer and took a series of large gulps. He set it down as quickly as he picked it up. "That was perfect love, I'll have another."

"I was expecting that," Peggy laughed as she turned and reached into the fridge for another beer.

"Big day, mate?" The stranger on the end inquired.

"Pardon me?" Robert was slightly taken aback by the stranger's forward friendliness.

"I said, did you have a big day today, mate?" The stranger was smiling and tipped his beer toward Robert as if to suggest a silent toast.

"Yes, I guess you can say that. A big day, a long day, but aren't they all?"

"Been out diving?"

Robert looked right at him, tilting one eyebrow with suspicion. "Yes, what made you guess that?"

"Oh, I'm sorry, let me introduce myself." He was tall man, and Robert noticed his new shoes. The scent of expensive cologne filled the air as he walked closer. Peggy couldn't take her eyes off him. "My name is Drake," the stranger said as he held his hand out to Robert.

Robert reciprocated with a stiff, firm handshake. On rare occasions, strangers would stop by this island, anchor out for the night on their way somewhere. But there was nothing very notable here on this island, nothing beside the old remains of a Navy dock. No reason to make a point of visiting.

"You here on some kind of business, Drake?" Robert was already well into his second beer. He looked over his shoulder to check on the boys, not that he thought they would go anywhere else.

"Are those your friends over there?" Drake pointed his bottle toward Brent and Eugene.

The screen door creaked open and Russell stepped in. Fresh out of the shower, his thick, dark hair was still damp. He waived to the brothers and then walked up to Russell and the stranger.

"Everything OK at home?" Robert turned his attention to Russell.

"Just perfect. I love her so much, Robert." Russell blushed and grinned. "We're not gonna be out too late…right?"

"Yes, right," Robert said as he turned to Drake. "And please excuse me, it's time for…."

Drake automatically turned to Russell and extended his hand. "Drake, the name is Drake, and your name is?"

Russell locked eyes with Robert for a moment before he answered Drake, which he did cautiously. "Russell, the name's Russell," he replied to Drake.

The two gave each other an equally firm handshake. Russell was determined to be the last to let go as he examined the gentleman.

"Yes, as I was saying," Robert broke in, "our friends have been waiting for us over there." Robert motioned to Peggy for another round with a few circular hand signals. "It's time for me, or Russell and me, to join them—and it was nice to meet you."

Russell extended his hand to Drake, expecting to shake in a "nice to meet you" or something like that.

Drake didn't look down at Russell's extended hand or even acknowledge it. He simply ignored the gesture and reached deep into his pocket.

"Here, let me take care of that," Drake pulled a large wad of cash out of his pocket. The money clip caught both men's eyes, as well as the amount of crisp bills folded in it. A large, distinguished gold coin of some sort was set on the perfectly polished silver money clip.

"Wow, is that real?" Russell couldn't resist asking.

"Yes, it is." Drake held out the silver clip with the unusual gold coin the size of a half-dollar artistically embedded into it. He showed it off to the men while he peeled off bills, winking at Peggy. "This clip was given to me as a gift, a special gift from my brother." Drake held it out, pointing to it as he carefully watched Russell and Robert's reaction to seeing this medallion.

Robert and Russell couldn't help but look at the medallion in amazement; they were hopeful they would find their own piece of gold. Neither of them had ever actually seen a real coin of such value or knew what they were looking at.

"I appreciate your offer, but I'll get this round," Robert said.

Russell and Drake looked at Robert as he pulled his small amount of folded cash out of his pocket. Peggy hesitated, not knowing whose money to take, all the while not taking her eyes off the stranger, so mysterious, so handsome.

Robert pushed his money forward.

"Well, I'm not going to argue with you, bloke." Drake folded the bills he had extracted and put them back into the clip, leaving one out which he put down in front of himself. He shoved the square, tidy packet back into the deep fold of his Bermuda shorts pocket, no doubt safe from anyone else's hands reaching in.

"It was nice to meet you, Drake." Robert reached up to his forehead with his right hand, mocking a salute as he walked away.

Russell turned to walk away, took a few steps looking back over his shoulder and shrugging at Drake's apparent dislike of him. Russell followed Robert, playing it cool. "See you around, Drake."

"Yes, see you around, gentleman." Drake tipped his beer to his lips, savoring the last inch slowly.

"Would you like another one of those?" Peggy batted her eyes at him. "You here all alone?"

Drake looked deep into her eyes as he replied with a soft voice. He was a charmer. "No, thank you my dear, I've had enough. And yes, I am alone. For now...." He winked at Peggy and she blushed a deeper red than before, her lips parting once again to a grand smile as she self-consciously lifted her hand up to her mouth and let out a nervous giggle.

Robert and Russell walked over to their two waiting men and sat down. The boys had already tipped through a few too many beers and were drunk. They were making Robert more nervous than usual, he didn't want any of his men to draw attention to themselves. And now, a quite mysterious stranger was on their island.

"Whaddya say, boss?" Brent's eyes were small red slits.

"I say we all go home tonight and we'll talk tomorrow."

They looked back at him confused, as if he was speaking a foreign language.

"Buut...but, boss?" Brent slurred his words as he spoke. "We, uhh, we, just got here!"

"Yeah, boss, just like this morning, we're here and you want to leave early again, what the hell's going on?" Eugene drunkenly reiterated.

"I think you've been here a while already," Robert leaned forward and lowered his voice, "And stop calling me fucking boss, at least not here." Robert leaned further forward and further lowered his voice, now a whisper, "Look, this place is just too crowded for me tonight." Robert was moving his eyeballs in the direction of the new stranger who called himself Drake, hoping Eugene and Brent would get the point. Then Robert looked back over his shoulder to see if Drake was still chatting with Peggy. He was, but seemed to be saying goodnight to her. Robert turned back around and looked forward as Drake turned and began walking toward them.

"Goodnight, gentlemen," Drake sauntered up and nodded to them as he stopped. His approach was like a cool mint breeze, the scent of the air announcing him. Coupled with his unusual good looks, he had a way of turning the heads of both men and women.

"Good night," Robert looked up and smiled.

Drake nodded, then walked out the flimsy door constructed of a wooden frame and cheap netting to keep bugs, not people, out. Drake stopped out front and slowly lit a cigarette as he contemplated his next move. He blew out the flame on the match as if he was hoping a wish would come true. As he did so, he looked back into the bar and nodded his head again, slowly, before he walked away.

****

"Who was that guy?" Russell asked Robert.

"I don't know. He was here when I got here. I don't like it."

"Like what, boss?"

"Damn it! Stop calling me that!" Robert was exasperated. "Look, I'm sorry, but we should meet at my home, not at my place here." He looked at each of the men to see if they all understood that this was a change in plan, as they always met there at this bar. In fact, Robert called this bar *his place* as it was practically his second home. "Tomorrow afternoon, around one o'clock, my house. This place just doesn't feel right for meeting, I feel like someone's listening here."

"Who's listening?" Eugene was drunk, trying to put the pieces together.

"Quiet, Eugene. Explain it to him later, OK Brent? Take him home and we'll see you tomorrow. Russell, go home to that pretty wife of yours." Robert finished his beer and stood up.

Eugene and Brent, still not sure what had just happened, stared back.

"Goodnight Peggy!" Robert waved at her from across the bar.

"G'night luv! See you tomorrow," she waved back

"See you tomorrow!" Robert went out the screen door.

7

Robert headed toward the dirt road he thought maybe he'd just seen the stranger take. A few moments later, Robert stopped and listened for footsteps. He didn't hear anything, and saw no sign of Drake. It was as if this man had simply disappeared into the night.

As Robert continued walking up the road, he did have the feeling he was being watched. It was dark, the moon was out and high up, but only a slight sliver. There were very few lights on to illuminate the surroundings and occasional homes dotting the sides of the road. Tied up goats were quietly grazing in the dark empty lots between the homes.

Almost to the end of the narrow road, Robert still found no sign of anyone. Up ahead, he would be given a choice of two roads, both of which went nowhere for a long time. A goat bleated out in the night. Robert turned, his hands in his pockets nervously jingling change. Keeping his cool, he slowed down and held his breath to listen again for footsteps.

A slight breeze blew up the road. The palm fronds overhead shifted with a wispy eerie sound, making the hairs on Robert's arms stand on end. His training and intuition told him he was being watched. He felt it, he knew it. But he just couldn't figure out where the watching was coming from. Robert said to himself that he needed some kind of alibi, a reason to be up this road, just in case someone was watching him and asked.

Up ahead was the home of Mr. Johnson, a bedridden man in his nineties. It was said he had fathered twenty-six children, twenty of them from his inside wife. It was also rumored it was his inside wife that put a hex on him and left him in pain and bedridden. Robert noticed a light on in Mr. Johnson's front room.

Robert had met Mr. Johnson on several occasions while accompanying Moses to his house with his weekly "medicine" which consisted of two quarts of vodka and three quarts of rum from the town. If anything, Robert thought he could get away with going up and knocking on the door, acting as if he had reason to be there. He was completely confident Mr. Johnson wasn't going to get up and answer the door; he could then walk away as if his mission were complete.

****

So Robert walked up the dilapidated concrete path toward Mr. Johnson's front door, and knocked. Then the unexpected happened, the door opened! Robert had not thought about who might be there or of who took care of Mr. Johnson. To his surprise, a beautiful, petite young lady was staring up at him, locking her eyes on Robert.

"You want somting?" She looked at him half angrily as she wiped her hands dry on a tattered dishtowel.

Robert's mouth, unable to form a word at that moment, hung halfway open as he tried to think of a reply.

"Someone's at me door? Now? Damn it!" Robert could hear Mr. Johnson yelling from his room.

"Uh, it's just me, Robert, Mr. Johnson...." Robert spoke over the head of the young woman who stood there in the doorway with her hands tightened into fists, each hand resting on one of her hips as if they were in holsters. She was just waiting to come out and punch. The expression on her mouth and face revealed suspicion and aggression.

"Robert? I don't know no Robert. Lucinda! Who's at me door?"

The young lady took a step closer, her frown turning to a scowl.

Robert visualized her as a small dog that could do some serious damage to his ankles if he said the wrong thing. This Lucinda was feisty, yet so cute you wanted to pick her up and snuggle!

"I'm sorry ma'am, I didn't mean to...." Robert found himself stepping backward as he spoke. He found himself taking in her beauty more with each step he took back.

Lucinda quickly filled the gap between them with a step forward.

"I mean—I'll come back, later," Robert added.

"For what?" She asked without skipping a beat.

He was at a loss of words for once in his life. Somehow this woman, so forward.... *Wow, think, think, think!* "I was looking for someone, an old friend, Moses."

"Not here, haven't seen dat mute boy in a long time now." Her eyes pierced through him.

"Thank you, ma'am." Robert turned around and started walking away slowly, hoping Lucinda would stay behind and back off.

The door shut loudly behind him, blasting into the still of the evening, the sound reverberated down the street. As Robert walked away, he could hear behind him a muffled yelling match between Lucinda and Mr. Johnson, something about just who was at the door.

Robert stepped his pace up, walking away from the house. He had already forgotten what had led him up to Mr. Johnson's door in the first place. It was something about that Lucinda, he was intrigued by her. There was something about the passion in her face as she looked up at him with those beautiful eyes. He found himself wanting to know more about her. He found himself saying her name over and over in a melodic way as if he was intending to break out in song. "Lucinda, Lucinda, Lucinda...."

8

Robert awoke early the next morning. He had work to do. He needed to find a boat of his own, one that could hold himself and all his men, as well as their equipment. On an island such as this, there were limited resources, few running boats, fewer dollars to buy them. And even fewer secrets could be kept. He had to be careful.

In town, people woke up slowly. Some started with setting up their daily vegetable stands piled high with green coconuts, papayas, and bananas, all before the heat set in. Others got to work repairing their fish nets or lobster traps for the day. Robert thought he would start his day down by the dock, a good place to start.

All but one of his men were used to close submarine quarters; they knew what they might have to be capable of to get the job done. Each man except Robert had enough cash in his pocket, so that when they pooled their money together, they could find a vessel that would work for them.

At the end of the dock was a beautiful newer yacht, stunningly maintained, over seventy feet, maybe eighty. Several very tidy men in nautical uniforms were tending to her. At the back of the stern, lounging at a table with cocktail glasses, was the gentleman Robert had met last night, Drake. He was sitting with two other men, and they were in a heated conversation. Each of them was neatly dressed in crisp white cotton with dark navy details. Large dark sunglasses half-covered their faces. *Impressive display of wealth*, Robert thought as he turned and walked the other way, not wanting to be recognized.

The conversation grew louder, and he could hear the words "stupid" and "double-cross" stand out as he walked away, trying not to be noticed. All three men stood up, one throwing his hands up in the air. When their attention turned and they noticed Robert walking down the dock, the conversation quickly halted and all three of them walked silently into the cabin of the yacht.

"Did you find what you're looking for?" A recognizable voice shouted from across the parking lot. Robert looked over. The beautiful petite-framed lady, Lucinda, was waving at him and walking toward him. Surprised not only to see her, but that she was so friendly, Robert consciously reached up and ran his hand through his hair in a half-attempt to train it as she moved closer.

"Hello! No, no problem. How are you? My name is Robert, by the way." Robert was blushing. A feeling stirred inside as he looked into those dark eyes that were looking right back at him. He reached his hand out to hers, taking it ever so lightly and gently shaking it as if it were going to break. He found himself nervous around her beauty, intrigued. He couldn't stop talking.

"I didn't know anyone else was living up at Mr. Johnson's."

"He's old and I have patience," Lucinda said, her eyes never leaving his. "Did you find this Moses, your friend you spoke of?" She reached out for Robert's hand, brushing her fingertips against his. "Aren't you going to ask me out for breakfast?"

Robert naively looked back over his shoulder, just to confirm she was talking to him as opposed to someone else.

"I would love to accompany you for some breakfast. I was just taking care of some business."

"Business. Robert, business is so boring." Again she brushed her fingertips against his, slower this time, as if she were dangling a piece of bait in front of a fish, waiting for it to bite. The second time Lucinda's hand brushed against his, he felt his insides melt further. He was surprised he was feeling something. There were years of ice built up around his broken heart, shattered beyond repair, closed for any business except pumping blood through the body.

Inside a large tattoo atop his shoulder were the words *Never Again*. After all, in his heart, men were men, and most women were whores. He preferred the company of men and the camaraderie of a common goal.

Lucinda knew just what to say to Robert to get him to let down that wall around his heart, to open the gate to himself. She knew just where to touch Robert to open it. A wave of passion would leave them both out of breath, and intertwined in their dreams.

"Let me take you somewhere cozy, and then you can buy me breakfast."

Before Robert knew it, he was in her trance, following her, his hand in hers on the street. "Your hands, Robert, you are a man of work, I can tell. Let me give you some leisure." She reached up with her other hand and rubbed his rough hands with hers.

Deep down, Lucinda was stirring feelings Robert had dismissed, put away, and refused to ever feel again. His insides began to melt at a faster pace as she continued to playfully touch his hands. He found himself wanting to say yes to anything she asked for, including for his undivided attention all day long. In return she gave him all of herself and her own undivided attention.

****

The next morning Robert woke to an empty bed, the curtains still drawn in the tiny bedroom. He couldn't tell what time it was. He climbed out of bed and found his pants. There was a window three feet away. He reached over with his right arm and pushed the curtains back. He heard the front door open and close in the other room; he peeked out to find his lovely Lucinda. He walked over to the counter where she had prepared cut papaya with key lime squeezed over the top. She lit a match without saying a word and ignited a burner on the stove top, placing a small pot of water on top of the flame.

"There you go my love, my salty sweet! Just like you." She put a center cut piece of papaya in his mouth, the tang of the key lime hit his tongue. She reached for his right hand, sensually putting his index and middle fingers her mouth, enjoying them slowly.

He was in a trance, caught up in the come hither look in her deep brown eyes. Her dark curly locks, springing softly, framed each side of her naturally beautiful face. Her lips were full and moist, a permanent deep shade of pink. Her skin was dark with perfect delicate features, as if each one were cast in unblemished porcelain, right down to each fingertip adorned with a perfectly coiffed fingernail. It was a joy to have these fingers reaching out, touching his chest. He was never going to let her go.

"Noo, you are the sweet one...." Robert guided her soft hand with his to a plate of papaya. She picked up a piece of fruit, he guided her hand back to his lips. First starting with the papaya, he took it all in, licking her fingers and smacking his lips. After a while, he tried to break his eyes away from hers. "Sweetheart, I've got to get home."

"Oh, no! What's home? You are home, here with me, baby." She held her hand out and guided his eyes around the room. "Don't leave."

Reaching down for the bottom edge of her bright cotton tank top, he pulled it up over her head to reveal her breasts as she leaned forward into him.

"Stay with me...."

VOLUME TWO: RAPTIS TRILOGY

****

<u>9</u>

Russell reached Robert's house just in time to see him drive up. Robert was not alone. A young, beautiful woman was in the passenger seat. You could see her hand reaching across to Robert's thigh, gently stroking him as they came to a stop in the gravel driveway.

"Well, I guess that explains last night? Did you stop to think we might have wondered?" Russell was terse. Eugene and Brent had come by his house very late last night, explaining they had not seen Robert and had been expecting him. They had been very drunk and it had taken way too much effort to try to explain to Russell's wife why Eugene and Brent would be concerned with Robert's whereabouts. It was almost a disaster, but Russell had saved the day by getting rid of Eugene and Brent, telling them Robert was looking for them elsewhere, some place none of them had heard of.

Lucinda was looking at Russell, her brown eyes locking onto his. He blushed and dodged her gaze as he looked at her beauty; it was almost hard for him to look at. She was indeed so beautiful she seemed to glow from the inside out, her bright white teeth rays of sunshine. Before Robert could get out of the car or say a word, she stuck her hand out to Russell.

"Hello, my name is Lucinda."

Russell took the offering of her delicate hand and awkwardly shook it. "Yes. Hello. Russell."

All caught up in his surprise at her forwardness, Russell found himself stuttering for words as Robert walked up.

"Russell, this is Lucinda." Robert wrapped his arm around her waist as he spoke, pulling her in close as if to claim her as his, all his.

"I'm going to make myself at home while you two men talk." Lucinda was smiling as she looked at them both. She winked and walked away, all the while examining her surroundings. A plywood house with old wooden windows fit the "how cute" she said aloud as she walked around the back.

"What in the hell are you thinking?" Russell was upset, he wanted to yell at Robert but kept his volume hushed. "You brought a total stranger to your house?"

"Not a total stranger," Robert retorted

"Twenty-four hours makes you inseparable?"

"Russell...." Robert stopped short of finishing his sentence and pursed his lips. "I haven't felt this since...." He couldn't finish his thought, it was too hard to even say her name. "I think I love her." His attention floated to behind Russell where Lucinda was standing.

Disgusted, Russell flung his head and his eyes back as far as he could. "Not now, not overnight. Eugene, Brent, and I deserve better than this. They were worried sick about you."

"Probably worried drunk, knowing those two."

"Doesn't matter, we're all down here and the clock is ticking, tic-tok, tic-tok. We can't afford to not have you focused."

Robert looked away. He knew Russell was right and he was usually the one who lectured Russell and the others about staying focused. Not even Russell's wife was allowed to know anything. Basically, all she thought they were there to work on was some sort of housing development. It was going to be a boomtown, they had told her, a new destination.

58

"She doesn't know a thing." Robert looked Russell in the eyes.

"Hmph." Russell wasn't quite convinced. "But did you find anything out about Moses? I saw him briefly yesterday, he didn't even acknowledge me."

Robert was standing there, facing Russell. But Robert had pretty much left the conversation and was deep in his head. It was all coming back to him. He was so enthralled, so taken with this woman, he all but forgot what he was supposed to be doing.

Lucinda's voice woke him up. "Robert darling," she stepped up and put both arms around him as if they were tentacles bringing him closer. With this, she got his immediate attention. "I have to use the girls' room, you know, the head. Can I go find it?" She looked up at him coyly.

"Yes, of course dear, go on. I'll be there in a minute."

She walked away with a distinct rhythm to her hips, hoping both men were watching.

★★★★★★★

"OK, let's meet up in three or so hours at the bar, we'll have a drink." Robert clearly wanted Russell to leave.

Russell was rubbing his chin as he listened. "And then what?"

"We'll exchange information on what boats might be available. Remember, we'll be out there for five days, four of us plus equipment." Robert didn't tell Russell about seeing Drake talking with those other gentlemen on the large yacht the day before. Robert was all but shooing Russell away with his hands, body movements, and words.

Russell clued in, but with protest. "OK, I'll go, and we'll meet up later. We'll all have some info now to move forward, I hope you will as well."

Then Lucinda stood at the doorway smiling, always that smile. She was so beautiful. Robert let out a sigh then a slight chuckle. She turned out to be a delightful contrast to the spicy, aggravated woman who answered Mr. Johnson's door that other fateful night.

Robert and Lucinda went inside. Robert locked the door and led her into his small stark dwelling. Miscellaneous pieces of diving equipment and tools filled one side, all in an organized manner. There were steel diving tanks, fins, and a lot of hoses.

Lucinda gazed at the amount of equipment.

A military issue single cot with two sheets was pushed up against the wall. A small round table and two chairs graced the other side. A little sink which double-dutied as both bathroom and kitchen sink stood in the corner. Robert pulled a curtain back revealing a toilet in a small closet space and blushed as he pointed to it.

"Not as comfortable as your place, I'm afraid."

"Oh, it's just perfect for you, right?" Lucinda was still smiling as she walked past Robert, unable to keep her fingers away from his stomach. She took the edge of the repurposed bed sheet and tugged it closed. With the curtain closed like a veil of secrecy, she rolled her eyes at Robert.

Robert began to shift from one foot to the other like a young boy, wondering how he was going to break away from her magical hold at least long enough to complete the job he was on this island to do. One side of him needed to break away, the other side didn't want to and somehow couldn't.

Soon Lucinda emerged with a new curiosity. "Why you have all this, Robert?" She asked, gesturing to the wall of diving equipment.

"Oh, I'm sure I told you, I was in the Navy. An officer on a submarine." Robert tried to change the subject as he turned her the other way, toward his single cot. "Sorry, not so cozy over at my place. How about I take you back to town and then we can meet up later tonight? Would you like that?"

"Take me back to town?" She pressed her body up against him and looked up into his eyes. "I want to stay with you, your place isn't so bad!"

"I have some work to do, then we can meet up. I was supposed to do it yesterday and forgot once I laid eyes on you!"

"Work is boring. That makes me sad. What is your work anyway? What is it you're looking for?"

"Right now, work for me is finding a boat, just the right boat."

"Maybe I can help with that," she pouted. "Then we can stay together."

"You don't worry one bit now," Robert said as he kissed her on the forehead. "Let's head back to town, then we'll be back together later."

VOLUME TWO: RAPTIS TRILOGY

****

<u>10</u>

"Robert, listen to yourself! You have known this woman *three nights*, and now you're saying she has found us the perfect boat? She knew we were looking for a boat?" Russell was waving his arms as his voice grew louder. "You know what *my* wife thinks we're looking for?"

Robert looked down to the ground and kicked at it with his right foot while enduring the lecture.

"My wife thinks we're looking for a fucking tractor! That's the story you have me feed my wife!"

"Russell, look, I'm sorry. Listen to me though." Robert reached up and put a hand on each of Russell's shoulders, squaring them off as he did. "All of our problems are solved! This is going to happen! And quickly!" Robert didn't give Russell a chance to interrupt and went on, "She has a house, it's hidden off the beaten path, with a small lagoon even. No one can see us, we can relax, we'll have a thirty-two foot dive boat with gas tank capacity and decent cabin space. It's a house that most of us can stay in as we put this plan together! Think about it, we could be out there by the next full moon!"

Robert's excitement was almost more than Russell could handle—it always was. That's how Russell had ended up there in the first place. Robert had been so excited about some sunken treasure, some gold coins, had said he had proof the treasure was there based on the stamp on the back of the plate.

Robert told the story quite well: Missing and never found, the old wooden ship had never been expected to be over this far off course. It must've hit the reef jutting up right below the surface for miles out of nowhere. There were for sure old tales of pirates setting off tall torches propped up from the reef to attract vessels sailing on the outer perimeter, coaxing them over to treacherous reefs only to run aground. And all this was true.

"You trust her? I don't. It's too clean, it's too convenient. Come on, think about it, a dive boat?" Russell was wary, very wary.

"It's not hers, it's her uncle's. He died. It's there, she doesn't want to stay out at his place by herself so there it sets. It's perfect."

"She's too perfect, I don't like it. Besides, how does this even seem fair to you? My wife Imelda is home alone, so lonely and she gets left out. She's upset with me, Robert, I don't want to lose her."

Robert didn't hear Russell's concern about his own wife and simply went on while still pressing his hands on Russell's shoulders, "Lucinda is perfect for me, Russell, I don't want to lose her." Robert was looking hard, right into Russell's eyes, challenging him. Then he went on, "Look, this is *my* plan, Russell. Not much of my money, yes. But remember, I was the one to figure this out, befriend Moses, turn all this into a reality instead of a dream. If you choose to leave, go ahead." Not letting Russell lose eye contact, Robert stood firm as he put this ultimatum out there. Robert now had everything he needed, and if Russell didn't like the way he wanted to do this, then Russell could take his eight hundred dollars, and his wife, and leave.

Russell let his shoulders relax for a moment as it all soaked in. Robert released the grip of his hold on Russell long enough for Russell to move sideways away from Robert's grip.

"That's the way it is, huh?" Russell took two more steps back and turned.

"Russell...come on...Russell...." Robert's voice took on an edge, a begging tone, as he watched his friend Russell walk away.

VOLUME TWO: RAPTIS TRILOGY

****

11

"OK men, here she is."

The men climbed out of the jeep with their eyes fixed on the white floating beauty at the end of the dock. It was everything Robert had said it was, for sure large enough and still floating. But as they moved closer, it became a little less than they had been told it was: it was in need of paint, had some rotted wood, only a suggestion of upholstery here and there, exposed wires, and few functional electronics.

"Plenty of room," Russell said as he stood with his back to the stern trying hard not to smile. He reached down to help Robert up, and together they pulled up the hatches to expose the engine compartment. Robert handed Russell the key and instructed him to turn on the battery. There was a click, click, click, then the fan in the blowers whirled on, blowing away any accumulated fumes which could result in explosion from a tiny spark of the battery.

Lucinda came down to the dock carrying a large container of guava lemonade and a stack of thick glasses. Guava lemonade was a specialty her mom had taught her. Watching her walk down the dock, Robert wiped his hands on his pants and climbed out of the boat, leaving the details to the others.

Russell turned the key. The engine resisted loudly with three chugs until slowly she turned over, light gray smoke blowing out the back exhausts. All three men clapped as the engine of the old boat, which they were already jokingly calling the *Ol'*

Wife, established her rhythm. They all were smiling at their success.

Robert's arm had found its way around Lucinda's waist now.

****

This compound of Lucinda's was perfect. Concealed from the rest of the island where no one would think to look, the men felt safe there in their need for silence and privacy. Each man had his own expertise to help bring the *Ol' Wife* to life for the opportunity of a lifetime. Eugene focused on the electronics, Robert and Russell on the engine, and Brent worked on painting, repairing, scraping the hull. Lucinda joined in and helped hand sew the interior curtains.

Timing for their trip was everything. They had to catch the full moon. Under the full moon, the crew could work twenty-four hours round the clock to unearth the treasure. This was crucial: they had to act quickly before anyone else detected their secret. The amount of wealth they had potential to unearth could attract many who would try to take it.

Robert put years of planning into motion to make this happen, and now here it was. This was it. His only regret was the loss of his friendship with Moses. Yes, he did use him, but he had developed quite a fondness for the young man. Robert had taken Moses under his wing to gain his trust. Now a smile spanned Robert's face as he thought of Moses, at least for a moment. But it was replaced by a greedy grin. *Ah yes*, Robert thought, *we're all going to be rich beyond our wildest dreams.*

****

The last piece of equipment they had to load onto the boat was an air compressor. They hoisted it into the back end. This was needed to fill the diving tanks, but there was another reason they needed a compressor. When they were diving, they were going to attach a long tube to it to pump air down below to a large-diameter pipe. Then the air would shoot up the pipe to the surface, taking the sand with it, revealing the treasure.

One day to go, and the *Ol' Wife*'s final details were coming together like pieces of a picture puzzle. Working in their usual cohesive, disciplined manner, the men were again the team they'd been before. Now the boat's engine was oiled and tuned, its exterior sanded and painted, the algae scrubbed off, the electrical wires retraced and brought to life.

Lucinda came down to the dock with another large jar of guava lemonade for the men as they worked, as she usually did this time of day.

"Robert!" she called out. He looked up and smiled. Completing the final turn of his screw driver, he put it down and climbed out of the boat as usual, to be right next to her.

"I must go into town for some final supplies, I won't be long." She smiled at him, looking into his eyes while pouring him a cold drink.

"Honey, you know the rules. I'm sorry but they also apply to you. They apply to everyone. No one goes anywhere alone. Groups of three. Remember?"

"I know, but this is just a quick minute, baby. My girlfriend, she's going to get suspicious if I don't show up as promised. I don't have a way to contact her out here."

"Hmm, give me two hours and we'll go together, OK? That's not long." He leaned down and kissed her cheek, expecting the situation to be understood and closed.

She smiled sweetly without a reply.

"OK, back to work." Robert finished his drink and set it next to the jar Lucinda had left on the dock. He climbed back into the boat as he watched her swing her wonderfully shaped hips back down the dock and up to the house.

Russell was quietly biting his lip. The chip on his shoulder was growing heavier each time he watched Robert with Lucinda. For some reason he had to sacrifice his own and his wife's happiness. His wife was not allowed to know anything. So Russell had sent his wife home to her mother's house for three weeks. She was upset that she couldn't come with him, and suspicious he wouldn't come home. Adding to the pressure was the fact that there wasn't any easy way to communicate with her, only the short wave radio was available, and that was only when both parties were ready. The bigger elephant in the room was the fact that there were four men out there at Lucinda's, one compound with four men and only one woman. It was frustrating for all of them.

Robert had met this new lady, this Lucinda, the woman of his dreams. But now suddenly this Lucinda was being included in *their* dreams. There was never before a woman included in what they were doing. Russell's wife of a year still had no idea what was going on. She was always kept half in the dark about things, which was made worse by a language barrier. But Russell and his wife loved each other dearly. Russell treated her like an exotic princess.

So who was Lucinda to be so special? With all Robert's talk of secrecy, safety, why was she here? Who was she really, just a pretty face? Just a woman making Robert feel like the captain in bed? None of them knew.

******

Working bent over, deep down in the engine compartment, Robert's head banged against the upper side lip as he heard the jeep engine start off in the background. By the time he got to his knees and to a window, he could see the jeep climbing away up the hill, up the long driveway. Looking around for a quick headcount, all the men were busy at their jobs. Everyone was there. Lucinda had left by herself.

To his left, Robert saw Russell's wary eyes watching the jeep disappear up the hill. Russell too was taking a visual headcount, confirming in his head that Lucinda had left on her own. Russell's eyes moved over and locked onto Robert's.

Eugene and Brent looked over at Robert and Russell, then at each other.

"Oh, you have her under control, right brother? Right?!" Russell's voice rose a notch with each word. "You repeatedly say my wife can't be trusted, *my* wife!" He was visibly pissed. "I can't say anything, and now this?"

"Settle down now, Russell. Look, we wouldn't have any of this," Robert motioned around the length of the boat to the dock and up, "we would be nothing without her."

All the men stood there silently as he spoke.

"I don't like it and don't like it one bit." Russell stood his ground. "Something about that woman, about her energy, she's gonna bring you down, she's gonna bring us all down."

"Yeah," Brent chimed in, "who is this lady? Can we trust her?"

VOLUME TWO: RAPTIS TRILOGY
****

12

Three hours later, Robert was waiting in the driveway when the jeep came down and maneuvered into the parking area. Lucinda was all by herself behind the wheel. The car stopped and she climbed out as if nothing had happened. Robert felt completely betrayed, and was practicing mental control of his anger. His first instinct was to take his rage out on her—how could she do this to him?

But Lucinda knew exactly how to work Robert. The first thing she did was lock her eyes on his as she walked up to him, doing her best to disarm any foul emotions he might be feeling.

"I'm sorry, baby." She touched his stomach with her warm hand, knowing just what to say and how to say it. "I told you I had to go, my friend just wouldn't understand if I didn't show up. You don't want to draw attention, do you? She would come looking for me."

By now, Robert's insides were beginning to melt further as the tips of her fingers reached into and tugged at the top of his shorts.

"You don't understand the suspicion you put me under. You should have waited. I told you, two more hours, no problem."

"I know, honey." She stood on her tip toes and kissed his cheek

"No, I mean it." Robert's voice rose a notch to somehow make her realize the potential consequences of her actions. This could affect them all, she seemed to show no regard for the others, Robert told her. Robert went on, "These guys are my brothers, we have all been together for years, years of planning our things. Now they think you could ruin everything we've worked for, that you could draw suspicion and hurt us."

Lucinda reached for the button holding his pants up and slowly twisted it open as she held her eyes locked on his.

"And what do you want me to say, darling," she said as her fingers massaged closer to his pelvis for a much intended purpose.

"I'd like to believe you, Lucinda, I really would." Robert's gut, his instincts, were telling him something different from what his hormonal brain and pelvic area were telling him. "What did you and your friend do when you saw her today?" He cocked his head backward to take in the full expression of Lucinda's face.

"Oh, you know, we did hair, caught up on gossip."

"I thought you said you had to get more supplies?" Robert looked her up and down now, noticing her hair looked just the same.

"Oh yes! Look!" She pushed away and swung her hips extra slow as she walked toward the jeep. Leaning in, she pulled out two large bunches of red bananas, round, plump, full diameters, almost ripe.

Robert looked at the bananas, confused.

"We'll need these! In the sun, these are very good for you!" She held them up as if they were an answer to the universe.

"Yes dear, we already have bananas packed and ready."

"Well, then we have more, you can never have enough." She walked by him toward the house. Conversation was over. Lucinda was done answering questions, answering to anyone for that matter. Lucinda did what Lucinda wanted. Halfway to the house she stopped and looked back at Robert.

"Are you coming? Now?"

The other men, still in their different stations of repair and packing of the *Ol' Wife*, could see all this from the distance. They watched the two in silence, glancing over at each other now and then. Russell could barely look as they saw their friend, their leader, get sucked into that spider's web. Regardless, they were committed and following through: if they were successful, each one of them would be a very wealthy man upon his return.

****

At five o'clock the next morning, the crew was already down at the dock. Lucinda was standing next to Robert. The men quietly packed their personal belongings, each one not wanting to break the silence and calm of the morning. They were focused, ready. There was not a cloud or a bird to be seen.

Russell couldn't take his eyes off this Lucinda. He hadn't trusted her before and now his suspicions had been confirmed by her antics yesterday. You don't break the rules in a situation like this.

With a turn of the key, the boat's blowers whirred on, doing their job. The men looked at each other in anticipation as it took several minutes for the blowers to work before they could turn over the engine and be on their way. Eugene was at the bow holding the line and Brent cast off the stern. The *Ol' Wife* turned over with a rhythmic purr.

With a nod, Russell put the boat in gear. Together they pushed off the dock and made their way out to the open side of the island. The calm of the protected water turned into a slight windward chop as they maneuvered out of the sheltered lagoon. With a push of the throttle they were approximately one and a half hours away from their destination.

****

The open sea turned choppy as the full moon tides exchanged between deep waters and shallow reefs. These tides caused strong currents that slowed the ride down. It was two hours before they reached their destination. They checked and rechecked their coordinates. They made sure one among them was on guard at all times, scanning the horizon with high-powered binoculars, ensuring they were all alone.

13

The shallow water was calm on the leeward side of the reef jutting up to the surface. The pure white sandy bottom made the water a crystal turquoise blue, like a sparkling gem. They tossed the anchor in and it set. Robert was the first to jump in and swim to the bottom. The others quickly followed. There it was, right where they had left it.

Once all the men were back up on the surface, Robert quickly demanded their attention to get to work. "Men! Let's move! God has graced us with this fortune, let's make the best of it, just as we have planned. We're ready: Russell, start up the compressor engine as soon as we have our grid marked and our pipe is in place. Eugene, bring out the recovery basket and put the pulley in place."

One by one, the men made a quick dive to the bottom, bringing up their first souvenirs, booming up to the surface with laughter and swimming to the stern of the boat. There it was, just as promised: the treasure, the sunken treasure.

******

Brent perched on the bow with binoculars. On the lookout, he was scanning the horizon in three hundred sixty degrees every two minutes, watching, watching, watching. Eugene manned the pulley, bringing the lift basket down to the bottom and up with the treasures. Russell ran the compressor for the air lift and filled the air tanks.

Robert was the first one to suck the sand away with their own invention, that large-diameter tin pipe they had fashioned. It

VOLUME TWO: RAPTIS TRILOGY

****

was fueled by the air they pumped down through a long hose to the bottom of the pipe, the rushing air lifting sand up and away, excavating a hole that revealed more and more gold. The tin pipe wouldn't last long in salt water, but it would manage fine for less than a week.

When down below, Robert would fill the basket until the air pressure in his tank became too low to breathe. It would then be time to switch turns with Russell, who would then switch with Eugene, and then Brent, each one taking turns. The men dove, cleaned, repaired, and watched the horizon. And Lucinda's job, against the will of the others, was to record, catalog, and stash the treasure. Somehow Lucinda had been allowed to join them, a development all but Robert continued to wonder about. How could this have been allowed?

The men had carefully calculated in advance just how much gasoline they needed to bring along on this trip, just how much was needed to run the compressor full time the whole time, and to fill the scuba tanks, and to supply air to the underwater sand siphon they'd rigged.

****

Throughout the days and nights, they took turns climbing into the cabin of the boat and taking long naps. Each man was too excited with his newfound wealth to sleep very long. It was all coming together. The less they slept, the harder they worked, and the more sleep deprived they became. But everything was going so well.

"I think when we get back we should hide the treasure and make a second trip out here, because there's so much!" Russell was overwhelmed at the amount of gold bars and bullion they were bringing up, just as he had promised the men.

But the close quarters, along with the lack of sleep and fresh water, were wearing them down. They had to be careful about everything now.

"One more day and we'll have it, we can do this. Once we get back, if one person catches wind of this, it's over. If that happens we might never get back here alone again."

VOLUME TWO: RAPTIS TRILOGY

****

<u>14</u>

An exhausted Brent put the binoculars back up to his sore eyes and scanned the horizon. He had started out doing this so carefully, diligently, at the beginning of the trip, but now he was weary. And his eyes were burning from the sun glaring back at him through the lenses of the binoculars.

The men worked through that last night tirelessly, stepping it up, doing what it took at the end of this trip. Lucinda had agreed to learn how to work the air compressor pump so they could double up on the manpower below. She manned the pump and the pulley so two men could be down at the bottom together, two filling the basket at once. So she too now was tired, she too now wanted this to be done soon. But done well of course....

While he and Robert were down below, Russell felt relaxed knowing Eugene and Brent would be above on the boat to keep an eye on Lucinda.

They had all been together in these close quarters for three and a half days. At the end of this night's work, they were scheduled to go back to the island and divvy it all up. So now they were close to done, close to having it all. For sure their job was almost complete, and they were rich men.

This time together in close quarters had taken an obvious toll on Robert and Lucinda. Lucinda had stopped looking Robert in the eyes days ago. Robert had grown too tired to notice this or even her lack of touch, that touch he had fallen so in love with not long ago. Russell had definitely noticed the growing distance between them, but was too tired to voice his suspicions. After all, this trip was close to done.

Russell was basically dreaming of his own life and future with Imelda, and it would be a very rich future. Russell was already living this next part of his life, this wealth, in his mind. Things had gone so very well on this trip. No worries about anything, just treasure! Besides, it had been three and a half days out there and after all, there was no sign of pirates anywhere. Success was in the bag.

****

Eugene was the first to see what he thought was movement on the horizon. He held the binoculars up close to his eyes, squinting, peering. Had he noticed an unusual movement on the horizon, a rogue wave? No. Everything had been going just as planned, not a worry in the world. Eugene looked to see who else was on the boat. Robert and Russell were underwater. Lucinda was in the back stern of the boat filling a scuba tank. Brent was taking a nap directly below him, where he had tucked himself into the bow trying to sleep, away from the continuous howl of the compressors.

Eugene stomped his foot three times, and then stomped again. He was afraid to take his eyes off the movement on the horizon. It *was* movement, it was. It was clear, whatever it was, and Eugene now had his suspicions. It was coming closer.

Eugene kept stomping over and over with his right foot.

Brent finally emerged from the cabin below, rubbing his eyes as he faced the bright sun.

"What the hell? It's my break shift. I'm trying to get some shut eye, I'm so tired."

"Come here quick, look!" Eugene shoved the binoculars at Brent and pointed to the north, "See?"

Brent squinted, and was quiet while he looked hard.

Lucinda had her back to the men as they pointed and stared out to sea.

"Lucinda! Lucinda! Call the men up, now!" Eugene shouted.

Lucinda remained with her back to the men, not budging.

"Lucinda!"

She remained still.

It was clear now that a vessel of some sort was coming right at them, and it appeared to be moving in at a fast speed. Eugene had to alert Robert and Russell ASAP.

"Brent, don't let that movement there out of your sight! I'm diving in to call up the men!"

Eugene quickly climbed down from the bow to yank on the pulley system on the side of the boat. Then he ducked into the cabin. Immediately inside to the right, tucked on a shelf there, he picked up a windup travel clock that was attached to two wires. Three quick turns of a brass key extending from the back and click, the surprise of a lifetime was set for two hours from now. He looked at his watch. Two hours. Eugene took two steps to the port side and flipped off the air compressor, then to the starboard side, deciding to dive over and alert the men.

Lucinda stood motionless. She knew what was coming and never turned around.

Eugene was down at the bottom of the ocean with several quick kicks. He pulled at the men below, with no mask or fins he couldn't tell who he was tugging at. The air flow to the sand sucking tube had been cut off and the men were waiting in confusion for the air to rush back down to them. With Eugene flailing in their faces, they thought this was about the condition of the air compressor which had suddenly shut off. Out of breath and trying not to panic, Eugene shot for the surface.

Now Eugene could hear Brent shouting at Lucinda and the sound of a boat rapidly approaching. Again he dove for the bottom. He quickly reached Robert and pulled at him, lashed at him trying to get him to surface. Almost out of breath, Eugene screamed out underwater. Robert and Russell looked at Eugene and then each other. Eugene again shot for the surface and gasped for air.

Eugene could hear that boat coming close now; he couldn't see it on the other side, only hear it. Robert surfaced next to Eugene and was also trying to catch his breath. Russell heard the sound vibrating the water below as he surfaced. Trying to digest the situation all at once, Robert called out to Lucinda in fear for her life, but he didn't hear back.

A single loud shot rang out of the chaos of yelling. Then there was a thud. The men treading water looked at each other: someone had been shot!

Brent dropped down, sprawled on the bow. One shot in his chest from a high powered rifle was all it had taken. Blood splattered and dripped down the side of the bow where the men hid in the water.

"The trap is set." Eugene whispered to Robert, who nodded yes in response.

The approaching speedboat was there now. There was a bump as it came up right alongside. On the other side of their boat, Robert and Eugene stayed hidden in the water at the bow, out of sight. Russell stayed hidden deeper down, under the water, watching them and taking forced, focused breaths from his regulator.

Robert and Eugene listened for voices on the speedboat, trying to make out what the intruders were saying.

They boarded from the speedboat at the starboard side of *Ol' Wife's* stern. For the first time, waking Robert's senses, Lucinda's voice pierced through the growl of three or four other men. They couldn't make out what she was saying, but all men shut up afterwards.

The two men in the water looked at each other, wondering what to expect from the quiet. Russell watched from below.

Then Robert and Eugene looked up. They were staring down two rifle barrels aimed right at them, each pointed at their respective foreheads. Robert could hear Lucinda's voice nonstop in the background, she wasn't pleading for her life. She was talking about her life, and the difficulty of it all the last couple of days.

Two shots rang out: the end came in a bright flash of light as Robert and Eugene looked up at their assailants, unable to maneuver, unable to duck. There were no more thoughts.

****

Eugene sunk, twirling in slow motion to the bottom. Russell looked on in horror from below, watching as Eugene's limp body sank, green ooze seeping, twisting upward. Fish raced over from nowhere, pecking at the flesh, examining the remains. Russell numbly kept his great panic under control; he'd seen even worse in the war.

Robert's upper body bobbed just below the surface, buoyed up slightly by air in his buoyancy vest. What remained of Robert's face gushed blood, pooling on the surface and floating with the current as the rest of his floating body dangled beneath.

Russell could see his old friend was dead. With Eugene laying on the bottom and Robert dead on the surface, Russell had to assume he was the only one left.

Gazing upward at the two hulls, he realized his options were limited. He grabbed a handful of coins and began to swim the opposite direction under the water, hoping no one was noticing the bubbles he was exhaling rising to the surface. He heard splashing above and looked up. Two men were swimming downward with scuba tanks on. Russell looked at his pressure gauge, saw that his tank was almost empty, and knew he was no match to try and swim away.

Russell saw the men swim down to the excavation site and begin to toss the remaining gold coins into the basket. For some reason, they weren't concerned with him. Maybe it was just the two men who didn't care that he was still alive. But Lucinda, she might mind. And she would still be on the boat. Russell's emotions began to race at the thought of her. But he had to focus to stay alive, and not fall prey to these feelings that could freeze him.

Russell slowly ascended to the surface, coming to the surface right in front of the bows of the two boats, being careful not to get smashed as the two hulls bobbed together. Before he could look up he could feel a presence. So he looked up. It was that slick man from the bar the other night, Drake, with a rifle pointed right at him.

Russell exhaled, trying to sink under the surface. He heard the shot ring out and felt the hot pierce of the bullet going through his shoulder. He continued to sink, breathing air from his scuba tank as he assessed the damage to his shoulder; it stung and he was bleeding....

Almost out of air and wanting to conserve some, Russell kept himself focused and carefully surfaced close to where the speedboat was tied up to the *Ol' Wife*. He took a breath very quietly, absolutely no gasping could happen here. Afraid of who might be in the strange boat, he had to be careful not to be seen, he had to check to see if anyone was there. He winced as he lifted his head and looked—no one was there.

VOLUME TWO: RAPTIS TRILOGY

****

<u>15</u>

Russell hid on the other side of the speedboat, trying to keep from coughing as he silently struggled to catch his breath. Reaching for his right shoulder, he felt the warmth of blood, and the excruciating burning pain. He had been shot, yes, and it seemed the bullet had gone all the way through. He squeezed hard with his left hand, trying to stop the bleeding, trying to contain the pain.

Russell waited, listening for the men to come looking for him. But he could hear that their conversation was elsewhere. It was as if they didn't care about him, or maybe they thought he was dead or dying. Russell decided that they thought he was dead and gone. As he listened for sounds on the *Ol' Wife*, he heard the air compressor crank on, and the hiss of tanks filling, and the splashing of the water, suggesting the men were going in and out as they dived for more and more treasure.

He could hear Lucinda's voice talking rapidly now. She knew everyone's names. They were talking about the treasure. "The medallion, get that medallion." Russell could hear that she wanted a medallion. The other men talked about preparing to leave on the workboat, the *Ol' Wife*, as Russell and Robert had fondly called her, with the treasure. They wanted to leave the speedboat behind. Russell listened closely to all this. And he listened for that English accent he heard, trying to distinguish it from the others.

Russell could only hope the disaster protocol had been set. If it was, then sometime in the very near future, that *Ol' Wife*, the boat Robert and the guys had prepared so carefully, was going to explode into tiny fragments. The cargo would go straight down to the bottom, immediately. This disaster protocol plan had been designed that way, with plastic explosives Eugene had taped around the hull for just such an occasion; it had been Russell's specialty when he was in the military. Russell was positive Eugene wouldn't have left the boat exposed without setting that clock.

In no shape to swim, there wasn't anywhere to hide in the middle of the sea from an explosion but behind the speedboat. He bobbed on the surface resting, gathering strength for the unknown.

Looking around the corner, Russell could see only two people on the *Ol' Wife*, Drake and Lucinda, and concluded that the others must be busy underwater, still dragging up treasure. So although the pain in his shoulder seared into him, he had to focus himself to do what he had to do now. He stealthily climbed up the speedboat's back transom while Lucinda and Drake, on the other boat, were looking out to sea the other way. Then he slithered into the stern and hid against the side wall, noticing the trail of blood from his shoulder. Just then, he heard the sounds of men climbing back out of the water onto the *Ol' Wife*. It sounded like the crew were all quite satisfied the job was almost complete.

Russell scanned the speedboat. There wasn't anything left on it, no personal effects. *Nothing, that's strange.* He saw the empty ignition key hole under the steering wheel and followed the taped wires underneath with his eyes. Maybe he could start the boat without the keys and get away. Hopefully far enough away so when the *Ol' Wife* did explode like a rocket, he wouldn't be in the vicinity.

He could hear all four men now and could distinguish Drake's voice in there. They were talking about leaving. He heard mention of explosives and prayed whatever those explosives were they were not his disaster protocol. *But what else could they be talking about*, he wondered. He prayed hard that they hadn't found the carefully hidden timer to the carefully set explosives he'd set up on the *Ol' Wife*. Russell thought he had better make his move before they came back into the speedboat. He inched his way up to the ignition switch, grimacing from the intense pain in his shoulder, wincing silently with each slow move. He stopped for a moment and looked up. He found himself looking right at one of the men who was untying the *Ol' Wife*, now ready to cast away from the speedboat.

"Well looky here, we've got a hero."

Russell lay paralyzed with fear looking up at a rifle barrel staring back at him. Two other faces peered over the side at him, laughing. One of the men had the keys to the speedboat and dangled them for Robert to see.

"Looking for these? Oops!" The man pretended to drop the keys into the ocean. "You can have that boat, if you can get it going!"

Risking everything, Russell gathered all his strength and leapt for the keys. Surprising everyone, he grabbed them away from the laughing man. Russell landed hard on the side of the speedboat with a painful scream and loud thud, grabbing his injured shoulder.

All the men began erupting with laughter.

Russell was confused as they finished pulling up anchor, casting away from the speedboat. They didn't bother to come after him or the key. They had planned on leaving the speedboat there all along, but the keys too? It wasn't making sense, they left him with the keys. Maybe the speedboat just didn't have enough gasoline to make it back to port. And the

Ol' Wife was probably too burdened with the gold to tow the speedboat along with it.

For a moment Russell enjoyed the relief of not being chased. His gut relaxed and he chuckled out loud as he thought of what those gentlemen were in for, enough explosives to sink that boat in a one second flash. A vision of Lucinda's dark eyes darting in a flash of panic filled his head and he smiled a faint smile. But the smile turned back to pain as his thoughts moved to Robert, his dear, dead friend who wouldn't listen. They had had his back, but he wouldn't listen. Sure enough, it was that Lucinda who brought them down.

Russell smiled again, thinking sadly that Robert's paranoid tendencies would still pay off in the end. Even with the best laid plans of the English guy, Drake, they were not going to get away with it. Plan C was in motion, the *Ol' Wife* about to explode. Then, as soon as he could gather strength, Russell would have this speedboat running and would simply follow the direction of the explosion from the *Ol' Wife*. He would then retrieve what was rightfully his, now all his, all alone.

He lay on the wet floor of the speedboat, the pain in his shoulder blinding. He could hear the *Ol' Wife*'s engine turn over as the men were preparing to leave the dive site. They untied the ropes holding them to the speedboat and pushed away. Two of the men turned around and watched him as they sped away, their laughing faces rushing away now.

****

The explosion rang out with the blast of a large bomb, the impact first hitting Russell's eardrums, bursting them both inward from the pressure.

Russell's mangled body flew high in the air like a rag doll, then dropped down and floated among the burning debris, each burning piece dropping out of the sky into the ocean like a colorful fireworks display.

Splashing down into the middle of the burning sea, Russell had surfaced next to a hot piece of metal that then burned into his side. Half conscious, he inhaled salt water as he gasped for air. Coughing out the saltwater obstruction, his sides shot pain like white lightening up into his eyes, it all hurt so fiercely. He felt like his chest was constricted and he couldn't breathe even a bit without intense pain. He tried to control his breath and exhale slowly.

Reaching with his right arm it stopped half way, as far as it would go. Looking at his arm with his blurred vision, he saw his hand mangled beyond recognition. He briefly closed his eyes, he wanted to sleep, to go with it while he didn't feel the pain of his body. No pain now, it was a dream, it had to be.

The salt water in his nostrils alerted Russell awake, and he opened his eyes. With a long inhale he leaned back, attempting to float with his face upward. The stars in his eyes flashed bright white again. His legs began to sting, he couldn't see down to see just what was wrong.

A large part of the burnt out bow floated up to him, upside down, as air trapped underneath kept it afloat. Several cleats were still attached. He reached up with his usable hand and held on to one as a handle. A white rope floated into his vision. He risked letting go of the cleat and grabbed the rope. Shear adrenaline helped him reach up with the rope and twist it around the cleat.

Using his mouth, he coaxed the end of the rope through his vest and pulled at it inch by inch with his teeth. He was out of energy and let his body go. The rope did its job, his head was held up above the water line as he closed his eyes again and rested, hopefully drifting off into a long, long sleep. Every inch of his body throbbed with pain. His head grew heavier by the minute. He couldn't hear anything but the loud ringing in both his ears.

Something was dangling on his cheek, moist and round, he brushed at it like a fly only to have it land back, bouncing against his cheek. Leaning his head forward as much as he could, he used his left eye to glace over and confirm his suspicions; it was his right eyeball dangling out from the socket.

He leaned his head back and shut his eye while drifting in and out of consciousness, drifting with the waning moon's swift currents. He barely heard the next and final massive explosion, the *Ol' Wife*. He missed the raining fireworks. His eye was shut. He couldn't see the black smoke rise up as the hull of the boat was instantly ripped out. He missed seeing how she sank within seconds, taking everyone with it. The smoke quickly extinguished with the *Ol' Wife*.

The ringing in his ears was so loud he couldn't hear the sound of the two stroke engine drawing closer.

PART TWO

IN ONE EYE

1980s

VOLUME TWO: RAPTIS TRILOGY
****

<u>16</u>

"Wow Mitch, what on Earth made you think about coming out this way? There's nothing out here!"

The Boston Whaler sped across the flat dark blue sea with Mitch at the center console. They had the day off work, and it was the perfect day for exploring something new: a large reef out to the northeast, twelve square miles of beautiful, mostly virgin territory. Few ever bothered to go out this far, and for good reason. It was a two hour boat ride, and dangerous in the wrong conditions. History recorded numerous shipwrecks in that area back in the days when explorers were getting into the New World, and recent history showed the same. Every year or so, a sailor would blow off course in a north wind and unexpectedly come upon the shallow reefs.

"Wait until you see, Terri. I've been looking at this spot on the charts for some time now." Mitch had a new boat, his new toy. Immaculately clean, totally outfitted with every electronic feature available, he was beaming with pride behind the wheel. This new boat was yet one more means of propelling Mitch forward with speed. "Now we can really explore, these large gas tanks hold enough to get us just about anywhere and back." He patted the center console as he spoke.

"Look! Look at that!" Terri was like an excited kid at the front bow, pointing ahead to the distinct bright turquoise and dark blue line. "Wow! That comes up out of nowhere!"

"I know! That's where we're headed!"

"Unbelievable, look at how beautiful that is, Mitch, the contrast between the two blues, shallow and deep all in one view, unreal!"

"The chart shows it runs for about eighteen square miles." Mitch was in his element. He had the wind in his face and he was exploring something new. Yes, he enjoyed his days off with a vengeance. Most days he had to spend in the office behind a desk with a pencil in hand, pushing, moving, and erasing numbers, mind numbing numbers all day long. This was a great break.

"I've never paid attention to any of this out here, Mitch. It's so far away from anything, really. So unprotected." Terri looked in a three hundred sixty degree radius, seeing that way off to the right was a mountain peak and far off to the left, the point of another island.

"Lots of island history and folklore out here, Terri. If my insurance company knew we were out here, they wouldn't like it at all, so many shipwrecks on the reef out here. Start keeping your eyes wide open now, stand at the bow." Mitch brought the throttle back several notches. The boat slowed down as they approached the shallow turquoise water line. Now they were looking down at bright white sand on the bottom fifteen feet below.

"Watch for large coral heads now, they'll start popping up out of nowhere...." Mitch slowed down another notch as the water grew shallower. "Maybe we'll get lucky and see a canon or an anchor, you might find an old bottle or two!"

"Oh yeah, maybe this will be the day I'll find that old Pusser's Rum bottle for my collection." Terri's grin couldn't expand any wider as she thought about it. She was ready to jump in anywhere.

The sun was straight above. At this slower speed, with no overhead canopy to slow Mitch's new baby down when he wanted to speed, they were really warming up out there.

"Incredible, Mitch, thank you." Terri looked out to the horizon, taking it all in. "How many lobsters do you think we'll find out here?" Terri turned and winked as the two looked at each other and laughed with excitement.

They inched closer to the large reef looming before them. The bright turquoise suddenly got brighter, whiter, with large groupings of bright yellow-gold staghorn corals reaching above the surface in many areas. The brilliant yellow, blue, black, and orange reef fish were dotting and darting through the coral branches like blinking Christmas lights.

"Where do we stop? It all looks terrific!" Terri was already hot and ready to jump in.

"Let's toss an anchor out and snorkel around. We can take a peek." Mitch let the boat drift to a standstill and the two looked overboard to the sandy bottom. A large school of fry swam through right below them, with several mackerel darting in and out of the synchronized group as they swam for their lives.

"Maybe ten feet?" Mitch took a guess.

Terri tossed the anchor and gave it a tug. Once it stopped moving she was satisfied. They were both ready to jump over and cool off.

****

Terri was in the water first, adjusting her mask and looking under the surface at the virgin territory waiting for them to explore. She was glad the school of fry had moved out, as fry attract other bigger fish, sniffing around at the signals of fish distress. Lately, Terri had found herself with a growing fear of the larger fish, the ones in the shark family. She would never reveal such a fear to anyone, but was beginning to constantly fight it back. Her theory was, if getting bit by a shark was one chance in a million, what happens after you've spent a million hours in the water? She had been feeling her odds closing in. She couldn't help but search out and read random stories of shark attacks and then obsess over the circumstances of the attacks.

Looking into the coral, Terri saw two big lobsters looking up at her. She called through her snorkel to alert Mitch. "Mnnph! Mnnph!"

Mitch knew what she was saying without the words. He swam over and watched her dive down and point.

Terri came to the surface with a plan. "Did you see that? Want to go diving right here? Do you notice how the depth just drops right off on the other side of the reef? It looks really deep!"

Mitch was listening, enjoying Terri's exuberance over her find. He didn't have an opinion about the dive spot one way or another, he just loved to watch Terri. She was so beautiful, such a natural beauty who didn't even seem to know it. Mitch loved her.

Terri and Mitch had been like two peas in a pod since the day they met, some years ago. And these best friends spent as much time as possible together. Terri was young, beautiful, bright, athletic, a master diver already, enjoying her adventurous life and the freedom to do as she pleased, freedom which she so proudly allowed herself. Mitch was older, fifteen or fifteen plus years older. He'd fallen very in love with Terri over the years and was now ready for more in his life than their scheduled evenings and days off together. *After all Terri has been through over the past year, she is probably closer to settling down now,* Mitch told himself. *She sure needs a calmer life. She sure needs me, but does she even know this?*

"Why not here, Terri? This spot looks just as good as the next."

"Yay!" She climbed up the ladder on the back of the boat and shook the saltwater off her hair, grabbing a towel and wiping her face dry. "I'm suiting up," she announced, leaning against the side of the boat and sticking her legs through her short wetsuit. "When you're ready, will you please hand the tanks down?" She put her back to Mitch as she talked, pointing, suggesting he zip up the back of her wetsuit for her. "You know how I get when the boat comes to a standstill and rocks." She reached up and pointed to her ears.

Mitch never said a word, he knew this. He was already at the back of the boat putting on his wetsuit. He zipped Terri.

"Thank you, you're the best, the very best," she said as she put her fins on. She sat against the side of the boat and adjusted the mask on her face. Looking over at Mitch, she smiled and blew him a kiss as she readied to back-roll off the side of the boat.

****

Mitch was a pillar of strength for Terri, who had never in her life wanted to lean on anyone. She was disciplined like her father, and greatly admired her dad's refusal to lean on anyone. Mitch never made Terri talk about anything she didn't want to talk about, he was just there for her unconditionally. It had been a tough year for Terri. And for Mitch too. Just knowing what Terri had been through had hit Mitch quite hard.

Her boss, Melvin, had insisted that she take a short leave of absence. And Mitch had supported Melvin's decision that Terri take a break after she had almost been killed by criminal drug smugglers. Sure, Terri had insisted she was just fine, but her actions had proven otherwise. Drink after drink, Terri's paranoia had plagued her as she tried to get that terrible movie playing over and over in her head to turn off, *that nagging memory of being drugged then dragged down into the sea and tied up to die there,* to go away.

Mitch had been happy for Terri when his friend, Melvin, had made her beach and dive manager, which is what she had always wanted to be. She was so skilled at diving and teaching diving, and dive manager was indeed what she would be when she came back from her leave of absence. Melvin had finally given Terri her chance, the chance she had begged for, the chance to run Melvin's big dive business, even with his reservations about her emotional strength at the time. But Melvin knew Terri could be strong as well as great for business ... she just needed a rest first.

******

Mitch wasn't far behind Terri as he readied everything for their dive. Soon their diving equipment was neatly organized and put together, tightly bungeed to the port side of the boat. Reaching down, he turned the handle on the tank. The high-pressure hose stiffened as it filled with the pressure of the air tank.

Mitch looked at the pressure, check. He pressed the button and heard the familiar sound of the buoyancy compensator inflating air automatically into the bladder, check. Picking up the mouth piece, he pressed on the front purge valve and air came out, check. He did the same for the other tank setup before lifting them overboard and letting them down to Terri.

Together, the two dropped down to the shallow bottom with their nylon bags and gloves. They were ready to take on the reluctant rosebush, to pull the spiny lobster out of the ground, out of its coral cave, by its roots.

Terri had the hunt down to a science. She stared the lobster straight in his beady black eyes. Lifting her one hand slowly above her head to the left, she wiggled her fingers, getting the lobster's attention. His eyes shifted toward the wiggling fingers on her left hand. She was keeping him captivated in a trance. Her right hand slowly came around, reaching behind the lobster for his opened back tail before he caught on.

Then the fight was on as the lobster retracted backward into Terri's hand. She closed his tail shut the best she could while holding on, pulling. Her wrists scraped against the coral as the lobster pulled back repeatedly with his strong muscular tail.

The secret to getting a lobster tail is that all of his strength is in the contraction, Terri had so many times told her dive class students. *The lobster has less strength when straightening the tail.* Terri reached behind the struggling lobster with her left hand and closed the large tail shut with her strong fingers as it resisted. Her right hand moved forward, holding the spiny jerky body and pulling him forward as he used his sharp long legs to grab, pull, and resist.

Looking over at Mitch, Terri smiled with her mouth full of regulator. Mitch held the mesh bag wide open as she carefully pushed the large spiny creature in backward while controlling his jerking motions. The lobster's strong, spiny long legs were grabbing onto anything it could reach, scratching at Terri's arms and wetsuit in a last-ditch attempt to resist capture.

****

17

What a day, six decent-sized lobsters, all males. And with 2000psi in their tanks left over and the water so shallow, it just couldn't get any better. So the two swam further down the reef, with the feeling they were looking at a seascape perhaps no one else had seen. Pristine and untouched, the beautiful coral was immaculate. Fish poked their heads out and darted around, protecting their territory. Mitch pointed to a wide gap in the coral that opened up ahead. It was a deep channel that went through to the deeper blue on the other side of the reef. He motioned to Terri, suggesting they swim through.

Terri was the first to see it out of the corner of her eye as she swam through the deep channel. The shiny silver was catching the angle of the light just right. It glistened from deep inside the large staghorn coral. She tugged at Mitch's fin in front of her and pointed.

Reaching deep inside as far as her arm would allow, she turned her head so she could reach a couple inches further without getting poked in the face by coral. But whatever it was that was shining was still beyond reach. Mitch was motioning with his hands to show Terri how close her fingers were getting to the gleaming silver object. But she just couldn't get there. She backed out of her position and released the straps holding the tank on her back. Removing the tank, she held the regulator mouthpiece firm in her mouth as she motioned for Mitch to come over and hold the tank close to the reef for her. This would give her all the room she needed to reach in and grab that shiny piece of silver.

She felt the sharp edge at the tip of her index finger and maneuvered the middle finger, taking hold of it like a pair of tweezers. Slowly maneuvering the shiny package to the center of her hand, she clasped her fingers around it. Her heart began to pound as her imagination went wild. She could feel it, hard, sharp, square, with something soft? Slowly, she retracted her arm from inside the puzzle of the sharp of coral. Together they looked, it was an old silver money clip, silver-ish with a gold-ish circular shape attached, tarnished and scratched by sand, but fascinating.

She handed it to Mitch as she put the tank back on. So random, a money clip, it must have dropped off a boat sailing by.... *Wait!* Terri looked down at the sand and saw something else, a round curve, stark white, unnatural. She began to fan the sand away with her hand, revealing a white plate. She held it up for Mitch to see. It looked old. Odd. Together, Mitch and Terri kept fanning the sand away with their hands, looking for another plate until Terri got bored.

****

"Whew! What a day, Mitch! What an awesome place, feels like we're seeing reefs no one else has ever bothered to look at."

"I know Terri, I can't believe it's taken us so long to get out here and visit these waters." He patted his new Whaler. "Now we have big enough gas tanks to get us anywhere."

The Whaler was just entering the small lagoon of an isolated key that they'd never stopped at before. Something else new this day. Together, they tied up to the small dock. They were one of two boats visiting this off-the-beaten-path island for the night. Few sailors would venture out to tie up at this dock. Not many reasons to come out this far. This was not really a vacation sailor's destination, it was so away from the ordinary, and no easy obvious fun.

They might exchange a piece of yesteryear with the other boat's party at the local hangout, tales of war, sunken ships, pirates, and woe. There were always drunkin' good times to be had in places like this, times with great conversation about days passed. People sailing for out of the way places like Locket Key rarely talked of the future, no one cared much for that. This key was where a hardy few would go, those who intended to really get away from it all and to be with those of like mind—if anyone at all.

This was a place for those with a true love for their lover, the sea. People who came here had to be only the saltiest of weathered souls. People like this guy, Russell.

VOLUME TWO: RAPTIS TRILOGY

****

18

Everyone had a story about Russell, but no one had ever been lucky enough to capture an image. This truly private man was an iconic destination for any sailor weathered enough to have heard of him. At Locket Key, he was the one man who had seen it all, as he himself always said. The added fun was that he was known to be as drunk as he was wise in years.

Old indeed now, and wiser than most, Russell's body was beaten up to the point he was hard to look at. Life had made this guy bitter and opinionated, and a smart and funny bartender. He could capture the attention of the saltiest of sailor with his tales of war and the seas he'd traveled. Looking past the obviously homemade prosthetics on Russell, he kept what was left of his body toned and in very fit condition.

Mitch had heard the rumors and stories of the one-handed, one-eyed bartender on Locket Key, and now they were going to meet him at his bar.

This was actually a bar Terri had never visited, which in Terri's mind was unheard of. She herself was embarrassed that in all her years out there, she had not visited this place so off the beaten path, the strange place other locals and friends had told her about.

****

Mitch had told Terri he had a special evening planned for them that night and thought the solace of this bar and its uniqueness, so like Terri's uniqueness, would be a perfect setting. So far, it had been a fabulous adventurous day, almost magical, like most times he spent with her.

******

Terri was in a great mood as usual, excited about the new pieces of treasure she'd found and full of herself with her newest adventure. She was ready to buy everyone a drink at the bar, and that was perfect because there were only two other people in the place.

She had thrown on the light long-sleeved denim shirt that had become the evening uniform she wore everywhere. To keep the no-see-ums and mosquitoes at bay in the night hours, she closed her eyes and sprayed her body head to toe with mosquito repellent. She gathered a rubber band around her long, half tangled blonde ponytail and considered herself ready for an evening. Mitch was always prepared with clean folded khaki pants and a tidy matching shirt. His short, receding hair required little or no maintenance. They were quite a pair.

The bar was constructed of two-by-fours, with plywood sides and a simple plywood and coconut frond roof. Walking up, Terri quickly noticed that, just as Mitch and others had warned, the bartender looked like he had been run over by a truck. She'd heard rumors about him, but had only half believed them, thinking the story was just getting bigger and bigger the more it was told. But by golly, they were right.

This man Russell had a large, old-style hearing aid attached to his strangely deformed left ear. A black leather eye patch, faded and weathered, was wrapped around his head, covering his right eye. At the end of one arm, a large brass hook was formed into a three-inch diameter circle. It was similar to that of the fairytale character, Captain Hook. But Russell's hook had been formed to be just the right diameter to slip down over a fifth of liquor. With just the right tilt and leverage, he could pour any drink with this handmade prosthetic while using his other hand like a puppet show while he talked, animated, drunkenly driving home his point.

When he let out a smile, his teeth were few and far between. He was the topic of many conversations, but pictures, evidence, well—they were never allowed, ever. In fact, Russell was known to be quite belligerent about this. He would not pose for photos or provide evidence of what he was saying and that was that. People's cameras had been broken, thrown in the saltwater and destroyed. This place was Russell's life and Russell's world and here you did as he said. Otherwise, there would be consequences.

When people asked Russell the wrong questions, they went unanswered, and the conversation was changed. But this sort of behavior only added to his great mystery. No one knew anything about him, beyond what he told in his own endless stories. There was never a last name offered, never any mention of his personal life. But Russell was always interested in you, where you were from and how you were enjoying your life. He was clearly someone who had morphed into yet another Caribbean character, perhaps not by choice, but out of survival.

"Two very cold beers, please." Mitch had planned on spending the night there with Terri, camping on the boat in their sleeping bags. There were very minor facilities at the bar, if you could even call them that. These facilities basically provided just a small bit of freshwater to wash your face, that is if you asked nicely. Freshwater was such a premium here, it was cheaper to drink and wash your face with rum rather than use whatever precious fresh water was somehow captured here on the island, or brought in from somewhere.

"This is right out of a Captain Hook fairytale," Terri whispered to Mitch as she tipped her beer toward him. He tipped his beer back at her and they clinked their bottles. "Can you believe it?" Terri whispered. She couldn't take her eyes off the bartender.

"It's been a great day, Terri, every day we spend like this is terrific." Mitch was looking Terri deep in the eyes. And now they both wore a nervous smile, but for different reasons. Terri had her hand deep in her pocket, turning, rubbing her new treasure as Mitch spoke. She wanted to pull it out and look again. Mitch was reaching deep into his own pocket as he was talking.

"Yes, well this is fun, Mitch, so fun. And you know me, I love to try out any new bar!" Terri was trying to lighten up the heavy emotions she started to sense were coming her way as Mitch looked at her so intensely. She was playing with the find in her own pocket.

Mitch glanced over at the other couple there and the bartender; they were deep in conversation at the other side of the eight foot bar. Ready to make his move, Mitch began to pull the little black box out of his pocket, it was time to reveal it to Terri.

But at that very moment, Russell the bartender swung around and turned his attention to them, limping over. "Well strangers, what brought you out today, plan on stayin' the night at the dock?" He asked them in a surprisingly gentle tone. "I do charge a fee you know."

Mitch's moment had been interrupted, so he shoved the special velvet box deep in his pocket.

Terri pulled the money clip out. It had an unusual large gold coin in the center. Old deteriorated bills were still stuck in the grasp of the clip. "Who do you think this belonged to?" She held it out for the bartender to see. "Guess somebody dropped it overboard!" She talked in a volume loud enough for everyone to hear.

The bartender turned his eye to it, and his eye lit up as he looked over.

The conversation had been skillfully changed. Mitch patted the little box in his pocket, hoping no one had noticed him slip it back.

But Terri had. However, for the moment if not longer, she decided to act like she hadn't. "We should try and remove those bills in this clip, see what they are. They look old, kinda different." As she spoke, Terri extracted the wad from the stiff clip and started fiddling with the moist paper, trying to peel one piece off like a wet beer bottle label.

The bartender was reaching for the piece and said, "Let me see that!"

Terri looked up at him. He had his good hand out, his fingers twitching with his large palm open, expecting her to immediately hand it over for his inspection. She was surprised and thought he was going to grab it right out of her hands! She became reluctant to let go, it looked so special. Looking around, she relaxed. After all, where could he go? And just how fast?

"I found this today, cool, huh?" Her hand moved in slow motion.

The bartender, Russell, snatched it away from her, quickly bringing it up close to his only eye. He began looking at it, inspecting it from every angle. Smiling, he handled it, turned it, and brought it up to his eye again as if it were a two hundred caret diamond set on ten pounds of gold, sitting on a priceless pillow.

Terri thought he was going to begin salivating on it. His intense interest was making her feel quite uncomfortable. She wanted it back in her possession; he was beginning to creep her out.

113

"Where did you find this?" The old man's voice changed. He sounded serious and gruff now as he got into Terri's face. He was still smiling, but with a different smile, a smile that felt rather sinister.

She examined this man, Russell the bartender, a little more closely. The intensity of his one bright blue eye, floating in a sea of broken red blood vessels, was reaching into her eyes for the truth. His face was outlined with deep wrinkles, leathered and weathered from the constant sun and perpetual alcohol meals. She could tell the eye patch was covering the result of a horrific accident of some kind. Looking back into his bright blue iris, she cocked her head slightly. She didn't trust this guy and nonchalantly put her hand back out to him, palm open. She wanted it back.

"Mmh, out diving today." Terri was cautious, his demeanor had changed. She did her best to talk to his good eye, not wanting to be rude.

"You did? When?" The old man turned the piece over and over in his hand, looking at it. He turned and started to pace the eight feet of the bar, back and forth, still clenching the clip, murmuring to himself. He stopped in front of Terri. "Young lady, you need to sell this to me right now, and don't tell anyone, no one! Has anyone else seen this?" His large weathered hand and his muscular fingers were still clamped tightly around it.

"Sorry, it's not for sale." Terri didn't like this guy's aggressiveness. She looked around the bar with suspicion. This was beginning to feel like the opening of a B-grade horror story. Here were four unsuspecting tourists on a small island in the middle of nowhere, where was the murder weapon stashed? She glanced at Mitch. "We don't even know what it is we have here, it's not for sale."

Mitch found a foot in the door of the conversation. He too was beginning to wonder about this over-the-top interest in Terri's find. "We'd want to identify that coin first, before we would consider any kind of an offer," he added.

The conversation being within earshot of the other couple sitting at the bar, curiosity pulled them in and over to look at the find as well.

Terri was looking at Mitch, raising her eyebrows, giving him the "We would?" look.

"What is it you found there? An old coin?" A middle aged gentleman who had been sitting off to the side held his hand out to Russell, also wanting to examine the piece. The ever-more intensely agitated bartender was reluctant to show the guy. So he turned away from this man and played down Terri's find like it was nothing. But he didn't let go of it. "It's a silver money clip," was all he said to this man, still not showing him.

"Five hundred dollars," Russell muttered as he came back toward Terri, much closer to her now as he whispered in her ear. His knuckles were white from holding on to this thing so tightly.

Terri was starting to feel confused. She really didn't know what she was going to do with this thing, but she did know what she could do with five hundred dollars. She looked at the guy, hesitating, trying to decide what to say.

"Terri, keep it, just keep it," Mitch insisted.

"Seven hundred dollars." The bartender was even more insistent now, bordering on desperate.

Mitch began nudging Terri with his knee, looking at her. What did this guy know about this coin? It must be valuable. Terri was feeling the same way. And this guy, Russell, was really making her uncomfortable.

"I just found it, today," Terri said, trying to de-escalate whatever it was that was escalating.

"One thousand dollars." Russell's offer kept going up.

"I'm going to keep it, but thanks for the offer." Terri stretched her hand out and wiggled her fingers at the man. She wanted her little find back in her possession. Old Russell saw her hand but didn't comply. So she continued. "I do have a really cool plate I found, if you want to buy that?"

"A plate? Yes, yes, let me see this plate." Russell's eyebrow lifted even higher as his interest heightened. "So where exactly were you diving today? Can you show me? Let's go tomorrow."

"Out on that outer reef, you know, way out there," Terri pointed.

"We went out to the Grand Key reef," Mitch tried to explain.

"Can you find the area again? Tomorrow?" The bartender was insistent.

This guy was quizzing Mitch with such an urgent tone, Mitch grew more cautious. What was all this intense interest and urgency about, Mitch asked himself. "Well, I'm sure—" Mitch began to explain.

"Mitch had it all planned out for the day," Terri interrupted.

But Mitch was done being interrupted for the night and continued. "We just picked the first place that looked intriguing. We were just out looking for lobsters." Mitch knew exactly where he'd been but wasn't going to say it.

"One thousand dollars, cash," Russell said as he leaned over the bar, practically whispering his latest offer.

Terri sat back in her seat to regain some distance from the two of them, this Russell and her Mitch. She grabbed her bottle of beer off the bar top while looking at them, smiling as she shook her head no. Then she stretched her hand out further toward the bartender, continually moving her fingers in a come hither movement, while shaking her head no. She just wanted her souvenir back.

Russell was reluctant to hand it back to her. When he finally did hand it back, it came with an ominous warning.

"Don't show or tell anyone, there are people who will kill for this. You won't be safe holding onto it." He was serious, dead serious, watching her with concern as she tucked it back deep into her front pocket. She took the warning with a grain of salt as she stood up and walked out, heading to the dock.

****

It wasn't long before Terri returned to the bar with the chipped white plate.

"Well I'll be damned." Russell was stunned. His reaction to the plate as he held it up was the same as to the money clip. He turned it to examine it, looking at the marking on the back.

"Look at the bottom, it has a cool stamp from England. I think this piece is real old, want to buy this? You can hang it around here somewhere? Only five hundred dollars," Terri said teasingly, looking over at Mitch and winking.

Russell was smiling so big he was almost laughing as he held the plate up closer to his eye.

"Sold! What did you say your name was?" Russell put the plate down and reached out with his one good hand as Terri put hers out as well. They shook on it as Mitch watched, half rolling his eyes and wondering why this old man was so interested in Terri and her finds. For poor Mitch, this was a game-over night; this old man had somehow singlehandedly knocked the wind out of his plan for a special night with Terri.

Terri, the perpetual dive tour guide, was the first to stick her hand out and introduce herself. "My name is Terri, and this is my friend, Mitch."

Mitch nudged her with his knee. The way this guy was acting, Mitch didn't want him to know their real names. But too late now.

"I'm going to buy this from you, Terri, five hundred dollars."

Terri's eyes widened and she looked at Mitch with a grin.

"But you have got to promise me, Terri," Russell brought his old face closer to hers as his breath hissed through his teeth. "You can't tell anyone about this, OK? I mean anyone. It's like you never found it." Russell's voice was low, hushed, now with an even more serious tone. "I don't want to scare you, but you have to know, this is dangerous. Real dangerous. Wouldn't want to see a pretty girl like you get hurt. Right?"

What the hell? Terri listened to the old man go on as she finished her beer. *Dangerous? Really.* This guy had no idea what she'd been through. Besides, what could be so dangerous about an old money clip with a gold coin and some old plate? They obviously weren't even from the same era. This guy must be off his rocker, way too much sun.

"Where did you say you were from?" Russell was all but ignoring Mitch, as most men did when Terri and Mitch were out together. Mitch had grown used to this, but now this Russell guy was wearing on him.

Yet Terri was soaking it up. She seemed interested in this interaction with this Russell. "From St. Todos, I'm a dive instructor there," Terri said, downplaying her big job there.

Terri had smiled with a portrait-like smile as she said her name, thinking this Russell would certainly have heard something about her, maybe seen her picture or something. He could have read the local newspaper when he picked up his supplies on the next island. The local newspaper, all of eight pages long, had had her picture on the front page the day her crazy co-worker had kidnapped her, trying to kill her. That had been a hard article to miss, especially when Terri would conveniently open a copy up for anyone who was even somewhat interested.

"Mmm, and do you dive out here frequently? I have been exploring every square inch of these waters, for years...." He winked his eye at her. "You should stay here for a few days, I can show you a lot more."

Mitch finished his beer and was ready to throw the bottle at the bartender to get his attention. This guy was enthralled with Terri, and Mitch didn't like it. *What in the world was this old man thinking?* Mitch nudged Terri with his knee again.

Terri was never one to turn down an invitation to go diving. But as she looked over toward the dock, she saw the third vessel out there and assumed that one was his. It was an old, barely maintained floating hull. She squinted in the dark, also noticing a crispy looking outboard which looked even older than this guy. She glanced back at his old weathered frame and his hand hook.

The total picture was not inviting. Anyway, Russell was way too much of a contrast to Mitch with his brand new Boston Whaler. It was possible—just possible—that this Russell could maybe be too much adventure, even for her.

Russell counted out twenty dollar bills on the bar top, twenty-five of them, then pushed them toward her, nodding at the plate.

"Sell me that clip, young lady…." He wouldn't let the idea go, he wanted that clip. "Sell it to me. Save your life." He tapped his fingers on the stack of twenty dollar bills, doing his best to scare her and tempt her with greed. Terri grabbed the cash with a smile, counted it out and shoved it in her front pocket next to the clip. The plate would have been cool to add to her collection of old bottles she found occasionally on the ocean floor, but it was easy to see it go for five hundred dollars.

"Thanks for the offer but I'm still holding onto that one. I'll take my chances." Terri winked at the bartender as he put another beer in front of her without her asking. He had forgotten about Mitch and the other customers at the bar. Mitch sat there wondering just how his special night with Terri had gone so sideways. It was now all about Terri and her new creepy friend, the bartender.

"Here my friend, this one's on me," Russell finally slid a beer over to Mitch without even looking at him. Russell simply couldn't take his eye off of Terri.

Mitch wanted to at least sketch out the markings on the back of that plate Russell had already tucked away. There must have been something about this plate that made Russell want to buy it. *Five hundred dollars, really? For a chipped plate?* Or was this crusty old sailor just trying to manipulate his way to the unusual gold coin in Terri's pocket? Or to Terri herself?

"You two better stay up at my place tonight. Did you see anyone else out on the reef today?" The old man was pressing Terri, insistent.

"Oh no, we're all set for the night," Mitch said, even more insistent.

Terri was curious about what this man's house looked like.

"I've got us all set up with a place to camp tonight," Mitch continued.

Terri looked at Mitch, puzzled. "You do?"

"Yes Terri, I do."

Mitch continued to nudge Terri's knee, harder. *Get on the clue bus!* Mitch was ready to leave this small island. He didn't really know where they were going to go, but he wasn't about to stay there.

VOLUME TWO: RAPTIS TRILOGY

****

<u>19</u>

The familiar clang of the bell on the back of the dive shop door announced Terri's arrival back on St. Todos. She was moving a little slower than usual with her sunglasses still on, evidence of the late night before. Terri had had most of Sunday to herself after she and Mitch had returned from their boat trip late that morning. Terri had told Mitch she was quite tired and wanted to rest, which was true. She was exhausted, having spent an uncomfortable night anchored out at some random cove they found after Mitch insisted they leave Russell's island that night.

Of course, instead of resting yesterday, Terri had ended up downtown at her favorite watering hole. She spent the rest of Sunday meeting new friends, laughing, telling stories while eating and drinking to excess. Her new friends insisted on driving her home that night. She couldn't remember what time they left.

Terri had woken up to find a taxi cab parked in her driveway. The driver had said he was sent to pick her up and take her to work. How could she refuse? She had first wanted to go to her car. Then she wanted to swing by the pier for a bowl of goat's milk soup, so spicy it makes every orifice in the body run. Terri had always said that this soup was an efficient way to wake all of her senses up at once. But the taxi driver had insisted that he was sent by friends, he wouldn't disclose what friends, and that he had been told to take her straight to work. Terri was sure that Mitch was behind this.

****

At the dive shop, Terri found everyone busy getting ready for the day, cleaning and preparing for the tourists, only ninety people today. Terri loved days like these, slightly hung over but no problem. She had had a terrific weekend with much to talk about. Today would be small dive class groups, no pressure, and everyone should be in a good mood.

"Good morning, Terri." Donna was the first one to great her.

"Good morning, good morning, looking good!" Teri coached as she shuffled across the sales floor, trying to stay out of everyone's way while they worked. She was ten minutes late. She knew Melvin wouldn't say anything about it this morning.

At that moment, Melvin stuck his head out the office door and looked straight at her. He had watched her arrive on his video monitor. "You're late." Melvin had that look on his face, that look she well recognized.

Terri looked over at Donna with an animated look of surprise on her face, tossing her hands in the air, trying to be funny.

Melvin didn't think it was funny. He didn't even smile or change the serious look on his face when he next said, "You have company," nodding toward the inside of the office.

****

Stepping into the office, Terri saw the two very handsome, young, clean-cut men she had met at the bar last night. They were sitting down with Melvin. They both stood up as she walked in and put out their hands to greet her.

"Hello Terri," one of them said. They were both standing up straight, at attention, smiling widely at her. They were so alert, such a stark contrast to Terri that morning, wiping the perspiration off her forehead with the back of her hand, her head still a fog. "We've been talking with your boss, Melvin here."

"Hi guys...." Terri was surprised and apprehensive to see them. "Didn't think I'd see you again—I mean, not so soon!" Actually Terri had thought she would *never* see them again. Now here they were this morning where she worked?

"Well, we really did enjoy meeting you last night, Terri, listening to all your stories." The taller of the two young men turned to Melvin. "We understand she's quite the local hero, you're lucky to have her on your team."

Melvin looked over to Terri as she stood there, late for work, her hair still uncombed, red in the eyes, not quite up to dive shop management's—to Melvin's—standards. Melvin released the air out of his lungs, slowly, through his nose.

The sound caught Terri's attention. She knew the signal, and there would most likely be some explaining to do later on.

"Really? Well thank you, we feel...lucky...to have her here." Melvin tapped his fingers on the desk and turned his attention to Terri, cocking his eyebrows and shooting her a look.

Terri's mind started to scour itself for the possibilities here.... *Uh oh...What did these guys tell Melvin? And what did I say to these guys?*

"These gentlemen are from Archaeology Unlimited. They have come to me requesting your services. Your services? Terri?" Melvin looked both confused and irritated, but aimed his unhappy face in a direction only Terri could see.

Terri stood there trying to digest what Melvin was telling her. Archaeology Unlimited? Her services? What services? She was trying to remember what these guys had been telling her last night—and what she might have been telling them as she drank more than she'd meant to. She turned to the men. "Yes, I'm listening. Go on. My services you say? What would those be? I mean, do you need a dive instructor? A dive master? Someone to show you around?" Terri plopped down on an empty chair. She was tired after last night. *How could these guys look so refreshed*, she wondered, *didn't they drink as much as I did?* She couldn't even remember their names!

"No, we need a photographer and feel you are the right one for the job." The taller one spoke up.

"Why me? I mean, I'm flattered.... Really?" She sat up straight and adjusted her posture. "I could do that, yes. Photographer." Terri looked over at Melvin, smiling wide and nodding her head yes.

"We will be in this area here for less than a month, doing an archaeological exploration. Our company believes it works best for us when we come into new areas to recruit locals, people who know the area, people who are connected, like you, Terri. It helps gives us a good story and draws attention to our projects."

"Which are?"

"Right now we're about to do a survey of Grand Key Reef. It's about a two hour boat ride east of here, pretty much out in the middle of nowhere."

"Oh yes, I told you guys, I was out there this weekend," Terri said, feeling like this was making some sense now. She had been eager to confirm they indeed had the right girl, and yes, now she knew, yes she must have talked to them about Grand Key Reef last night.

Melvin watched Terri as she went on and on with all this. *What on Earth is she doing*, Melvin asked himself impatiently.

"Oh yes, there's a lot of folklore about that place out there, right? Shipwrecks, lots of shipwrecks. I think I showed you my find last night, a gold coin on a clip. That reef, that's out where I found it." She smiled as the men agreed, feeling good about herself, important to these men.

Melvin rolled his eyes, thinking that any minute Terri's head would tip over, it was so big with ego.

"Well, you'll like this then, because we've planned a survey with all kinds of modern underwater search equipment, and we need a photographer."

Melvin was looking right at Terri now. He intervened to move the conversation along, as he knew how it was going to end.

"Basically, Terri, what they are asking me is this: They want to hire you to go out diving with them for a month."

"All right, Melvin! Cool. Yes, I want to do this! Yeah!" She looked over at the two men, trying to stop herself from jumping up and down with excitement.

"Cool for you, Terri. But who runs my dive shop during one of our busiest months while you're gone? I'm going to have to say no, Terri. I'm sorry, but right now you're irreplaceable to me. I can't let you go."

"But...but—"

"Besides that, Terri, is the fact that you're a woman." Melvin already had his backup excuse in place. "I'm sorry, but the man-woman ratio for this job they're talking about is too askew for my comfort. So I've offered them Jim."

Terri stood there speechless, those five words going over and over in her head in slow-motion, *I can't let you go.*

Melvin braced himself for the response.

"What do you mean, I can't go? These guys want to hire *me*, right guys?" She looked at them, trying to get them to agree, the mental rolodex turning and turning in her head as she tried to remember their names.

The two men from Archeology Unlimited sat there silently, just listening and watching all this.

"There are several guys here capable of running this joint without me, Melvin! Jim is one of them!"

"Terri," Melvin stood his ground, "I said no, I'm sorry." He knew what was coming next, and all he could do was stand there and watch.

"I can't believe you're saying no to me, Melvin! I feel like quitting!"

The two men looked at each other, waiting for her to stomp her foot like a child, and throw a tantrum.

"Now Terri, settle down, get out there on the floor, get to work and we'll talk this out after work today."

She pursed her lips, trying to keep her mouth shut while looking over at her new friends. She was happy to have them, now that she felt she did not know who her friends were any more. *Certainly not Melvin.* Terri wasn't used to Melvin saying no to her. He didn't do it very often, especially not this past year. All that had happened had been rough on both of them, and they'd had very hard decisions to make.

After the old beach manager, John, died last year, his wife and co-manager, Kathy, had left the islands and done so quite abruptly. This was pretty much as expected given not only that her husband had died but that he had been murdered (by the people who had also tried to kill Terri). Kathy had gone back to the States, leaving the shop for Melvin and Terri to run on their own. At first Terri had tried to run the beach all by herself, saying she could do it all.

But bravely showing up on that beach to run things so soon after she had been kidnapped and then almost killed had proven more than she could handle. She had been having visions of what she had been through, and bouts of fear, PTSD even, and refusing to talk about it. During that time, Terri had preferred to go home to her little bungalow after work at night, sit there in the dark and drink a beer, and then another, and so on. Mitch would show up looking for her and she would send him away telling him she was too tired to talk. She hadn't been doing well at that time, which is why she had been told to take a leave of absence.

****

"Sorry guys." Terri didn't bother looking at Melvin or responding further as she half stomped out of the office. She was mad and there was work to do. This just wasn't fair. She was the one who had found these guys, or they had found her. Either way, they were *her* connection.

Terri realized she hadn't even had a chance to show off her treasure to Melvin, the old coin with clip she had found out on the reef.

Twirling the clip in her pocket, she continued on out of the office, ready to show it to anyone and everyone who might ask her how her weekend had gone. She could feel the five hundred dollars cash still in her pocket, already burning a hole in it. She found herself walking over to the photography section of the dive shop, ogling the toys while everyone around her worked.

****

"Thank you, guys!" Terri told them all collectively as she watched them work. Some of them acknowledged her, others kept looking down and continuing their tasks. Not all of them were happy with her management style. They were used to working with her—but next to her, not under her.

But now Terri was on the other end of the spectrum. She never saw this change in their attitude coming, not with these guys, her friends. But it all shifted now that she was becoming their boss. Both Melvin and Mitch had warned her about this possibility. She had refused to believe them. "These guys are my friends," she had insisted.

No one working in the dive shop asked about her weekend.

<u>20</u>

The two men were standing across the street from the dive shop, watching, waiting for Terri to walk out after work. They stood there quite casually in their elegance, the vision of sun, sand, and sea, their hair bleached blonde from the sun, neatly cut and groomed, with bright white smiles. The collars on their monogrammed polo shirts were flipped up all around in a classic yacht club look. Expensive sunglasses covered their eyes.

Terri saw them and headed over.

"Terri! Look out!" The tall one called out as she started to cross the street waving at them. Right then, a car was coming around the corner and speeding down the small two lane roadway. Terri, who had already started across the street, kept moving, running toward the men and narrowly avoiding the car.

David stepped forward and grabbed her as the car sped away.

"What the hell? Fire trucks don't even drive that fast here! Who was that?" Terri waved her fist at the car as it sped around the corner. "Fuckin' tourist in a rental car!" Her adrenaline rushed through her body and she broke out in a sweat.

"Careful, now." David still had his arms around her. "You almost got hit!"

"I'm OK." Terri said this as if nothing had just happened. "Hey, I'm sorry about my boss. You won't believe how upset I am, haven't talked to him all day."

"Let's not worry about Melvin." David released her, then gave her an unexpected peck on the cheek. She turned bright red. These men were so friendly, even after her boss had given them a definite no.

"We haven't given up on you, Terri," David continued as Matt nodded yes. "You're the one we want on our team."

"Me? Your team? Really?" Terri had had fun talking away at these guys last night. But at the time she never dreamed she would see them again. Men on sailboats, here one day, gone the next, sailing off to the next port of call. But here they were, searching her out, asking her to work for them, wow. She reached for and twirled the money clip in her pocket, and smiled as she listened.

"We think we will want you for more than a month, longer."

Terri listened harder as she examined them up and down, noting their European clothing and expensive boating shoes. Those shiny gold Rolex watches blinked at her.

"Hmm." That option hadn't even entered Terri's mind. *Hey! I love my job. Quit? Wow, I can't do that. I worked so hard to get it!*

"We're a new company, Terri, hiring select people, the best of the best, you know, someone with brawn, brains, and beauty, capable of being in front of a camera." They stood there, perfect posture, like a set of twins on a TV show.

"Well, I was a stunt double for a Coca-Cola commercial once," Terri naïvely told them.

"We're talking about television, Terri, interviews, you know, National Geographic kind of publicity. We want to, our mission statement is, to bring attention to the archeological mysteries these oceans have to reveal."

∗∗

"Wow, like a real TV show?" Terri's eyes grew big with imagination as she went off into dreamland.

"Come on, can we take you out to dinner? Let's talk."

Terri was tempted, oh so tempted, and she was hungry. But she was expecting Mitch to drive up any minute as she had planned to go eat with him, just as she and Mitch did every Monday evening, and most Thursdays. It wouldn't be fair to Mitch to say yes to these guys, not on a Monday night.

"I would, but I'm expecting a friend of mine, Mitch, to show up here any minute. We're supposed to go eat...." Terri was fishing for an invitation for Mitch to join in.

But these men didn't bite.

∗∗∗∗∗∗∗

Mitch saw Terri talking to the men. Mitch quickly reached into his pocket, feeling for the little felt case there to give him the confidence he needed for that night. *It's time to propose to Terri,* he said to himself. Mitch parked at the dive shop, crossed the street, and walked up to them.

"Hi, Mitch!" She gave him a quick hug and peck on the cheek. "This is David and Matt."

The men exchanged greetings as Terri continued, "We were thinking of going out for dinner tonight, Mitch, you want to come with us?"

Mitch and the two men were each taken aback, but Terri had decided to take things into her own hands. Each had had a much different night planned. Terri could see Mitch growing anxious and breaking out in a minor sweat over the idea.

"I had reservations for two, at the La Masion tonight." Mitch looked directly at Terri, giving her his best clue.

Terri looked down at her attire. *Shit, La Masion? I'm not dressed.* But she responded aloud and with excitement, "Wow, Mitch, La Masion? French food tonight? You didn't say that, Mitch! Sorry guys," Terri said looking at David and Matt. "Maybe tomorrow night?"

Mitch put his arm around Terri, trying to usher her away.

"Sure Terri, we'll catch up with you tomorrow, after work, OK?" They were so cute, so handsome.

Terri stepped forward and gave each one a quick hug with Mitch glaring on.

"I'm looking forward to it! Tomorrow night, after work!" Terri had to turn her head to get the last words out, as Mitch had taken her hand and started walking her toward his car. He didn't care if he did appear rude. Terri had forgotten that this was their regular dinner night out, with him, with just the two of them.

****

"Gosh Mitch, you didn't have to be so rude." Terri broke the silence as the two of them drove away in Mitch's car.

He kept silent.

"I just met those guys last night. They're my new friends, David and Matt." Terri began to pout.

"That's great, Terri, and how long have you and I known each other? We had a date and you were ready to blow me off!"

"A date?" Terri was confused. "But, ah, I thought.... I'm sorry. I just wanted to talk more with those guys, Mitch," Terri stopped herself short of further explaining because Melvin was Mitch's best friend. She didn't want any word to get back to the dive shop that David and Matt were offering her a job. At least not right now.

"When it comes to me, you only think about yourself!" Mitch was clearly hurt and upset.

Terri thought he was just jealous that she was talking to someone else. But all she really wanted to think about now was having a beer, an ice cold beer, and then another. She didn't want to talk about anything. She felt her mind being pulled in too many different directions. Maybe she just wanted to go home, but she wasn't even sure about that.

"I never thought of it that way...." It was clear to Terri that Mitch was hurt. She didn't want that, and this wasn't the first time she had hurt him. But it was all pretty innocent, she'd just wanted to know more about this job offer. *And since when do Mitch and I go out on actual "dates?" What's up with that? He's my best friend, but that's not a dating thing, is it?*

Silence a moment.

"Mitch?"

"What?" He was irritated with Terri, trying to move past it. But his expectations for the evening had been shattered, and he couldn't let it go. Not again.

"Honestly, I'm tired and now I've lost my appetite. I just want to go home, Mitch." Terri was sad and confused now. She was arguing with her best friend and didn't want to be. She loved Mitch, but her love for him was different from the love he had for her. She wanted to be by herself in that dark unlit room back at her place, drinking beer after beer, then going to bed and throwing a light sheet over her head. She had to think.

"Yep, no problem." Mitch turned the car around and headed back to the shop. The car windows were rolled up with the air conditioner on, keeping the enclosed environment at just the right temperature.

Terri looked out the window. The congested street of small faded stucco dwellings in the small town gave way to the waterfront. The city lights began to twinkle as the sun was gently descending in the west. Warm pastel colors of the tropical sunset were enveloping all who watched, as if a soft, newborn baby blanket was covering them.

Terri rolled the window all the way down, ignoring Mitch's grimace about the air conditioner being on, and stuck her head out the window. She stared into the sky.

Mitch looked forward, both hands on the wheel, questioning his sanity over his feelings for this woman. Beautiful, fun, fascinating, talented, a great diver to boot, what more could a man want, but totally absolutely impossible. He pulled up and parked next to her car.

"I'm sorry Mitch. Thursday, OK?"

"Sure, Thursday...."

Terri could barely look at Mitch as she got out of his car. All this control stuff she was feeling coming from him, what was that? She skipped the usual hug goodbye that night and shut his car door.

He waited for her to pull out of the lot before taking off.

<u>21</u>

Terri was halfway home when she noticed the dark colored car following behind her. It was making all the same turns she was. When she turned right up the hill, the car was still behind her, also turning right up the hill. All alone, she noticed herself breathing faster with anxiety. Was this car really following her? *Really?* Vaguely, Russell's weathered face came to her with his ominous warning of danger. *Ridiculous, this hinting to me to stay away from this treasure hunting world or something like that. What in the beck is he saying? Is he just trying to be important or what?*

But was it ridiculous? Terri suddenly wondered. She hadn't been able to make sense out of whatever that crusty old Russell had tried to tell her, if it was anything at all. Maybe it was just the ramblings of an old lost and wounded man.

When she saw room on the side of the road, she pulled over and motioned the car to pass her. She saw that the windows were tinted. It was so dark that she couldn't see much about the car or who was in it as it passed. The car simply drove on, slowly, heading in the direction of her home less than a mile away. Terri felt the hairs on her arms stand up as she looked out ahead of her. The sky had turned very dark, no light to speak of. She was scared to go home. She couldn't help but think of that man Russell again, and now she couldn't get Russell's face out of her head.

Terri thought about what she should do now. If she drove to Mitch's house, she would have to tell him she felt she was being followed. He would be concerned again, and that was the last thing in the world she wanted. The last time everyone got up in her business and overly concerned, she was forced to take time off, told to "go away and relax," to "come back fresher." Many of them were still telling her this.

She made a u-turn and headed back to her second home, the dive shop. It had a locked gate and front door, no one could get her there. Her heart was racing as adrenaline pumped through her, she just couldn't turn it off. She pulled up to the front of the shop, imagining in her head that the dark car was not far behind. She looked around for anyone watching.

Ready, set.... Terri looked behind her and quickly opened the car door, got out, and slammed it shut. She rushed to the gate, fumbling with the padlock. Afraid to turn around and look, her adrenaline was pumping at full force as she tried to shove herself through the half open gate, opening it as fast as she could without even pulling it open all the way. She choked back panic as she lost track of the front door key, then found it, put the key in, turned and pushed it open. Then she pulled the door firmly closed behind her.

Panting, she tried to focus on anything she should pay attention to. *But what? What is this?* Terri counted as five cars passed by, but this was not surprising as this was a popular waterfront road.

In all this, while she had been getting through the gate, running into the shop, shutting the front door, Terri had missed spotting the dark sedan out front in the middle of the row of parked cars.

<u>22</u>

Terri was at work on time the next morning. She had slept in the back theater area, stretched out on a bench. She hadn't really gotten much sleep, she'd been tossing and turning all night. She had this strange feeling she just couldn't shake. She knew she was being watched, followed. But who was following her? Who was it? Could this really be about that money clip that guy Russell had wanted to buy?

Terri was scared, yes. But she was actually more afraid of telling anyone about her suspicions.

She tried to pay attention while at work and to cover up her distress, but the change in her demeanor was noticeable. Her pace was slow, she looked stressed. She couldn't escape the thoughts forming in her head.

****

Melvin was determined to ignore Terri's moodiness this morning. He said no word to her and did his best to keep his shop rolling as she stood there in the middle of her crew. Finally Melvin had to go talk to her and see how she was.

Terri swung around startled, her hand in a defensive fist as Melvin put his hand on her shoulder.

"Did you get the line up started yet, Terri?" Melvin questioned as casually as he could.

He had entered the fog of thoughts in her head. "No, I thought you asked Jim to take care of that," Terri retorted, regretfully.

She wanted to take this retort back the second it came out of her mouth, as she could never stay mad at Melvin.

"In my office...now!" In front of everyone, Melvin marched her into his office and sat her down.

"I've had enough of this, Terri, and I'm going to put a stop to it right now." He was looking her in the eyes. But now he could see that something was wrong, real wrong, he could tell. "Terri, have you had a drink this morning? What's going on with you?"

"No, Melvin!" Terri was insulted. "That happened just that one time! OK? You sent me home, I dealt with it. No! I haven't had a drink this morning!"

She was so defensive that Melvin could tell something big was up. If it wasn't a drink, it was definitely something else. He knew Terri well, and had felt protective of her from the minute they met back in Acapulco. So young, so naïve, but such a great diver at such a young age, a real natural. He'd watched and guided her as she did a considerable amount of growing up out on these islands, mostly alone.

"OK, I believe you." He really didn't and had a concerned look on his face. "I'm going to be straight with you though, Terri. I'm sorry, but you're going to have to get over this thing about that job. And if it helps, they don't want Jim, he's not going."

Terri looked at Melvin. He had his serious face on, she hated that. She hated the choices running through her head right now. She wanted to bolt and run as fast as she could, away from Melvin, away from Mitch, and most of all, away from whoever was following her.

"Jim's not going? Yes, that does help...a little...." Terri tried to smile, to lighten the mood as she told herself, *He must have talked with Mitch this morning. Ahh, that's it, they had breakfast together.* She had been dodging Mitch now for two days. But now she could see that Melvin's expression wasn't changing. He was set in what he was saying to her. "OK, I'm sorry." She kicked at the carpet, looking at it while she talked. But she wasn't really sorry, she was scared. She wanted to tell Melvin she was feeling nervous again, like someone was following her, that she could feel it. But she chose not to say anything about this to Melvin for fear he would send her home to the States.

Terri thought about the awesome photographer position that the archeological guys had offered her. At the same time, she looked around Melvin's stark office: Older paneling with two outdated desks, the carpet worn but clean. His award-winning underwater photography graced the four walls everywhere; he had a real talent for capturing the moment and in fact had taught her everything he knew about it.

So familiar this office felt to her, like a second home. She looked at the phone he let her use now and then to call home and check in. No one else around there had a phone so far as she knew, except for Mitch. If you wanted to use a phone, you had to try your luck at a local phone booth, usually close to a hotel lobby or downtown where everyone could hear you. Terri thought about this now and wondered if she truly could leave the warmth of this office. Could she really leave the home she had created for herself here, the community she loved so much? She let out a long heavy sigh.

"Now please, get back to work." Melvin hated to be so hard on her but felt he had to nip her attitude and behavior in the bud before it got any further out of control. Coming in late, half hung over, having the other guys do the lifting, shuffling—and they were starting to voice their opinions about her to him.

She had been feeling untouchable the past year, above any consequences for her actions, somewhat of a princess in a Terri-like way. As a good boss, Melvin felt he needed to do some disciplining to keep her attitude in check. This was a job after all, she got paid for it, and paid well.

<u>23</u>

At the end of the day she walked out the door alone. She was not very surprised and actually a little relieved to see her two new friends again, waiting across the street at a bait stand. They were clearly keeping a respectable distance from her boss, Melvin.

"Hey, Terri! Stay there!" The two men shouted from across the street, looking both ways twice and watching for the dark sedan before crossing to her.

"Hi guys! Sorry about last night. Geez, Mitch thinks he owns me or something."

The three of them together let go a slightly devilish laugh, the kind of laugh you have when you know there is intended trouble to be made.

"No problem, Terri, is that your boyfriend or something?" David inquired.

Terri was taken aback by the question. *Boyfriend? Mitch?* "Noo, no, no, no, no, I don't have a boyfriend, no, me? I just like to have fun!" She didn't want to appear to have any anchor attached to her, she was ready to float. And she was.

"Great, we're having a small get together tonight on our ship, we want to include you."

"Tonight? Yes!" That would do the trick, she gave a small jump to her toes without leaving the ground in excitement. She was so animated, the two men looked at each other. Was she always like this?

VOLUME TWO: RAPTIS TRILOGY

****

Just then her fellow dive shop employees began walking out the front door of the dive shop. They were getting off work. Some crossed the street and walked over to her as she was talking. They wanted to invite her out with them that night, to which she told them thanks and maybe tomorrow. She thought she heard others among them murmur to each other, "No, don't invite the boss."

Terri and the two men, David and Matt, just went on with their conversation.

"Well, perfect, leave your car here, we'll take you."

Terri wasn't ready for that part, she took herself everywhere.

"That's OK, David, I got it under control, I'll be there."

Terri finally agreed to let David drive her home. She really didn't want to be by herself and David wouldn't have it any other way. When she got there, she looked around her small bungalow. It had been a few nights since she'd been home but something seemed amiss, her stuff appeared to have been moved around. She tried to take this surprise with a grain of salt as she showered and changed her clothes six times. Looking in the mirror, trying to make her straight hair look like something, she eventually put it in a ponytail.

David smiled at her as she stepped out into the small front room. "You look real nice, Terri."

Terri blushed. David was so handsome. Perspiration beaded up across her forehead and upper lip. "Thank you."

******

Matt greeted them with the dinghy to shuffle them to the ship. She saw it for the first time, anchored in the harbor, huge, grand. More than she thought it would be. Terri started to relax inside. Time to party, have fun with no worries.

They stepped on board to a sea of people, dressed in all different attire from very fancy to very casual. Terri felt underdressed as usual. She looked around, scanning the faces, not recognizing any of them. They looked great through, and everyone there was laughing, drinking, talking, all appearing to be enjoying themselves. There was a man in a sheik's turban with a large woman of obvious means over in the corner. He was laughing, dressed to the nines. *Wow, look at the wealth.*

Terri turned to the first person who looked her in the eye and stuck her hand out for a shake and some meaningless conversation. "Hi, my name is Terri." It was easy for her, meet and greet, the perpetual tour guide, she did it all day long at her job.

With all these mystery guests, she ate and drank all night, almost non-stop, to the point of excess. She was surprised that several of them had actually heard of her at the dive shop. She felt welcomed. And indeed it seemed the party was designed that way, to make her feel at home, offering her drink after drink. Then there was the cabin below, on a lower deck, where people in the know, which appeared to be everyone, would slip off for a line or two of cocaine to keep the party rolling.

From the first time Terri told her heroic story of coming this close to dying and of the bad guys being shot, the guests couldn't seem to get enough of her. She became increasingly animated and eventually very drunk as she was telling her story over and over to anyone who would listen through the night. According to whispers from David and Matt, she was apparently being introduced to potential investor after potential investor, all big time, all wanting to hear about her, asking her over and over about her diving adventures.

"Why, just last week I discovered a new dive site, a very old plate and a piece of silver with this gold coin out on the reef, the same reef these guys are going to work on." She told them about the old plate she had sold to that crazy bartender out there. She pulled out the treasure she had in her pocket one more time for all to see. She always had the treasure ready as she carried it with her everywhere.

"Oooohh," the crowd was impressed and curious, asking question after question.

"I don't think the two pieces are related, but I did tell my friend, Mitch, that we've got to get back to that place and explore some more! And look, that's what these guys are doing! What a terrific coincidence!"

"I really think this is meant to be, Terri. Are you enjoying yourself?" David was at her side, coming out of nowhere, his arm around her waist.

"Tell me, Terri, who is your boyfriend, do you have one?" One gentleman there abruptly asked this. Terri was caught off guard again. She wasn't used to this kind of question, especially when from complete strangers. Her two new friends, Matt and David, started chuckling out loud.

"What guys, what's so funny?" She gave them a look as she pulled away from David.

"Mitch, Mitch is your boyfriend." The two started laughing again.

A wave of humiliation began to creep over Terri; she did her best to dodge it. "No, he's not!" She defended herself with a bright red face. "Mitch is a really nice guy, he's my best friend."

"Whoa! Touchy much?" David joked with her as her new friends continued laughing, egging her ego on. They laughed like there was some sort of inside joke.

Now she didn't like the way they were making her feel. *What's so wrong with Mitch?*

"Terri," David went on, "all these tales, all these adventures, you are such a beautiful woman." David stepped closer and put his arm around her waist. "Such a shame to waste it on, well, an office worker?"

"Hey, that's not fair, he's an accountant!"

The crowd continued with their light chuckles no matter what Terri said.

"Don't you think you deserve a life filled with more…life?"

The small drunken crowd of strangers who had gathered around began to clap and agree with Matt, as if on cue.

David strengthened his grip around Terri's waist, drawing her closer.

She looked up and carefully examined his tall chiseled upper body and his bright blue eyes which were looking down at hers. He was so strikingly handsome, like a model, or a movie star or something. Then she glanced around at the crowd of strangers who were still laughing, drinking, having the time of their lives. This was a different crowd, a whole new league.

The strangely quiet but friendly waiter came to her side. He had a small round platter filled with tall glasses of champagne. She reached over and picked up a glass flute, gladly accepting his bubbly offer. *I* **can** *do this! I can be with these people!*

<u>24</u>

Terri didn't know when the party ended.

She woke up alone in a lovely upper forward cabin. The early morning sun shone through the large round porthole and onto her face. At first she couldn't remember where she was or how exactly she had gotten there. She looked around. Her clothes were strewn here and there and there was a robe draped on the nearby chair.

It all came back to her. A sudden soft gentle rock of the ship from the wake of a passing boat set off her internal alarm. She wasn't sure what to expect as she stood up, she didn't want to embarrass herself with any symptoms of a hangover or motion sickness … especially not nausea.

Terri quickly dressed, then groggily made her way up the gangway. It was quiet, no one was around. She wanted to sit out on the bow, greet the morning sun, and wake up.

A tall muscular man, a local islander she assumed, the waiter who brought her that champagne the night before, and now she realized maybe also the ship's cook, appeared out of nowhere with a platter of colorful fresh fruit and juice. He set it on a table in the open galley on the back of the boat. It was beautifully arranged. He smiled, motioning her to eat and drink.

"Thank you, I wish I knew your name, you're so smiley, so friendly!" Terri sat down and picked at the fresh fruit, focusing on the horizon. Her body was dehydrated from all the drinking she had done the night before, and she had to wake up because she had to be at work back at the dive shop soon, in less than half an hour. But she was dressed in her evening clothes. That was all she had with her, so she had no choice but to go to work in them. That was no big deal, as once she got to work she would be in her bathing suit in ten minutes flat. It was all the flack she was going to get from anyone who might see her when she tried to sneak in late.

Matt walked in and sat down.

"That's Moses, did you get introduced last night? He's a local guy, recommended to us. He doesn't speak but seems to understand everything we say, huh Moses?" Matt was pointing at the gentleman with his index finger as he spoke looking at him, then turned his attention to Terri. "Good morning, sleep well?" He reached down and picked at the fruit as he motioned for Moses to leave the area.

So what if he can't talk, he talks with his eyes, he's beautiful! Terri was drifting in her head, hung over and foggy. She really liked her new friends, but sometimes they said and did things that didn't sit quite right with her.

"Hello? You awake?" Matt jostled her knee, waking her out of her daydream.

"Yes, I think so, gorgeous stateroom, sunny, spacious…. I wasn't planning on spending the night, should I be embarrassed?" She couldn't look at Matt until he answered with light laugh.

"Not at all, not at all, what a great time. Everyone really enjoyed you!"

Terri looked around to an empty ship. It was just Terri and Matt now, there was no one else around. She imagined everyone else still asleep or lounging decadently in their individual staterooms as Moses served them each breakfast there, one by one.

"Thank you, I really enjoyed myself. I've never been to such an opulent party before."

"One of the perks of working with this company."

"Wow, so cool…. Speaking of work, I have to get there, back to the dive shop." She looked at her old Seiko dive watch.

"Oh yes, the dive shop. Back at it, I suppose." Matt patted Terri on the knee before he stood up. "How many cruise ships today? Quite a business, day in and day out."

Terri stood up and followed him to the back transom.

"I'll take you back to the dock, do you have anything? A purse or something?"

"Oh, no, I don't carry a purse, I have a habit of leaving them behind." She patted her front pocket, "I'm good to go. Where's David?" Terri looked around wanting to say goodbye.

"I took him to shore earlier today, he had some errands. Step in."

The engine started right up and Terri pushed them away from the back transom.

******

As they left, David peered out the window of the ship's office with another man, an older man, Walter. David wasn't in the mood to deal with Terri this morning; Matt drew the short straw of a bet to get rid of her. David had agreed to do what he could to lure Terri to the ship, but frankly, she just wasn't his style.

"Mmph, what a damn mess," David murmured to the older gentleman standing next to him as the dinghy sped away. "I hope this works."

"Yes," the older man said sternly, "you'd better make this work, you haven't been able to get your hands on that medallion or the coordinates like you promised. That stupid girl, she doesn't even know what she has. Do not—and I mean *do not*—let her out of your sight," he commanded.

"She carries the thing on her body everywhere she goes."

"Yes, it appears she does. I want to be out on that reef now. That must be him following her: we have to move faster! We have to keep ahead!" The man then sat down behind his desk, red faced and angry, looking down at a chart, motioning David away with a gesture of his hand, a kind of wordless "go do your job."

25

The work day seemed to Terri to go on and on forever. She called out group after group on the megaphone. She lifted full scuba diving setups onto the table, each weighing thirty-five pounds. She coached people as she put tanks on their backs, sending them off in groups with their instructors for their thirty minute underwater tours. Between every setup, she glanced around the parking lot for anyone new, anyone watching her. She could feel that someone was.

The day felt extra hot and humid. The customers, everyone, seemed extra agitated, pulling at Terri every which way with questions and demands. The asphalt parking lot was hot, the white sandy beach looked unusually worn. Terri looked down at a used cigarette butt, picking it up, carrying it to the trash can. "Fucking cigarette butts," she said aloud, "they buy 'em, have to have 'em, but can't find a trash can as they stomp their cigs out with their feet. Pigs." *Mmmm, just way too many tourists, they don't care about our beach. ... What kind of adventure is this for me? Our same old Disney ride, over and over and over again....*

"Are we going back to the ship soon?" An oversized, sweating, sunburned mother with a pink visor and two kids slathered white in sunscreen was the latest at Terri's side. Just like the others, this woman had to know what next when. Everyone wanted to know silly details today. *Cripes, you've come to a beach in the Caribbean, sit down! Relax! Soak it in, you'll be back to your cubicle doldrums or your same old house on the same old block before you know it!*

"Your bus will be loading up soon, when the next two groups come out of the water, ma'am," Terri answered with a calm smile.

Terri leaned back against the truck and watched the small groups on the beach. Each free moment between the tourists, she found herself thinking, thinking, thinking. *Are you going to do this for what, another twenty years? Then what? Marry Mitch and make little Mitch babies? Is this what you want, really? Or, is it what you're doing just for now? Isn't there more than this? Sheesh, I'm still so young. Married? I can't get married! I don't want to get married! Why is Mitch trying so hard to propose now?*

****

All Terri wanted to do today was lean against the truck and brood about her life which she was realizing had become a monotonous bore. No wonder she was nervous. She looked out and watched her fellow instructors, trying to imagine them five, ten years from now. They won't be here, maybe one or two will, but for the most part they will move on to the next phases of their lives, whatever those may be. Career? Married? Children? Be back in the States, move home closer to their families? She tried to count how many friends she had that had already moved on to next phases of their lives. *Too many*, Terri told herself.

Kevin walked over, catching her deep in her thoughts.

"What's up? We done with groups for the day?" He shook the saltwater off his hair and body, shaking drops of water all over her like a puppy trying to make her smile.

"Thinkin', thinkin', thinkin', my friend. Just two more groups. Here, we're on group fourteen." She handed him the megaphone, gesturing him away with her hands, suggesting he go do it while she went on thinking, which really was her brooding about her future.

"Me? You're handing me your megaphone?" Kevin was animated and playing around with her, still trying to make her smile. No one liked this mood she was in.

"Yes, now go do it." She looked out over Kevin's shoulder as he stood looking at her, trying to make her smile.

"Look, someone just popped up," he said as he turned around.

Terri and Kevin saw that one of the instructors out in the deeper part of the tour was on the surface with a beginning tour diver. But right then his arm went up high in the air waving back and forth, a signal for help.

Terri and Kevin took a few steps closer to the edge of the beach as they watched the lifeguard placed out on a center rock dive in and swim toward the help signal. The lifeguard reached the two divers within seconds. Terri watched as he raised his hand straight up in the air as well and waved. Another signal for help.

"Stay here," she told Kevin who was holding the megaphone. "Actually, go bring everyone out of the water on the further side of the beach and please do your best to keep them busy." She trotted out to the water's edge and dove in, swimming out to the three divers floating on the surface out there.

She reached them quickly.

Henry already had the man on his back and was performing mouth to mouth. "I think he had heart failure," Henry said between breaths of air. "No pulse."

Terri rose her hand straight up and waved, they needed support on shore, stat.

A worried Cindy popped up and down nearby. She had left the rest of her class down there under the surface.

"Cindy, just go down with them, stay calm, be happy, round them up, then just keep them all swimming for shore! Now! Cindy, go! Now! He'll be OK, we've got this." Terri could tell by Cindy's wild eyes she was shaken up. But with not a second to spare, Cindy put her regulator back in her mouth and descended down to the remaining tourists. Those tourists had, at Cindy's signaled instructions, stayed waiting down there while Cindy had ascended with the man in distress.

Henry had the tank valve and was already swimming for shore with Terri swimming next to them, continuing mouth to mouth on the way in. Still no pulse.

Johnston, the bus driver, already had his CB radio in action, alerting the police for an ambulance and help. Kevin had gotten busy loading up a bus full of tourists and sending them back to the dive shop. Their tour was over before they even figured out what was going on.

Terri and Henry got the gentleman to the shoreline and up on the firm sand where they could perform CPR. Kevin ran to their side with a bottle of oxygen. They began CPR while continuing mouth-to-mouth. His skin was pale white as they pressed with hard, even compressions on his chest while blowing air into his lungs. Still no pulse.

"Oh my God, not this guy. Kevin, come take over for me." Terri had just realized who it was they had on shore. She motioned with her eyes for Kevin to come in on the other side and take over chest compressions. Maybe, she thought, he could push harder through the man's multiple layers of fat. She stood up slowly, removing the rental camera still attached to his wrist with the band, no one noticing. She trotted to the surf bus, to Johnston who was standing by with the CB radio.

"Dey commin', Terri, dey commin' fast for you, hold on."

"Crap, Johnston, I'm upset." Terri loved Johnston, she could tell him anything.

"It'zzz hard, Terri, God, He takes us when He wanna us, not necessarileee when we wanna go. We neva ready."

Terri looked at him, wondering how he could be so philosophical at a time like this. She wanted this man to live, but deep inside she knew the outcome. She could hear the distant wail of a siren coming toward them.

"Thanks for having this end under control, great job Johnston." She gave him a tender pat on the shoulder and he nodded with pride as she turned to walk back. Earlier that day, she had ridden with Johnston to pick the tourists up from this guy's cruise ship, one whole bus load of tourist divers. And this is where she had met this man whose life was now on the line.

****

Part of the fun of her job was to convince anyone on the snorkeling tour that they too were capable of going underwater for the ultimate adventure, scuba diving. She had found this gentleman all by himself. He had been all done with any shopping excursions and had been glad to do something by himself while his wife went into town shopping with new friends she'd made on the ship.

It hadn't taken long for Terri to win his trust and convince him to go scuba diving. She'd rented him a camera so they could take pictures of him underwater, pictures to show off to his wife when she got home. His wife would be so proud of him, Terri had insisted.

****

Terri found herself praying this gentleman was going to be able to go home. She knelt down beside him as they performed CPR, holding his hand, talking to him.

"You're going to be OK, Jack, I know you will be."

The others looked over at her and kept going. The ambulance pulled up and a stretcher was at their side, the professionals knew just what to do. He was cold and clammy white, still no pulse as they attached an IV, taking over chest compressions while lifting him on to the stretcher. He was in the ambulance and wailing away to the hospital within minutes.

"I've got to get back to the shop, Kevin. Wow, that was hard, you OK?"

Cindy's group was walking up from the shoreline, just finishing with their tour as the ambulance pulled away. The group walked up to Terri collectively after having their tanks removed, all concerned for their fellow diver. Cindy was looking at Terri's eyes, wondering if she would ever hear the truth from Terri.

"He's going to be just fine folks. A little scary, I know, but trust me, he's going to be just fine." Terri had a confident smile on her face as she stood there with the man's rental camera still wrapped around her wrist, assuring everyone that all in the world was good, not a care in vacation land.

After they all walked away, Terri told Kevin to wrap the beach up so she could be on her way to the hospital. Melvin would be there. She opened the driver's side of her truck, tossed the rental camera onto the passenger seat, and jumped in. While absent-mindedly staring at the rental camera, she reached under the seat and pulled out a warm bottle of Morgan David Twenty Twenty. The Morgan D. was tolerable when warm, and it had a blackberry lozenge scent to cover itself from detection, Terri figured. She opened it and stealthily took a long sip before replacing the cap and putting it back under the seat for safe hiding.

****

Terri drove straight to the hospital.

Melvin was inside consoling an older lady, the gentleman's wife. Melvin looked over at Terri through the glass door, she knew right then and there it wasn't good.

She took a deep breath before entering. Poor Jack did not make it, just as Terri suspected, and his wife didn't understand why he would go scuba diving against her wishes.

" 'Snorkeling Jack, go snorkeling, you're not a kid!' I told him." She was crying as a friend stood next to her, consoling her.

Terri stood there paralyzed, with her mouth shut tight as she listened, feeling this lady's grief. Terri knew why her husband Jack had gone diving. "I'm sorry, ma'am."

The lady turned and looked at her.

"I was on the beach with Jack, we did everything as fast as we could." Terri was never sure when to stop talking but decided that was a good place for now. She didn't want to be the one to explain how Jack ended up on the scuba tour against his wife's wishes. After giving condolence, Terri excused herself and drove back to the dive shop.

****

She brought the rental camera in without anyone noticing. She went into the back and removed the film from the camera, Jack had taken thirteen pictures. She could take this camera and hide it from his wife and family, but should she? His wife was so upset he went diving, this would be a constant reminder.

Why do this to that poor woman? Or, Terri figured, she could find his envelope with his personal belongings, which he had left behind, and slip this camera in there. Maybe his wife needed to see he actually had it in him to do something against her will and to follow his own dream. Terri decided to look for his envelope.

Donna walked up. "Sorry about today, Terri, what a year...." Donna wasn't sure what else to say. In Donna's eyes, Terri always seemed so brave yet so fragile.

Terri's brows were furrowed with thought as emotions swirled in her. Terri too was sorry, sad, frustrated, and upset as she thought of poor old Jack putting his trust in her when she said, "You'll be glad you did, Jack!" Now her words resonated in her head. She patted the envelope with the film in it, decided to put it on Melvin's desk. She gave Donna a sad smile and headed for Melvin's office.

Terri didn't want to talk. Cindy, Henry, and Kevin had left early for the bar, and she would have loved to join them, just to be with them. The other instructors were gladly picking up the extra work so that their friends could go plunk down at a bar somewhere and digest the day with a drink. Terri was management now and was discouraged from fraternizing with the other instructors the way she used to. This was part of the deal, this being a manager now. But now she yearned for the company of her old friends.

****

Terri left the shop alone, ready to go home.

But then David and Matt called out to her. Just as they had the day before, they greeted Terri outside of the dive shop. She glanced up and down the road and at the parking lot, looking for any strange cars and for Mitch. She hadn't seen or talked to Mitch in three days now.

That morning, Melvin had appeared to be avoiding her. He had been gone from the shop, hadn't been around to answer questions, not that she had any. And not that Melvin had any, maybe.

But now Terri didn't want to answer any more questions about the day or herself or anyone, not now after her trip to the hospital. Mitch would have at least a hundred questions for her and a lot of concerns. This was probably her chance to avoid both Mitch and Melvin that night. She knew they cared about her, a lot, and this was great, but sometimes it was too much.

So there were her new friends, waiting for her.

"Hi Terri," David said, smiling at her.

Terri found herself glad to see David and Matt as she didn't really want to be alone.

"Come out to dinner with us tonight, we've got a surprise for you."

She still was wearing the clothes she had worn the night before, and the day had all but drained her. "Well, I'd love to guys, last night was so much fun, holy smokes, do you have fun parties! But gee…."

They all shared a laugh.

"It's just that I haven't been home since yesterday, I've had a day and a half today that I'd rather not talk about, and I've got a big day tomorrow. How about you guys come on up to my place, we can hang out a while." Terri ran her hand through her tangled long blond hair, simulating a hair brush the best she could.

"Nah, come on, don't worry about any of that." David handed Terri a neatly folded shirt.

She opened it up, it was her favorite style. A long sleeved, light blue denim button up, with a collar. It had a pocket on the front with the cool *Archaeology Unlimited* logo embroidered on it. "Thanks guys!" She immediately put it on over her clothes, perfect fit. She ran her hand over the logo and smiled at her friends. It was a great gift, she let a smile out of the corner of her mouth.

"Hey now," David stood back arm's length and looked her up and down. "That looks great on you! Perfect fit!" He slowly reached up and ran his hands around her collar, making it stand upright like theirs. "What's up? Tourists got you down?" David pinched her cheek. "Come on with us, you know we'll have fun."

David's arm was around her now. She felt like putty in this man's hands and would do whatever he asked. He was so strong, something about him made her feel safe. She was beginning to feel like one of their team as she buttoned up her shirt. Terri wanted to be distracted from the pain of her day.

"Come on Terri." David moved his hands down both of her arms while looking her in the eyes. He took her hand, suggesting they walk together. "We have someone we want you to meet. He's anxious to talk with you."

"Meet someone else? Who could that be?" She found herself walking with them against her better judgment. She was physically exhausted and couldn't shake the thought of Mitch looking for her and not being able to find her. The guilt was building up, but she went with David and Matt now.

The three strolled through the grand hotel lobby.

David was still holding Terri's hand, leading her as they walked out to the dock where their dinghy was tied up.

Reggae music streamed from a cassette player on a nearby docked sailboat where a charter captain entertained his guests, getting ready to take them on a sunset dinner sail around the large harbor, eating, drinking, watching the stars and the town lights come on.

VOLUME TWO: RAPTIS TRILOGY

****

<u>26</u>

The rubber zodiac dinghy was slick, sixteen feet long, bright yellow with a center console. With a low profile, it sped atop the water. The wind was in Terri's face, and a light mist of spray from the bow began to wake her up as she felt transported to heaven. They were so low that when looking up, any vessel appeared larger than life. They approached their ship, so big, so grand.

"You didn't tell me dinner was on your ship," Terri said. "She is a beautiful sight, isn't she? How big is she?" The closer they got, the more impressed Terri became. These new friends, this grand ship, all this was beginning to feel familiar now, maybe like a second home.

"Yes she is, one hundred and fifty-six feet," Matt smiled. They pulled up to the back transom and tied the boat to a railing. David held the dinghy close, motioning for Terri to step out of the rubber boat and back into their world. And what a beautiful world it was, with its vases of live tropical flowers placed on tables just as in a fine hotel lobby.

The evening hours illuminated the back deck with a warm glow. Terri was unusually speechless as she stepped on board with David holding her hand. This wasn't a party, she was going to meet someone. *Wow, this is what you read about in magazines!* The grief stricken thoughts of the day were being pushed aside as she walked aboard the beautiful ship.

The floors were neatly cleaned, the wood perfectly oiled and maintained; every detail of the brass shined without a smudge or fingerprint anywhere. It was as if that party never happened the night before. But somehow it all began to feel different tonight, businesslike, stark and sterile, almost too clean.

Terri pulled the top of her denim shirt closed as she felt a cool breeze hit her. The men walked her up to the top deck which was enclosed with glass and had a three hundred sixty degree view. It was spectacular. Everything, including the navy blue carpet, appeared brand new.

There was someone sitting in the middle of the room, waiting to meet her. He stood up as he heard them walk in.

"Ah, finally, Terri," the gentleman walked up to her, meeting her halfway as she was ushered in. "Welcome aboard, it is my pleasure to finally meet you."

She felt as if she was in a fairytale, and being greeted by a king. He was older, so graceful, so classy, she thought.

"I trust you had a good time last night? I'm sorry I missed you and the party," he said.

The party already seemed like a year ago to Terri, so much had happened between then and now. She couldn't help but let out a yawn. "Thank you, yes, your guys here throw one heck of a party." Terri let out a brief girlish laugh as she looked at her new friends. She reached her hand out to shake this older man's hand. Now her excitement kicked in, her second wind hit.

He reached out and grasped it lightly, giving it one light shake, as if she was insisting on the shake. Then he lifted her hand gently to his lips as he gave the back of her hardworking fingers a light kiss. She was salty and her clothes were wrinkled from the day before. She tried her best to smile, feeling so out of place.

"My name is Walter, I am the owner and the CEO of this company." He guided her hand back down and gently let go. "I'm sure my men filled you in on what we are doing here." He spoke to her in a very businesslike manner.

"Yes, yes they did." Actually, Terri still didn't quite understand what exactly they did. She thought all this archeology talk sounded fun and looked like something she could want in on. Maybe this was exactly what she needed, diving with no tourism for a while.

"Shall we eat while we visit?" Walter raised his hand and waved to the gentleman dressed in a white coat standing in the distance.

Terri looked over at the man in white. It was the tall handsome local with the beautiful smile, Moses. Terri recognized him from the night before and waved. He disappeared and came back within moments with a platter of beautifully prepared food, peeled cooked shrimp, fruit, crackers, cheese, and caviar, setting it down directly in front of Terri. She dug in, hungry after such an exhausting long day, her body numb.

"This is so delicious! Thank you!" she managed between bites.

"You like that, Terri?" Walter smiled as she dipped another shrimp. "Those are just a few appetizers before dinner tonight, pace yourself," he said politely. "Thank you Moses, you may be excused."

Terri nodded as she shoved another cracker topped with cream cheese and caviar into her mouth.

Moses retreated back into the ship, leaving them alone, never saying a word.

Terri watched to make sure Moses was inside and the door was shut, before she whispered to Walter. "Does that guy ever talk?

I mean does he just not talk? Or can't talk? Or is he not supposed to talk while working? I don't get it?" She was feeling a bit nervous now. Anxious and fidgeting in her seat, she couldn't sit still and was looking around, trying to stay awake. This was all so formal to her.

Walter sat there with his stoic face, listening to Terri nervously ramble on. *Just like Matt and David said, five minutes and I already want to slap her.*

****

Terri didn't yet know for sure that Matt's great uncle, this man, Walter, was from somewhere in Europe, as his accent, if he had one, was sort of vague, indecipherable. This Walter appeared to be a man of great wealth and perhaps even greed. And of course, Terri had no way of knowing that Walter was one of three brothers, one dead and the other at war with Walter over the treasure lost with their dead brother.

Some time ago, a few decades back, the three brothers had watched those foolish sailors do all the work of finding the treasure for them. Then the brothers had swooped in and taken the treasure as planned—that is, until the plan had backfired and the boat had exploded. The one brother, Drake, had been killed and the treasure had been lost back to the sea.

The two remaining brothers had, for quite some time now, watched the one man who had survived Drake's takeover and the consequent explosion, old Russell. This Russell guy had doggedly searched for that treasure, year after year. They were actually glad Russell had survived Drake's attempt to kill him, as they hoped Russell knew in which direction the treasure had gone. But after all this time, it sure seemed that Russell just didn't know. Or did he know he was being watched?

They searched and searched the large reef, never finding the lost treasure or their brother. Each wanted the medallion for his own collection. But more important to them was the cargo on that old ship, identified by the plate specially made for that voyage. The stamp on the back of that china was one of kind.

"How long have you been working at the dive shop now, Terri?" Walter was saying.

"Six years."

"Wow, that's a long career, congratulations."

She didn't quite understand what Walter was talking about, this long career thing. It was just her job, and sure, she loved it! "Thank you, I love my work. I have loved the ocean since I was a kid. The dive shop is living my dream!"

"Oh yes, I understand you're quite an accomplished diver for your age. You're driven, a leader, not afraid of a challenge. Impressive." Walter smiled as he skillfully pumped Terri's ego to the point he thought he would have to ask David and Matt to hold her head up it was so big.

"Oh, well, I love to learn and love to teach as well. Did they tell you about how I almost got killed? That I was the one who discovered the killer?" Terri sat up, positioning her posture straighter, ready to tell the story one more time.

"I'm sure someone mentioned something about that," Walter shrugged and tilted his head to the side. "I'd like to talk to you about something else."

"OK.... What can I do for you?" Terri sat back, her sails momentarily deflated. It was obvious this slightly pompous Walter wasn't that impressed.

"I heard your boss's main concern was that you would be the only female on the boat for a month. He didn't feel, let's say, comfortable with that." Walter was tapping his mouth with his index finger as if he were thinking of a way to get around Melvin.

Terri was game and put her two cents in.

"Well, he may not be comfortable with it, but I don't have a problem with it at all." She looked over at Matt and David who were off to the side, grinning. Last night was a ball and she saw plenty of other women and people around. "I feel totally safe out here." *This does feel different tonight, though. Am I being totally stupid? Out on this boat alone?*

Terri looked around for her smiley islander friend, Moses. He was gone. David was sitting next to Matt on the other side of the table, not next to her. Nothing felt particularly comfortable right now, but then again it was a very uncomfortable day all the way around. *No one ever mentioned this Walter guy before. He's so dry. I wonder if he's on the ship all the time? Where is everyone else now?*

"Well, we have many famous people involved with our explorations. I believe you met some last night, it was sort of a bon voyage party, you might say. Benefactors, supporting us as we explore new, potential archaeological sites, they all wanted to see the new ship. We intend to explore some Mediterranean sites after we are finished with our project here, doesn't that sound exciting?"

"Ooh!" She was impressed. "Those people I met last night?"

"I'm sure some were there, yes Terri." Walter leaned forward and looked right into her eyes as he spoke, his voice a notch louder as the sales pitch began. "I'm going to cut right to the point, Terri, we want you on our team, and I'm willing to do what it takes."

Terri stared back. She wasn't ready for that. *An actual job offer? Tonight?*

"We're the real deal, I think you will further your career and meet some pretty interesting people working with us," David interjected.

"Now. It has come to my understanding you have found a unique treasure out on that reef." Walter pushed the food tray aside to reveal a map of the reef under glass.

Moses appeared out of nowhere, seamlessly picking up the platter of remaining food and moving it to another location.

"Yes sir, I was just out there a few days ago with my friend, Mitch, looking around. We were looking for a canon or maybe an old anchor.

"Mmm, interesting…and did you find one? What exactly did you find?"

"Well, I found an old white porcelain plate with some cool old English stamp on it. And this." Terri reached into her pocket and pulled out the money clip.

Walter sat upright, resisting the urge to grab it out of her hands. *There it was.* He kept his composure. "Oh, how unique, may I see?" Walter already had his hand out and a jeweler's loop up to his eye to examine it. Terri handed it to him. He held it close, smiling as he looked at every corner. "Can you take us back to this spot, Terri? Maybe we could find more of those porcelain plates you spoke of. Where is the one you found? At home?"

"No sir, I actually sold it to this old guy on some little island way out there, he offered cash. I took it." She didn't tell him how much she got, she was so proud, five hundred dollars. Now this guy was holding on to her other prize way too long. She held her hand out, suggesting she wanted it back. He looked at her with a blank face, hard to read, staring her in the eyes. She could tell he didn't want to let go of it. She kept her hand out. "He wanted to buy this too, but it's not for sale."

When Walter didn't hand it over, she lifted up out of her seat and took it right out of his hand, quickly sticking it back into her pocket.

Surprised, Walter looked over at the boys. Then he turned back to Terri. "Yes, well let me ask you again, can you take us back to that spot?" Walter was looking right at her now, waiting for an answer.

Her two friends sat across from her, nodding their heads in unison. They looked pretty spiffy in their neatly pressed uniforms of khaki pants and embroidered polo shirts, their matching Rolex watches still winking at Terri as they caught the light and glistened. She wanted one. "Well, sure I can, I can get you back there if that's where you want to start." It just came out of her mouth, she had no idea where that spot was on the reef. How was she going to get that info out of Mitch? He was going to be so upset with her.

"Yes Terri, we hope to find more of those plates you mentioned, with stamps on them, yes?"

"The stamp on the plate I found looked like a crown. Wish I would have traced it before I sold it—"

"That sounds like the perfect spot to begin our expedition. Shall we have a toast, then eat?"

"Why not?" Terri raised her glass.

"To the start of a great expedition!" Walter looked at Terri. "We leave in three days," Walter announced as they clinked their glasses, all four of them, each one of them smiling.

Terri unexpectedly accepted the new job offer, hoping the excitement would fill the growing hole inside her, or at least

****

make her feel safe. Her life at the dive shop had changed; she had reached her goal, what next? *This. This is next,* she told herself.

VOLUME TWO: RAPTIS TRILOGY

****

PART THREE

BIG DIG

VOLUME TWO: RAPTIS TRILOGY

****

27

"Melvin, wow, I don't know how to say this, you know I love you like a father. I would never want to hurt you. You were the one who took a chance on me, and this dive shop has become my family."

Terri went on with this goodbye as Melvin sat down, letting out a heavy sigh. They were alone together, early in the morning before anyone else arrived. Terri was having a hard time keeping from crying, her emotions were overpowering the words she had so carefully practiced.

She felt like she was leaving home all over again. She had to, she wanted to, and she couldn't wait, but this didn't make leaving easy. She loved her parents, and Melvin too.

Melvin had had a sense of what was coming. The last couple of days Terri had grown distant, quiet, and deep in her thoughts, unlike her usual self. He was only half surprised by this, but still he felt so deeply disappointed in her. He just listened, knowing that whatever he would say she would have six answers to. So he came up with just one question. "Have you talked to Mitch about this?"

Terri looked away and then down at the floor.

Melvin knew the answer before it came out of her mouth. She hadn't talked to Mitch in days, she'd been avoiding him, busy with her new friends after work.

She really didn't want to say it out loud but had to. "No, no I haven't."

They both looked away, opposite directions, in silence.

Terri broke the silence with more bad news. "Anyway, they want to leave here soon, they said three days."

"Three days? You're giving me three days' notice?" The sound of disappointment in Melvin's voice was glaringly obvious, it bordered on anger.

Terri couldn't look him in the eyes as more guilt began to creep in. This was short notice, too short, and she knew it. She tried to maintain her confidence as she looked over at the door hoping someone would open it and rescue her. "I'm sorry Melvin, I really am. It's just that—"

"I know, I know, you really, really, want to do this." Melvin just kept shaking his head in ever more disappointment as he looked at her. "I knew this would be too much for you, Terri, you didn't want to listen. Maybe you should take a break first, the break I've wanted you to take, a trip home to visit your folks or something. What about it?"

Terri squirmed. There it was, she knew it, they wanted to send her home again, to rest. "No, no I don't want to go home, Melvin. I'm OK, just ready to move on. Never thought I'd say it out loud." She was looking everywhere but at him.

"Well, tomorrow's Friday, and you're off. I'm sure you'll think of something to tell Mitch tonight." Melvin didn't want to look Terri in the eyes either, she already knew what he was thinking. Mitch was his closest friend, he knew how Mitch was going to be affected. Mitch loved Terri, he was serious about her, ready to marry her, and this was going to be devastating for him.

Terri knew this was going to be a difficult conversation with Mitch, but she wasn't prepared for just how hard it was going to be. Tears formed and began to run down her cheeks, she couldn't keep her voice from cracking. The excited girl in her wanted to grab Melvin and hug him in all her excitement, and to tell him about her fears of being followed and her fears of Mitch wanting to marry her, and how this move would solve it all. She was ready for something new in her life, something bigger. She kept telling herself this over and over, hoping she'd convince herself.

Talking with Mitch, now that was going to be harder than finding the words. How was she going to find the right time? The right words and the right feelings? She should have seen Mitch last night after her day at the beach, but she didn't, she went with her new friends. She was sure Melvin filled Mitch in on the details of the day. And Mitch probably drove to her house last night and didn't find her. This was all getting so complicated, she didn't want to think about it. She couldn't face Mitch's concern and questions about how she felt about everything, including about him.

****

Terri had promised her new best friends, David and Matt, that she would meet them again that night after she got off work. They loved her and wouldn't let her out of their sight. And now, she couldn't wait; they had promised her a night dive the likes of something beyond her wildest dreams, to coax her onto the ship again. After two nights hanging out on that vessel, she couldn't wait to return to it. This was the first dive they had invited her on, so she looked forward to it.

Matt and David were in the shop on the sales floor before the day ended. They had Donna waiting on them hand and foot as they spent money like it was growing on trees, buying extra diving supplies, two and three of everything. Masks, extra straps, bags, and more camera equipment. Donna calculated the huge commission in her head, smiling as she pulled more illuminating glow sticks from the back; they wanted all she had.

"Hey Terri!" Matt was excited to see her.

"Hi guys."

"Ever held one of these? Look." Matt reached into a bag he was carrying and pulled out one of several long narrow boxes. "We just picked these up at the post office today, special order." He lifted a box up to show Terri.

"Wow! Bang sticks? Heard of them, but no, I've never held one, cool!" Terri grabbed the box and opened it, revealing a long black cylindrical "stick" with a handle. She held it up, examining it closely.

David reached over, up close, right on her. He put his hands on hers as she held the stick and slowly pulled one part of the stick back as he stood over her, his head next to hers.

"What is that thing for?" Donna had never heard of a bang stick.

"Sharks, just in case, right? They won't like this shoved up their noses." Terri teasingly pointed it at Donna while trying to inch away from David's uncomfortably close distance around her. She didn't want people to see this at the dive shop. Not on the sales floor, she didn't want anyone to see, especially not Melvin.

"This is where you put the bullet, a 38 special, in this chamber right here." David pointed and pretended to put a bullet in, then together their hands slid the chamber shut. "See? It's that easy." David was right there, still next to her with his hands entwined with hers around the cylinder.

She looked up at him and smiled.

"When you push the head of the cylinder into something, it's like pulling the trigger on a pistol, bang!" David took her arm and reached it out, pretending to jab something.

Donna watched the two.

"Let me show you the important feature, right here, this bright yellow orange switch, the safety switch." He slid it back and forth, demonstrating.

"So that's how it's done." Donna muttered to herself, watching Terri practically fluttering off the sales floor with this guy.

"Let's go!" David patted Terri on the butt.

Terri couldn't help but give it right back to him, grabbing one of his firm butt cheeks and squeezing.

"I'm grabbing my gear right now." She let out an evil chuckle as she wondered just where she really wanted to go with that.

"Grab your gear, Terri, let's get out of here." Matt finalized the bill with a large wad of cash he pulled out of his pocket.

"I'm all set. Oh wait, I was supposed to make a phone call...." Terri thought of Mitch, who was going to show up there soon. With this thought, the pressure was mounting in her head to the point she herself thought it was going to explode. A cold beer would certainly relieve the pressure. "I'm going to shoot out early Donna, we're going on a night dive. I'm sorry, did I even introduce you to my new friends? Matt and David." Terri pointed to them, respectively.

Terri hadn't told anyone but Melvin that day that she was going to quit and move on. Already feeling ostracized by her old friends, she didn't want rumors. And now everything was happening so quickly. Terri really wanted to be the one to tell Mitch, really...well, kind of...oh not really, that would hurt way too much. She would count on Melvin to take care of that for her.

"OK guys, I'm ready to go, let's bring the bang sticks tonight! Sharks!" She teased as she grabbed her bag, all but pushing her new friends off the sales floor and out of the shop. The bell attached to the door clanged as it opened and they walked out. "This is going to be great!" Terri was walking fast, pushing the guys to move faster before Mitch showed up.

****

Ten minutes later the dive shop the door opened. The bell clanged one more time. It was Mitch.

"Hi Mitch," Donna was at her usual station, cleaning and putting together the rental cameras for the next day. She was always the first to greet. Now, barely looking up from what she was doing, she didn't have to, she knew who it was. "Melvin's in the office."

"Terri around? Haven't seen her in a couple of days."

"No, you just missed her, she left early."

"Left early? We were supposed to have dinner together." He was confused. It was Thursday, they always went to dinner on Thursday nights, Thursdays and Mondays at least.

"I don't know anything about that, Mitch. She left with these two guys, called them friends, David and Matt. I don't know, I never met them before. They just left about ten minutes ago, something about a night dive, sorry."

"Diving?"

Donna knew Mitch would be confused, she played it that way. She hated the way Terri treated Mitch, she thought Terri just took advantage of this nice guy. There were very few people, especially men on this island, that didn't drift like plankton in the sea, sticking to something momentarily until any small storm came, uprooting it, sending it floating along.

Mitch wasn't one of them, he was stable, a real rock of a man, the kind of foundation coral could grow on.

"Hey Mitch? I'll go to dinner with you," Donna smiled.

VOLUME TWO: RAPTIS TRILOGY

****

28

Terri and the two men arrived at the ship right before sunset. Doing her best to avoid her guilt over dodging Mitch, she was eager for a drink and some fun. No one could watch her out there, she felt safe. It was quiet on board, quiet as a ghost town as they made their way onto the ship and into the main galley.

"Moses! We're back!" Matt shouted in a demeaning way.

Terri cringed just a little.

Within moments the quiet man appeared with a tray, always smiling, never saying a word. On it was a selection of cold exotic beers and three frosty mugs.

"Help yourself, Terri." David reached over and picked up a beer. "Or, can I select one for you? This is one of my favorites." He was opening it and pouring it into a frosty mug as he spoke. Then he held it out, offering it to Terri.

Terri smiled at David. "Yes, fabulous, I'll have what you're having."

Matt poured his own beer. Together the three of them clinked glasses and toasted. The large engines on the ship rumbled on and warmed up.

"Where are we headed tonight? How about over to Bon Key? Great place to see seahorses this time of night."

"Moses, we're done here, ready to move on," Matt commanded a little belligerently.

The way Matt talked to Moses again made Terri uncomfortable, so she walked away for a moment. She went over to look at that chart of the islands that was lying under the glass of one of the tables. Matt and David joined Terri as she poured over this map and pointed out different locations for a possible night dive.

Both men continued to look over her shoulder. Matt pointed to the reef where he thought she had found her treasure. "Exactly where were you diving last week?"

Terri picked a spot and pointed to it, what did she care whether she was right or not? "I've got the coordinates written down in my dive log, I always keep track." Lying through her teeth to impress the guys, she knew she hadn't written anything down. "Right here is where we started. Where're you guys digging?"

"We have our team of archeologists providing us with the coordinates, appears to be in the same vicinity you're pointing to."

Terri laughed in her head, *Really? Same random spot?* She was actually quite clueless, had no idea where she and Mitch had found the plate and clip. She never wrote down coordinates.

"Your dive log? Did you bring it? Let's look!" David was too eager.

"No, I didn't bring my log." *Shit, it's in my bag, gotta' remember to hide it.* "Left it at the shop, I'll fill in tonight's dive tomorrow morning." Terri kept digging her hole deeper and needed to change the subject. "Where are we diving tonight? We're moving this whole ship to dive? Wow!" She went back to pointing to the chart. "This spot is close, I love this spot!"

"But you've been there before. We're going to explore." David was leaning over her, his cheek practically touching hers as they looked at the map together. "That's what we do."

She could feel his warm breath down her neck.

The loud clang of the anchor retracting reverberated in the background. The bright interior lights dimmed, and the running lights came on. The ship began to move forward. Terri looked out to the shoreline and saw the bright lights of the downtown, the dive shop area.

"Where is everyone tonight?"

"This is it!" David squeezed her waist. "Let's go where no one has ever been night diving!" David looked back down at the map.

Terri was feeling pressure to show them something different, so she studied the map.

"Well, uh...." Terri wasn't sure where to go, she was tired and usually let Mitch lead the way. She looked at all the spots and places where she and Mitch had explored. "Let's see," she said, "well, I have to be at work tomorrow, so that means we won't go far, right? Why don't we just go to Bon Key, we'll go around to the left here, check that out." She had her finger pointed to the spot.

"Boring, boring, boring, Terri. I expect a lot more than that from you! We're going over here." Matt aggressively put his finger in the middle of a channel between two small islands on the outskirts of St. Todos.

Terri looked up for the moon, wondering what the tides and currents would be like way out there at night. She reminded herself that the currents had been pretty stiff that morning.

Matt was looking at her, challenging her. He didn't like playing with girls.

She felt goose bumps running up and down her arms now. She was at a loss for words. She had never been diving out in that channel even during the day, it was deep, with ripping strong currents, *Why there?*

Matt's large hand slapped down on her back, waking her up out of her daydream.

"Come on! This is going to be great! You're playing with the big boys now." The men toasted each other, clinking their glasses. "Relax, have another beer, we're not going to be out there for an hour or so." Matt tipped his glass, finishing his first, then reached for another.

Terri questioned his actions. "Don't you think you should wait on that one till after we dive, Matt? We don't know what it's going to be like out there yet."

"Relax Terri, I can take care of myself, you worry about yourself." Matt's tone bordered on harsh as he replied, making it perfectly clear he felt it was none of her business. He wasn't fond of Terri, hated playing this game, and was now having a hard time holding back.

"Oh, OK, I just didn't know, you know, what the dive plan is and such." Terri was embarrassed for calling him on it, and was apprehensive about that night dive they were about to do out there. But she was trying to act like she did this sort of thing every night. "Why not the channel, wow at night, sure! This will certainly be an adventure!" Holding her glass up, she tipped it toward David and Matt and smiled. "Let's do this!"

The men tipped their glasses forward and let out a devious chuckle. Terri wasn't sure why they were chuckling but felt the need to join in.

She laughed a little.

29

David and Matt had graduated from the Commercial Diving Academy together; they had met there in their first month of class. Both had a deep love of the ocean and a competitive streak larger than a freeway. They had pushed each other through competition into total fitness and hyper-awareness of their surroundings. With both brains and brawn, that uncommon combination in their age group, they had quickly excelled in their careers.

Their first work had been in the harsh, cold conditions of the far northwest, deep, cold, swift moving water with a visibility of two inches at times: not for the weak of heart. One of their first jobs had been in emergency conditions. There David had found out how quickly trouble can arise. Two hundred feet underwater, he had become entangled in wire that wrapped around him with the current, while facing zero visibility with the negative buoyancy of his weight belt pulling at his waist through his dry suit. The fifty pounds of lead it had taken to get him down below thirty feet then felt like a three hundred pound anchor, an anchor wanting to drop. With his arms entangled, David had been unable to reach the quick release of his weight belt and was about to exceed his safe bottom time without completing his task. He knew Matt was twenty feet below him on his own task, but he did not have a visual.

It was Matt who saved David's life. Matt had come over to give his final OK signal, saying that it was time to ascend. It was then he saw that David was struggling in the tangled web of wire. Matt then risked his own life, risked getting caught in that giant web or exceeding his own bottom time by going in. Matt swam in and untangled David with the ease of an athlete.

Matt and David then made it up to their underwater decompression stop-off destination. There they tied off two more tanks, enough air to decompress the nitrogen out of their systems before surfacing. In the deep underwater silence, they spoke with their hands, both thankful and relieved; they had a bond that would never break.

Accumulating a lot of money by just focusing on work, they then moved down to the milder climate of southern California. Next they found themselves getting even warmer off the coast of Louisiana. Their impressive underwater prowess and strength came from hundreds and hundreds of harsh, cold, deep hours under all conditions.

The Caribbean waters were like a warm bath tub to these two, no matter what the time of day, night, or type of current.

****

Tonight, Matt had picked this unlikely spot just to watch how hard Terri would struggle to keep up. It wouldn't be enough to scare her off, just enough to check her ego when she played with these big boys.

By the time they reached the two outer islands, the stars were twinkling above in the darkest of blue sky just as the black night was fighting to take over. Terri was watching this alone with David. They were looking out from the port side, stargazing as they approached their destination.

****

Matt, who had been off somewhere on the boat for most of the ride, reappeared half suited up in his wetsuit with the neoprene arms dangling down at the sides. "Let's do this!" Matt was ready to roll.

The ship was slowing to a stop, in what looked like the middle of nowhere. The engines went into reverse and revved slightly before stopping.

The sound of the anchor dropping caught Terri's attention. "We're here!" Terri couldn't help but let out a slightly nervous giggle. She couldn't believe she was actually going to go diving that night, right there at this random spot. *I should be home in bed*, she thought to herself. *Hah.*

Unfortunately, neither her competitive side nor her curious side could ever say no. And now, diving in one hundred twenty feet of water at night in a channel, just for the hell of it, her first dive with her new friends…she couldn't say no.

"Come on." David grabbed her hand and led her back down to the transom where she had left her equipment. "Let's suit up."

But now Terri was growing more nervous and unusually quiet; everything about this was going against the tiny grain of reason embedded deep inside her. She considered herself an expert diver and here, now, red flag after red flag raised in her head. Still, she chose to keep her concerns to herself and followed. Soon they were all in their wetsuits and stepping into the dinghy.

It was dark. They each had a flashlight. The ship looming above looked haunted in the dark as they shone their lights up on it. It was so quiet out there, no one but spirits of the night were watching them. Matt sped the dinghy to the front anchor line, the strong surface current pulling the ship kept the chain taunt. Matt killed the engines and David grabbed the anchor line as they drifted toward it.

"Here's the deal," Matt explained.

Terri tried to be alert and listen. Finally, a plan.

David tied the dinghy up to the anchor line. Terri hoped he was also listening to Matt.

"We go in, follow the anchor line down, and all meet at the bottom, at the anchor, OK? It's approximately one hundred and twenty feet. We go down, take a peek around, find a monster lobster or three and come back up after seven minutes of bottom time, got that? We decompress at fifteen feet for five minutes."

Terri looked at her watch and a yawn escaped. *What?* "This should wake me up." She looked down into the dark water lapping at the yellow nylon dinghy and then back at the guys who were already putting their tanks on. She started to scramble.

"Don't forget, on the way up, five minutes and fifteen feet, you don't want to get bent out here."

30

Terri's stomach was growling and her head was growing light as she was growing more and more nervous. *Not a good mix.* She fumbled with her equipment while putting it on, having to correct herself several times. The guys were already adjusting the masks on their faces and were ten seconds from going in.

Hurry! Hurry! She heard their two splashes as she tightened her weight belt. She didn't want to lose sight of her buddies, who apparently didn't care if they lost sight of her. She sat on the edge and rolled backwards, holding onto her mask, adjusting it as she rolled into the water. The surface current swiftly swept her away from the dinghy. *Shit, I'm tired.* She put her face in the water. Looking down, she could see the illumination of her buddies' lights. She flashed her light toward them several times as she struggled to swim against the current on the surface.

Her regulator in her mouth, she was sucking hard to catch her breath as she swam, struggling not to go backward and to reach the side of the dinghy where she could hold on and catch her breath. She saw a line to the right laced down the side and grabbed it, relaxing, catching her breath as her body straightened with the current. She could still see the lights of her friends, they were waiting on her. She waved her light toward them one more time, feeling her resistance while trying to hide it. She wanted to climb back in the dinghy and forget about doing this dive.

She could see one light coming closer, it was David. He had let go of the anchor line and was coming to get her. His mask came right up to her and she could feel his strong grip on her tank. He asked her with hand motions if she was OK and she gave the OK signal back. He motioned with his other hand and then grabbed hers, swimming down toward Matt. Terri kicked hard to keep up with his powerful leg stroke, hers no match.

****

David pulled her down against the strong current, along the anchor line to Matt. He placed her hands on the line and motioned for her to grip it and pull herself downward. She held on until her knuckles were white. The two men began to swim on down the line against the current. Terri pulled and pulled and kicked against the current sweeping past her, but she couldn't keep up. They didn't bother to turn around. When she would turn her head to look out, her mask would quiver with the push of the current against it; she felt like it was going to rip off her face. She didn't want to let go of the anchor line to adjust her mask so she just looked down into the current and continued to pull herself along.

She could still see the lights below her as she stopped to slow her breathing and rest. Shining the light outward, a large silver tarpon swam up out of nowhere to investigate the light. Her body jumped as it took her off guard. She was so frazzled she couldn't even laugh at her own reaction. This wasn't fun. She focused the light back below as she began to pull and kick her way down.

Finally at the dark bottom, she looked at her watch and her pressure gauge. There was no time to stay down, she had almost sucked all her air down. Already, it was time to go up. What kind of dive was this? She looked around for her friends. She'd lost track of their lights a while ago. *Damn it, I don't like this!* Looking up, she started to ascend the anchor line as planned. She was trying to be brave, but this wasn't her idea of fun. She hated the dark and she hated surprises, and this was both in one dive.

Three kicks upward and her right fin stuck. She pulled, it wouldn't budge. Her body froze as her imagination began to take off, she was afraid to look down. She looked out for any lights, any signs of her dive buddies, trying not to panic. Suddenly, a rush of bubbles arose from beneath her legs and David came up between them out of the dark, his lights were turned off. Matt came up behind her from below, grabbing at her waist, looking at her with animated suggestions of laughing at her. They both motioned for her to follow them upward.

She met them at fifteen feet. They were both drifting out in the current, holding on to the anchor line. She found a spot to hold on directly above them. She knew she had only been at the bottom for less than a minute looking for them, *they're the ones who'd better hold on*. Seven minutes later and Terri was following the line back up, she had let her friends ascend ahead of her. Afraid to let go, she didn't want to drift off with that ripping surface current, in the dark, again. As her head popped above the water she immediately felt a hand under each arm, instantly pulling her upward and onto the boat.

****

"That a girl" David said as they sat her down. "How was that for a dive?"

Terri looked back at them, she didn't know what to say first. First of all, she hated the phrase "that a girl"— *What did that mean? Girls are less? Girls are weak? Just like a girl?* She wanted to spit, but she was too tired.

"Whoa, thanks for your help guys, I was more tired than I thought! Already put in a whole day at the beach today. Wow, am I tired." Terri was feeling like a weak little girl compared to these two men. Their first dive and she felt like an incompetent boob.

"Looked like you were having a time with that current, huh?" Matt helped her off with her tank.

"Caught me by surprise!"

"A channel, at night? Be more ready next time, aware of your surroundings." Matt was almost scolding her.

Terri was the one getting the lecture this time, but on the other hand, it was these two guys who just took off without her, never looking back. She sat there and took it, trying to be one of the team, but only found more excuses coming out of her mouth. "Sorry, I wasn't thinking, I was busy following—"

"We don't want to lose you next time! We've got to work on your strength."

"Yeah, right, next time, I'll be more careful!" *Strength, mmph, I'm really just tired!* She held on to her equipment as the dinghy quickly shot back to the transom of the boat. Terri wasn't tired, she was exhausted. Everything was hard, even trying to stand up at this point. This wasn't fun for her, it was stupid, crazy, and scary as far as she was concerned. She hadn't seen anything but that one tarpon that spooked her as she was busy choking back her fear of the dark. *This was diving with the big boys?* "This was great though, I had a good time, the best! Thank you!" came out of her mouth.

****

Moses was there with fresh drinks and a platter of fresh cut fruit as soon as they set foot on the pristine back deck. It was past nine now and they were still anchored out at sea. Terri was drained and tired, she just wanted to shut her eyes. Her mind drifted to the great friends she left behind for all of this fun, for enjoying the good life of constant adventure. *I wonder what Donna and everyone will be doing this weekend?*

"You look tired, Terri, Moses can show you to your stateroom if you want to freshen up. We'll have some dinner." Matt interrupted her thoughts as he was busy rinsing the dive equipment.

Terri wasn't paying attention to any of that work, she was used to Mitch doing it for her after their dive excursions.

"Am I supposed to rinse your equipment as well? Terri?" Matt questioned with a halfcocked smile.

"Can you? That would be great, I'm exhausted." With a slight wave goodnight, Terri followed Moses to her stateroom, not thinking twice that Matt was being facetious.

Oh boy, that same stateroom, plush, comfy, way nicer than anything she owned. There was a small private shower and sink. She was ready for bed, she couldn't think about eating. After her shower, she locked her door and slipped into bed, it felt like expensive goose down. She didn't bother to go back up and say goodnight to her new friends. She wanted this night to be over, right now. She thought of her old friends and wondered again what they were doing without her.

As she shut her eyes, drifting off, feelings of homesickness began to creep into her thoughts. She wasn't sure which home she was longing for. Was it her maternal home with her parents' care, or the home she created for herself, her own world? What was she missing as she prepared to cast off into life again....

She shifted her thoughts to waking up in this air conditioned room with the comfortable bed. She was out living on the sea, tomorrow morning the sun would be peeking in on her face through that wonderful window. Now that would make it all worthwhile, if she could just wake up to that view every morning. No more tours, just diving for treasure, adventure— *What a great life.*

<u>31</u>

"Gosh Mitch, I know, I'm jerk, a genuine jerk. I didn't know how to tell you, what was I gonna' say? I didn't know how to say it. Look, you're my best friend in the whole world!"

Mitch sat there looking at her, stunned, hurt, upset beyond words as Terri went on and on with one excuse after another.

She'd had to convince her new friends she had to go to dinner with Mitch that night as promised. This was hard to do, as they wouldn't let her out of their sight. But she insisted there was no way she could blow Mitch off again.

"I can't even believe I was the last one to find out." The hurt in his heart was sticking to every word he said.

"I know Mitch, I'm sorry. I got all caught up in it. I wasn't thinking of anybody but myself as usual, I guess. An archaeological company sailing around the world, finding sunken ships and treasures? How cool is that? Aren't you happy for me? I can't stay here forever, teaching diving, can I? These guys are so cool!" She was giving Mitch the best sales job she could muster under such pressure, but she was so nervous, she couldn't shut up.

He sat there looking so hurt she thought he was going to cry.

"And now you're telling me, you're leaving everything behind and sailing away on that ship in two days?" Mitch was exasperated and trying to wrap his mind around all this.

"I know, can you believe it? I have so much to do! My car, where am I going to park my car?" Fumbling for a piece of

****

paper and something to write with, she thought now was a good time to get organized, maybe she could even divert Mitch's attention by getting him to help. She had been doing her best to mute the enthusiasm which had taken her over. But she had things to do, and if Mitch wanted to hang out with her—

"I guess so, if you're sure that's what you want to do. Why don't you give it a few months though, make sure you like it, living on a ship, with your ears and all. Plus, you don't even know these guys."

"Mitch, what is there not to like, have you seen that ship? I've been out on it, several times now! Wow! It's really something, and comfortable, you should see my stateroom! It has a large window, more comfortable than my own bedroom! I can go to sleep and wake up looking out at the water, every day like a dream come true! I don't even feel slightly seasick at all in that big stateroom, that's how big that ship is!"

Mitch sat there unimpressed, listening to her ramble. How could someone be so impulsive about her life?

"They promised that every two weeks I'll have one week off to come ashore. I'll have that whole week off, pretty cool, right? We can go out diving during that week together, I promise."

"Well Terri, if there is one thing I do know about you, you'll go the distance and do what it takes to get exactly what you want." Mitch's voice was void of emotion. He was hurt and beyond disappointed in Terri. Mitch hadn't wanted to believe Melvin when Melvin said that Terri had given notice. Mitch expected to hear something this big directly from Terri. So Mitch had waited all day yesterday to hear from her. He had driven by her bungalow, no sign of her there. He had driven by the dive shop and found that her car was still parked there. But no Terri. She had just turned around, pointed herself in another direction, and forgotten all about him.

"Mitch," Terri reached out, putting her hand on his thigh, wishing she could put a Band-Aid on his hurt feelings.

"It's OK, Terri."

"No, it's not. I was a jerk, I *am* a jerk...I don't want to lose you! You're my best friend!"

Mitch sat in silence but Terri still couldn't shut up.

"I'm gonna make it up to you somehow," she reached out and squeezed his arm, trying to get him to look her in the eyes.

He took her up on the brief invitation of intimacy and looked her right back in her eyes, searching for her heart, her conscience. "Dinner? Tomorrow night? Just you and me?" he asked her.

Her head began to spin, so many details, so many things to do, so many people to tell, and then the packing. Did she have time for dinner with Mitch? Did she want to make the time? This was uncomfortable. But this was Mitch, her best friend in the whole world no matter what.

"Sure Mitch, dinner tomorrow night, that'll be nice." *Jeez, I can't believe that just came out of my mouth.*

VOLUME TWO: RAPTIS TRILOGY

****

32

Terri's last day of work at the dive shop, there on the beach, was the longest day of her life so far. A fairly busy day, she had already handed the megaphone over to Jim and he was busy replacing her. Everyone was gathered around Jim, instead of Terri, waiting for their next instructions, directions for what to do and where to be when.

Gosh, it's like they've forgotten about me already. You just wait Jim, you'll see what it's like. Terri watched from afar, then she walked out into the water to cool off. She swam out a short distance and turned to face the beach and continue watching. Everyone was busy working and there wasn't much for her to do except go through the motions, make sure everything was on schedule. She looked at her watch. *These guys are done already? They're going to be just fine without me, just fine.* She saw Jim busting out, laughing with half the crew, her old crew, loading the last truck. *Mmmm, wonder what they're laughing about?* Jim glanced over at Terri and then back at the guys. *Probably already thinks he's getting it done better than I ever did.*

Terri held her breath and ducked underwater. She felt like her friends, what used to be "her guys," were all laughing at her. She wanted to disappear. Under the water there was some silence, but she could hear the sound of the large surf bus engine starting up, ready to leave the beach with a load of very happy tourists.

At the end of the day, everyone was busy cleaning. Terri began to say quick short goodbyes to her friends as she passed them one by one in the shop, promising some a lunch and dive the next time they might meet, saying that if it ever gets too busy at the dive shop, heck maybe she could come in and help out sometime.

****

No one had much time to talk, and no one seemed to care. She knocked on the door and poked her head into Melvin's office. "Hi, Melvin."

"Come on in, Terri," he motioned for her to sit down.

"I want to thank you for being such a great boss, you taught me everything." A floodgate of tears opened as Terri professed her respect and love for Melvin; he meant the world to her, she was sad to leave. "And for being a great friend, good times!" She walked over and threw her arms around Melvin who remained seated, then sat back down as she wiped her face with the sleeve of her shirt.

"Thank you, Terri, I knew this day would come sometime, I just wasn't expecting it so fast, so sudden. You've been the best, Terri, it's been a pleasure watching you grow as a person and an instructor. I hope you don't stop teaching." Melvin opened his desk drawer and reached in. "I have a little something for you." He handed her a long slender box.

Terri tore open the wrapping like a little kid. *What?* "A Rolex? Melvin! You didn't!" She held it up, admiring the style before putting it on her wrist. One of his local friends owned a jewelry store downtown.

"Did you look at the back?"

Terri looked at the back of the watch. "It's our dive shop logo! Melvin, I don't know what to say." She stood up and threw her arms around him one more time. "I'm going to miss you so much, you have no idea."

He wiped a tear off her face with his thumb, holding her face and looking her in the eyes. "You be careful out there, big shot."

"I will Melvin, I will."

"You deserve that watch just as much as any hotshot sailor around here. I wanted to be the one to give it to you."

"Thank you, Melvin, thank you!" She held her wrist up, looking at it. The watch glistened with newness, she couldn't wait to take it diving. She was beaming with pride. Terri hated goodbyes more than anyone and most times refused to say the words. "I'll see you soon Melvin, I'll be back in two weeks, you'll be the first person I report to."

"And Mitch?"

"He's taking me out to dinner tonight, just the two of us." Terri looked down at the floor and kicked at it, an annoying trait of hers, before looking Melvin in the eyes. "You know I've got to do this, right?"

"Yes Terri, I know." He gave her a kiss on the forehead, murmuring, "Now go!" and pointed his finger to the door.

Mitch was waiting for her out front. He didn't even bother turning the car engine off. Terri strolled out the front door without seeing anyone. It was like they all had disappeared, she couldn't shout out a final goodbye, everything was happening so quickly. Didn't her friends realize she was actually leaving?

Suddenly, Terri had an epiphany: after all these years, today she had become "one of them," one more piece of plankton, just like those people she always talked about, floating off with the Caribbean current. Now she was the one saying goodbye, the one saying things like, "Hey, when I get back we'll do lunch, go diving." They never did come back and do lunch or go diving one more time, she had seen and heard it a hundred times before. *You learn to not attach to people here, you just enjoy them in the moment, because at some point they will drift away. And some go quicker than others,* Terri said to herself. *Well, everyone has let go of me already. Oh well.*

****

She stepped out of the shop and saw that yes, Mitch's car was already parked out in front waiting for her. She noticed David and Matt nonchalantly walking across the street and waved at them as she opened the car door.

"Hi, Mitch." Terri leaned over and gave him a quick peck on the cheek. "Hard to believe it was my last day, kinda weird."

"I bet. Are you hungry?"

"Sure, let's go have dinner. What's on your mind, I mean what were you thinking about for dinner?" She was already twisting in her seat, she loved Mitch but was afraid of being alone with him tonight. She had this funny feeling he was going to plead a case for her to stay here on this island with him. She was going to have to say no tonight, and no was the hardest word in her vocabulary.

Dinner was terrific, the conversation was light and reminiscing, it was more than Terri could have hoped for. Before she knew it, Mitch was paying the bill and suggesting it was time to leave, she was almost feeling rushed. Looking at her watch, she was only half drunk, it was still early, and she wanted another drink. Mitch was ignoring all her clues, he was so determined to leave.

"Well, I guess I do have some final details to take care of, best to get home on the early side." Of course she wanted another drink but she really didn't want to leave the comfort of Mitch's friendship right now.

"Yes, we both have big days tomorrow."

Terri was expecting the night to go on and on.

"Congratulations Terri, I hope you enjoy your new life ahead, I'm looking forward to hearing all about it when you get back for a week in two weeks."

Mitch seemed so formal, it wasn't what she was expecting at all, just as she was getting relaxed again around him. She was so worried about that little black box he had been carrying around in his pocket, afraid he was going to pull it out.

"Is your car at the dive shop, or do I take you home?"

She ignored the question and asked, "What are you doing tomorrow?" She didn't want the conversation or the evening to end, she was enjoying herself, but Mitch was already standing up.

"Oh, this and that, lots of work on my desk right now, taxes, all that boring stuff."

"I never said taxes were boring."

"Oh, Terri, I'm just teasing you. Let's just say I've got a full day at the office."

Terri had never asked him about his work. She knew he went to work every day, at an office, she'd seen it. She knew he was an accountant, worked with taxes, numbers, money and such, what was there to ask?

Mitch remained standing, it was obvious he was ready to go.

"I did drive in today. I'm going to pick Donna up tomorrow morning, then she'll drop me off. I'm going to let her use my car while I'm gone. She'll take good care of it. So I guess you can take me back to the dive shop." She was waiting for Mitch to offer to pick her up in the morning and take her to the ship, but he didn't.

This was it, no parties, no big woo, she was moving on and no one seemed to notice or maybe even care. She looked down at the brand new watch wrapped around her wrist—*Well, someone did care.*

****

Mitch drove up to the dive shop and into the small parking lot, pulling up next to Terri's car, which sat all alone. He turned the engine off and now it came time for the awkward goodbye.

Terri was quiet. She had hardly said a word all the way back.

"You OK, Terri? You don't have to go through with this if you don't want to. No one will think any less of you." Mitch had a serious tone to his voice.

"Yeah, I'm OK Mitch, homesick already I guess." Terri wanted to cry.

There was a loud banging hard on the side of the car which started to shake, startling Terri. It was Jim. "You left without saying goodbye!" He was almost slurring.

"What the heck! No one had time to say goodbye!" She stepped out of the car, so happy to see Jim's smiling drunk face.

"Come here, you." Jim wrapped his arms around her and hugged her tight, lifting her heels off the ground. "Come on, I've got a going away present for you."

TREASURE HUNT

****

"For me?" Terri looked over at Mitch and smiled. *Someone else did care!* She was thrilled. Jim took her hand and started to lead her to the front door of the dive shop.

"Come on in and I will get it. I was just coming down to the shop to get it, and then I was gonna come looking for you!" Jim reached in his pocket and was fumbling with his dive shop keys.

"Really?" Terri was blushing like a schoolgirl as she held on to his hand, following.

"Guess you don't have a copy of these any more to help me get this door open, huh."

"This present better be good." Terri was excited about Jim's goodbye present, and didn't want to sound impatient. But Mitch was standing behind her and she knew the inevitable goodbye to him was just being delayed.

****

Finally Jim got the key to work. The doorknob turned and the door swung open, and all the lights sprung on. Every one of her friends and acquaintances were standing there on the dive shop sales floor, Melvin in the middle shouting, "Surprise!" at her. *Wow!* Surprised she was!!!!!

Amazing, they did this without my knowing, Terri thought. She prided herself in noticing everything! All their cars had to be parked away from there, and everyone had to be quiet in the dark! They really wanted to pull one over on her. They really wanted to surprise her!

Showering Terri with love and good wishes, picking her up and carrying her on their shoulders in a parade, they even oohed and awed as they let her tell her stories one more time. She was queen again, for the night.

VOLUME TWO: RAPTIS TRILOGY

****

She had her friends back again, and now she had to leave. She forced them all up to her house so the party could continue.

<u>33</u>

"Welcome aboard, Terri." She looked up the gangplank leading her into the luxurious interior. "Is that all you're bringing?"

There were men there she didn't recognize as they squeezed past her. She stood there in a hung-over daze. They were busy going back and forth, carrying supplies of all kinds onto the ship. Water, food, many boxes. Moses was at the entrance pointing directions for where everything was to be put, unpacked, and stored.

"Hi, Matt, I do have more bags. I have another trip to make, just wanted to make this first trip easy. I was hoping—"

"OK, let me help. Walter is anxious to set sail, we've got all of our supplies loaded up already, and we're waiting on you." Matt reached down and grabbed the bag out of her hand, cutting her off, he wasn't interested in what she was hoping. "Let's go, go get your bags, we're ready to ship out soon." Matt was pointing the way back off the ship.

"Oh my, I'm sorry, I didn't know we would be taking off so abruptly. I had a few friends that wanted to come down and say goodbye. I was hoping...." Terri felt all alone. She was really hoping Mitch would appear this morning and help her. As much as she had wanted to ask him for help, she hadn't asked. But she sure wanted to show off her new home to anyone that would come down and look, although she wasn't sure who would show up this early. Anyway, she had just said goodbye a few hours ago. She looked down and patted the pocket, straightening the logo on her new denim shirt.

"Well, I hope you said goodbye to your friends last night, because we have orders to set sail as soon as you step on board."

Terri saw Donna across the pier, watching. She was pulled over on the side of the road, waiting for Terri to come get her last bag, then Donna would park and come aboard.

****

Terri trotted over and poked her head in the passenger side window, grabbing her last bags.

"Looks like they're leaving sooner than I thought, Donna, no time to say goodbye, or have you board the ship." Terri felt herself holding back a tear or two. She backed her head out of the car window and looked up and down the street, hoping to see that familiar BMW racing down the road, or any sign of Mitch's face.

"No time to park and come over? I was hoping to get a peek inside and see your new friends, Matt and David, again." Donna smiled at Terri, giving an exaggerated coy look.

"I don't think so, Donna, they seem to be in a hurry. Hey, thanks again, enjoy my car, be good to her and I'll be in touch in two weeks when I have that week off." Terri threw her a kiss and waved goodbye, heading straight for the gangplank. A new life was about to begin. Walking with a spring in her step, she looked back one last time before walking in.

Donna waved.

****

When Terri arrived back on board, she still didn't recognize anyone among all the working men, no one but Moses, that is. There were many strangers milling around and moving boxes, their shirts already soaked from sweating in the tropical heat at dawn.

Moses was busy counting and receiving inventory, so Moses pointed Terri to one of the new men to have him help her. This new man was gruff, unshaven, didn't have on any good looking logo wear. In fact, he smelled like he had been working outside for the last thirty hours, without stopping.

The smelly sweaty man never bothered to introduce himself and didn't want to know who Terri was. Terri followed the big guy down two sets of ladders to a cabin so forward in the bow she hoped she would remember her way back to the main galley. It was all a maze of shut doors, teak walls, and shiny brass. He pushed the small door open for her. The cabin was sparsely furnished with a single set of narrow bunk beds against the wall, one small desk jutting out from the wall, with a chair.

She looked around. "What's this room? Is this where I keep my extra stuff?"

"This is your cabin."

Finally, he speaks to me. But he must be wrong.

The other bag Matt took from her earlier was already sitting on one of the bunks. She looked at it, wondering if it had been opened for some reason. In her stunned silence, she could hear the water line lapping against the steel hull next to the head of her bunk bed. Her world began to close in as she found herself struggling for a long deep breath. The man's work stench began to overtake her nostrils and she fought back an unexpected wave of nausea. She looked around the room for a trash can just in case. The smelly man was blocking the doorway.

VOLUME TWO: RAPTIS TRILOGY

****

The room was much smaller than the other stateroom she had stayed in. This was a closet, and there were no windows or portholes to look out through! Terri heard two loud clicks and a motor engage. The bow began to rumble and the steel walls in front of her vibrated lightly as the engine revved, warming up. Another sound vibrated the room: the loud clang, clang, clang of the anchor chain banged against the other side of the hull as the men prepared the ship to cast off.

Terri looked at the smelly man in the doorway. "Are you sure? I stayed in a different cabin the other nights I was on board, it had a window." She looked around, then back at him, hoping he would realize his mistake. He just stood there without offering a word of advice.

"We've never met, my name is Terri." She looked up at the large man who was now beginning to look like the wet dog he smelled like. She stuck her hand out as a friendly gesture.

He ignored Terri's hand and reiterated to her without concern, "This is your room."

"Can you tell me where the shower, the head is?" She looked behind the door hoping to see an attached room.

"Down the hall." He walked away, not bothering to shut the door behind him.

She watched as his large frame lugged down the hallway, she never even got his name. *Crap, I hope that guy's not coming out with us.* She sniffed the air and gagged as the smell of that man lingered behind.

****

The large engines revved again as they readied for the excursion. The walls began to close in on her and her head was spinning. She couldn't get her bearings. The smell was overtaking her and she couldn't look out a window. "This has got to be a mistake—" Feeling closed in, she needed to get to the bow before any seasickness hit.

This was her first official day and already off to a weird start. Shutting her small cabin door behind her, she realized there was no lock. *Huh? No Lock?* Trying to relax, she headed upward to the main floor, the one she was used to. She was sure that David would get all this about the wrong cabin straightened out once they were done loading the ship: That guy she followed just didn't know who she was.

She couldn't remember her way out and up with all these shut doors. She was so turned around in this part of the ship. *Where is everyone?* Looking around, the hallways became noticeably stark, all the doors were noticeably shut. What was behind them? Who was behind them? Reaching down, she held a knob and began to slowly turn it. That door was locked. She tried the next, so was it, and the next, locked. *What the hell? No lock on my door? But all these are locked?*

The last door did open, and it revealed the stairs up to the next level. *This must be where we came down.* She went upward, looking for the galley and her friends. Everyone was gone. She sniffed the air. *Phew, those guys smelled bad, especially that last one.* The engines locked into gear. She stopped and held on as the ship took an unexpected quick jolt backward. But then, with another surge, they were gracefully moving in forward.

Looking out and back to shore, she could see that some of her friends did show up. She studied the group, hoping to see Mitch in the small, very small, crowd, but she didn't see him. Wildly waving with both arms, jumping up and down, she hoped her friends would see her final wave goodbye as the ship moved away. On the deck above she heard her friends, Matt and David.

"Thank God, we're finally on our way. This St. Todos, what a drag, such a tourist trap."

Terri stopped smiling as she listened. She looked down at the logo on her pocket and found herself agreeing. *Well, it is a tourist trap after all, and I have worked with tours for years, but not anymore!* Wanting to find her friends, she followed their voices up the outdoor stairwell.

Then she heard Walter's voice. His whole demeanor sounded different now, somewhat hostile as he said, "You men did an excellent job, you will be rewarded. Although I must say, with her ego it was almost all too easy! I thought it was going to take a lot more than that to pull her out of that dismal dive shop."

She could hear all three men laughing about her now. *What? Dismal dive shop? What a nasty thing to say.*

****

Terri looked out toward land. The land was getting further away as they were now leaving the harbor entrance. The ship began to gain speed.

Looking back at the bay's east point, she made out what she could swear was Mitch looking for her with a pair of binoculars. A tear ran down her cheek. If it was Mitch looking, she didn't want him to see her crying. Wiping her eyes, she found her way back to her room through the maze of shut, locked doors. Her room was completely dark with the lights out. She laid down on the bottom bunk bed and began to sob, her intuition telling her she had made a big mistake.

There was a light knock on the door. Terri choked her tears back and wiped her eyes with the bottom of her shirt before opening the door just a crack to peek out. It was Moses, he had a cold glass of water with a wedge of lemon stuck on the rim of the glass.

"Thank you," Terri managed to say from behind the door, not wanting him to see her swollen red eyes. Moses just smiled and nodded, then silently walked away.

VOLUME TWO: RAPTIS TRILOGY
****

<u>34</u>

"I'm looking, I'm looking!" Terri was at the top of the ship with Matt on one side and David on the other, looking out with binoculars, gazing across the vast reef. "It all looks so, you know, different from up here." Terri tried her best to converse with the guys. It used to be so easy, but now she was so bored and was feeling more and more isolated.

Matt and David were silent.

They had been silent with Terri since they set sail. She did whatever she could to be helpful and did what they asked, but she really had no idea where that spot they were looking for was. She really didn't know where she had found the plate and money clip she had showed them. It was their expedition, not hers. Certainly they must have had other plans before meeting her.

They never upgraded her room, those rooms were for guests only they said, guests like she was before she took the job. Now she was a worker, with worker accommodations, get over it. Their next suggestion was to shut up and put a bucket next to the bunk if being a land loving greenhorn wussy was her thing.

She decided to never ask again.

There was no alcohol either; a strict rule of Walter's. Terri wasn't ready for or aware of that rule, there had been plenty of alcohol around before, during the party and all.

Day six and she was so lonely, there was no one to talk to, or at least no one who would talk back. She did feel she had found a friend in Moses through their brief encounters. Moses would come down and knock on her door with that refreshing cold glass of water with the lemon wedge at the most convenient times. She liked to think it was because he cared.

Terri's one sided conversations with Moses grew longer and longer as she began to tell him her life story, including the various circumstances and events that had led her out there on this lonesome treasure hunt.

Moses always listened and smiled at her as she talked to him.

She began to find comfort in his beautiful wide eyes and bright smile. She was making a much needed friend.

"It was a tough decision, Moses. I love Mitch dearly, and it was hard to explain to him. He's my best friend, I love him like a dear pet dog."

She could see the expression on Moses' eyebrows change as he listened.

"OK, that didn't come out right, but you know, I'm a loner."

****

So far they had been lumbering the mother ship down the reef systematically, dropping anchor, getting in the little dinghy, swimming, swimming, diving, diving, and repeatedly asking her, "Is this it?" Is this it?" With these fifteen square miles of reef jutting up in the middle of the sea, she was absolutely clueless where Mitch had taken her. She was also clueless why this archeological company was so interested in her.

"One week now and that's all you can say? This is one simple spot we're talking about, Terri. You repeatedly said yourself you could show us this spot with a blindfold on. Each day we spend out here, Walter is growing more and more impatient."

"Yeah, well, I thought I could, all right? What can I say? I'm sorry! I keep telling you, it's all a blur to me now! I could show you a lot of other things." Terri didn't understand what was going on, it was hot and the days were ticking by doing nothing. She wished she had kept her mouth shut about her dive trip out there. They were doing nothing but obsessing about this particular dive spot. Her eyes hurt from all the glare, the constant looking through binoculars. And her ears were crispy red and peeling from the constant sun exposure.

Terri had a few questions herself. "I thought you were the experts out here on this reef, so why are you so interested in my find? What have you found? Why are we out here?" She was frustrated and done with all this and wondered what was so important. She knew this whole trip, this large ship, all this equipment, couldn't be completely focused around her one find, a random money clip and a plate they'd never seen. *Could it?* Matt and David had said they were surveying the whole reef.

This was just too strange, and now Terri's mind was spinning.

She was quite bored with this so-called adventurous job already. She was missing the quick action of the beach, tour after tour, and her friends, not to mention all those crazy tourists with their funny questions. She looked back out to sea, wondering if Matt and David would ever start digging on something out there like they had promised.

"What about a grid? Shouldn't we be setting up a grid of some kind?"

"We've got all that under control, Terri." David dismissed all of her questions.

"What is it you're doing out here?" Terri was rather defiant now, not understanding. She stopped herself from getting a little angry.

"You just keep looking for that spot, Terri, and if I were you, I would find that spot soon, real soon." Matt didn't even bother looking at her as he spoke, he just looked straight out to the open sea with the binoculars up to his eyes.

"Yeah right—" she giggled, trying to lighten the mood, "or what, you're gonna fire me? Or something?" She was hoping real hard in the back of her mind they would. Fire her.

"Something, that's for sure," Walter's deep voice came up from behind them.

35

A shiver went right up Terri's spine to the hairs on the back of her head. She was beginning to hate the sound of Walter's voice.

"I've been patient, Terri, very patient with you."

Terri's eyes widened as she turned around to look at Walter as he spoke to her. She felt like a schoolgirl caught giggling in the classroom during a lecture. Nervous, she couldn't keep her mouth shut. "Gosh Walter, this isn't anything like I expected, I mean, what are we doing anyway? I thought we were going to meet National Geographic out here, dig on a site, why so much pressure on me? I'm just the photographer, right? I haven't even seen the camera you were going to provide me."

Walter took a half step closer to Terri, looming over her as he spoke. "You have found something that belongs to me, Terri."

"What? I did? You can certainly have it back!"

"As it turns out, I already helped myself." Walter reached in his front pocket and pulled out the silver money clip with the large gold medallion, holding it up for her to see.

"Hey! That's mine!" She grabbed for the money clip as he easily held it up and out of her reach.

"You are mistaken. This is a clip I gave to my brother, Drake, a long time ago, a very long time ago." Walter held it up to her face and pointed. "Did you ever bother reading the engraving on the back?"

VOLUME TWO: RAPTIS TRILOGY

****

"Well, yeah, but, I didn't know." Suddenly remembering her precautions: "Hey! You had to go through my underwear to get that!" She put her hands on her hips with an indignant look on her face.

He chuckled at her feistiness. "Right here it says 'Drake, we did it. Walter.' See that?" He pointed at it with his beefy index finger. "Walter, that's me. Drake, that's my poor brother who died while searching for the third and last one of these."

"Really? How would I know any of that? Well, gosh Walter, you can have it, OK? I mean, if you would have told me that when we met, you could have had it a long time ago." Terri was so nervous, she just wanted to keep the peace, bide her time. In six days she'd be off this ship and not look back, lesson learned, her ego bruised, but glad to be done. Six days.

She didn't yet know all this was far from over.

"Thank you Terri, I do have it." He held it up and looked at, twisting it around in his fingers. "Unfortunately, that's not all." He moved his face closer to hers. "You found a plate as well."

He was too close. "I believe you have found my lost treasure and, you—" he poked his right index finger into her chest— "you are going to find it again for me."

"I sold that plate the day I found it. I don't have it, Walter, I…."

"I know Terri, you sold it to that repulsive Russell with his stupid handmade eye patch and round hook. We took care of him."

"What, Russell? You know him? I really don't know him, alright? We just spent that one night out near Locket Key. He gave me twenty-five dollars for that plate." Terri lied to Walter about the price, not wanting to raise any more of his suspicions about any more treasure. She was doing her best to distance herself from any reputation that old man Russell may have had.

"Let's just say, I know enough about him. For years, I cursed him being alive when he should've died, like my brother. But here we are. And it turns out to be you, of all people, who is leading me back to what is mine." Walter hovered over her as he talked. "You stupid girl, twenty-five dollars for that plate? Russell pulled one over on you! You found the tip of a treasure worth millions and millions of dollars. He found it for me once, and I took it!" Walter swiped his hand as if he were taking it again. It was the most animated she had seen Walter yet— "Only to be lost again, along with my brother Drake," Walter said gruffly.

"Well, I don't know about any of that, and now that you have that clip back in your hands, we're OK, right? Even though you went through my room—and you know what else—to get that clip, when hey, you could've asked, it's all yours. From me to you. I don't know where that dive spot is. The real truth is, I've only been out on this reef once, alright? One time and that's when I found it, pure luck." She looked at Walter with a cocky smile, wanting him to turn around and walk away. She was quite angry with herself that she hadn't seen all this coming.

"You *are* a silly character." He patted her cheek firmly, twice, as he spoke.

Her expression didn't change.

He leaned down closer into her face and got louder. As he did, his own face changed color, becoming a bright red ball of frustration. "But I'm afraid you are *not* getting the point."

Terri stood there like a deer caught in headlights. The back of his hand came down and cut hard across her cheek. Her face swung to the side as she lost her balance.

David stepped over and caught her as she fell, but only to hold her back up facing Walter. She stepped back on his toes hard with her heels.

"Let me go! You bastard!"

David squeezed her tighter as she struggled.

Holding her hand up to her face, Terri could feel the wetness, blood. The ring on his finger had cut through her cheek. Her face was stinging and beginning to throb. A knot began to form in her throat, and she couldn't talk. Terri wanted to cry but blinked her eyes to fend off the tears, refusing to cry or even release a single droplet. She swallowed repeatedly to stave off that feeling of panic and hopelessness welling up inside her, but she had nothing left in her mouth, which was too bad because she wanted to spit on David.

"Now, are you going to start remembering just where that channel was? So we can retrieve what is mine?" Walter lifted his hand up to strike again.

"So you mean...." The point was starting to sink in at least as deep as the cut on her face. The cut area was starting to swell as blood dripped from her cheek onto the stark white floor. "You mean there is no Archaeology Unlimited?"

Matt and David smiled as Walter responded so intensely he was tossing spittle into her face. He too was done with her. "Now you're catching on!" Walter looked out toward the reef for a moment and then swung back to face her. Reaching around and grabbing the back of her hair, he forced her to look out to the sea with him, his face close to hers as he spoke. "We have been out here looking for my brother, and our treasure, for thirty years now, and haven't found it. Yet, somehow you, you stupid girl, go out one time, just one time you say, and discover it?"

Again Walter pulled the silver clip out and held it up for her to see. "You had better start thinking, looking harder, praying to God, whatever it takes. The next time we put that anchor down and we don't find what we're looking for...." Walter let go of her, almost shoving her away as he reached into his back pocket and pulled out a little faded red book. He held it up, showing her.

"Hey!" Terri exclaimed, "My address book!"

"Why, yes it is, Terri, and every time we drop the anchor and you don't find *you know what—*" he said in a sinister, light, sing-song tone. He opened to a random page, pointing again with his finger "—someone," now six inches from her face, "is going to get hurt."

Terri stared out past Walter. *What? What? How did all this happen? How? Now someone is going to get hurt? Because of me?* She stood there as her heart sank. She had no idea how to find that spot. No idea.

VOLUME TWO: RAPTIS TRILOGY

****

<u>36</u>

"Melvin? There's someone out here looking for Terri. He won't give me his name and he looks...I don't know, scary."

"Scary?" Melvin stood up.

"You'll see."

Donna ushered Melvin out to the ragged old man standing in the middle of the sales floor.

"Uh huh," Melvin uttered under his breath as soon as he saw the man. The man's hair was long, gray, gathered in a ponytail. It was obvious he had been through some terrible accident, with a weathered old eye patch, and a faded scar reaching far down to his chin, and a brass hook fashioned into a circle in place of a right hand. He stuck his other hand out to Melvin as he walked up.

"Yes sir, I'm looking for an instructor gal, named Terri, I believe. Tall." He held his good hand up to the height he remembered. "Blond, beautiful, she said she worked here."

"Well yes, she did work here, until recently. May I ask who you are?"

"What? Did she move back to the States? Is she OK?" The old man became agitated at the news, and he wanted answers.

"What did you say your name was?" Melvin took a step back. He had never seen this ragged gentleman before, but there was something about him that rang familiar. Melvin tried not to stare. Had he seen a picture of him before?

The old man paused for an uncomfortably long time before replying, looking over both shoulders, as if someone could be listening.

"Russell, my name is Russell." He looked down at his callused toes poking out from his old flip-flops before gaining enough confidence to look Melvin in the eyes. "I met Terri out on my little Key, with her friend. I have the bar out on Locket Key."

Melvin remembered Mitch telling him about a weekend and a night on Locket Key.

"Yes, well I'm afraid she doesn't work here anymore, Russell. And as a past employer, I'm not allowed to give any personal information, I hope you understand."

Melvin was done but Russell was insistent. "OK, but what about telling me where she is, as a friend."

"I'm sorry Russell, I can't tell you."

"If she's your friend, I have reason to believe she could be in danger if she's not careful." Russell's one good eye focused in on Melvin's. Russell's intuition told him he was not being taken seriously.

"Yes, well I'm sure she will appreciate the message, I will give it to her the next time I see her."

"*If* you *do* see her again...." Russell scowled. "Or will the headlines report just another young lady missing, vanished?" He stood there staring at Melvin.

"Yes, well, I thank you for your concern. But now I must get back to work. It was Russell, correct?" Melvin stuck his hand out to Russell, he was ending the conversation there.

Russell didn't accept the hand offering, he just continued on. "You *have* to take me seriously. They've already been out to my island, ransacked it and beat the crap out of me. Took me almost a week to get here to tell her."

As Russell's voice grew more desperate, Melvin grew more irritated. He did his best to be nice, but now it was time to get back to work.

"Thank you again, Russell. But I don't feel I have to do anything. Now, is there anything else I can help you with, a new mask? Some new fins? Maybe brush up on some of your diving skills? If not, well I'm going to have to ask you to leave."

Donna, who had been standing nearby, took one step back behind Melvin. This guy, Russell, was beginning to act strange.

Russell let out a grunt of disgust before turning around, limping on his stiff right leg toward the door—but not without having the last word. "You better hope I find her, before they do."

With that, Russell left.

The door opened and closed, the bells rang out, issuing their warning, leaving Melvin and Donna both standing there wondering in silence: *What was up with that?*

Melvin looked at Donna and was the first to say it out loud. "What has Terri gotten herself into now?"

****

Russell left the dive shop with nowhere to go. He had thought it would be that easy: find Terri, warn her. Now she was gone. And it was becoming obvious, looking down at his grooming and attire, that no one was going to look twice at him or take him seriously. Well actually, everyone looked twice, but they all just kept walking, faster away.

Across the street from the dive shop was a larger chain hotel complete with its own public dock extending into the harbor. A bar perched out on the end. Russell had noticed it on the ferry ride in, passing it as they came into the harbor that morning.

Cruise ships were tied up to the dock, gangplanks all down, pouring tourists out by the hundreds. Surf buses packed full of these tourists were going every which way, pulling out of the large parking lot, cruising down the main roadways to their destinations for the day. All this was going on just as the town was beginning to wake up.

The commotion was enough to send Russell over the edge and running for cover. With cars whizzing by him at all of thirty-five miles an hour, all those horns honking, and scads of people shouting, walking, talking, pointing, closing in all around him, his head spun. There were people of all kinds, and children, lots of children. Russell realized as he stared how few children he had seen in the last few decades; they were rarely out at his hideaway. His world was so hidden, it made the island of St. Todos feel like the crowded streets of New York City at morning rush hour.

Russell tried to lift his head up, forming a visual in his mind of who he used to be, looking forward as he shuffled through the lobby of the hotel with his stiff leg. There were screaming children running around, mothers barking orders at them, telling them to be quiet and that if they would just stop running there would be fun soon. Everyone was clad in their bright, stiff, brand new, colorful matching beachwear like they were from a page in a magazine. And there were many other sounds and sights he had never seen before.

He could hear the conversations stop and the heads turn as he limped by. He could sense the hushed disdain and the children's silent whispers with questions as he passed. He moved as quickly as his leg would allow him on the slick marble floors. He had every right to be there, he told himself, even as it became glaringly obvious to him what he had become.

He found his way to the solace of the tiny bar out on the far end of the dock. Still early in the morning, only a serious few bent on a relaxing morning were settled up to the bar. His body began to release some tension as he felt on familiar ground. The young bartender, seasoned with years on the sea, greeted him with a smile.

"Fancy having you at my bar, mate! What'll you 'ave?"

Surprise at this kind greeting clearly showed on Russell's face.

The bartender tried again, "What brings you over to these islands mate? I've met you before at your bar on Locket Key, right?"

Russell extended out his good arm, feeling welcomed, feeling a little closer to the comfort of his home. "Thanks, let's make it a stiff one, OK? Tequila, straight up, anything you got."

The young man quickly complied, setting a large double shot down in front of Russell.

"This one's on the house with my pleasure." The bartender was smiling, feeling good about having a real local icon at his bar.

"Hey kid, I'm trying to find that gal who worked across the street, Terri, you know her?"

"Bloody slippery one that one is, mate. What'd she do now?"

"Just lookin' for her. If you see her, tell her I'm lookin' for her."

"She don't come in here often mate, but when she does, I'll let her know."

Tequila and stories began to fly as Russell sure did know how to entertain people. By noon a small crowd had gathered around Russell as he told tale after tale about what it had been like in the old days on the islands, before all this "cruise ship mania," as he called it, began to spoil his seas.

By two o'clock, Russell was clearly drunk and was escorted to the swimming pool by some of his new friends who started encouraging him to dive into the chlorinated pool. Their ulterior motive was for him to soak off some of the accumulated smell and grime. One more festive round of beers by the poolside and Russell was passed out, snoring on a reclined white plastic lounge chair.

****

By the time he woke up, his new friends had abandoned him for the next best thing. Brushing his hair back with his fingertips, looking at the clean pool, he felt alive, he felt human now. Surrounded by all these people, listening to the sounds of laughter and conversation, he closed his eye and remembered when. When he opened his eye again, he looked down at his dented brass ring and tattered pants. His soul was brought back to his reality. He was a freak to have fun with, but in the end, he was still alone.

Russell stumbled out to the street once again. His ferry didn't leave for another hour.

As Mitch was driving up to the dive shop, he found the old bartender on the sidewalk across the street. *There he was.* Melvin had told him earlier on the phone about the strange man with the eye patch and the brass round hook.

Russell was still half drunk and didn't recognize Mitch as he walked up to him.

"Hey! I heard you're looking for Terri."

Russell stood to attention immediately upon hearing Terri's name. He stopped walking and put his closed hand up to his forehead like a visor, to see who was talking. "I've got to get ahold of that young lady. Have you seen her?"

"What's so important? I'm one of her closest friends. We met at your bar when Terri sold you that plate."

"Yes! Yes! That's right, now I recognize you! That plate. There's danger, big danger. They're looking for the wreck again and I can't get out there. They've already ransacked my bar and home, and they beat the crap out of me." Russell was relieved to see Mitch and explain. Mitch would listen. He had to.

"What are you talking about, 'danger' and 'looking for the wreck again?'" Mitch didn't understand.

Russell's voice lowered to a hushed whisper as he answered Mitch's question. "The plate, it's from a lost wreck, with a lot of gold, a fortune in gold and more."

Mitch listened but looked skeptical. This old man sounded ridiculous. Terri simply ran off with an archeological dig. With his fifteen years on these islands, Mitch had heard so many stories about treasure and lost gold, but of course had never seen any. Nothing had ever been found. So Mitch was thinking Russell was telling just one more story, just another tale. "Yeah, well, that's what they all say." Mitch was unconvinced.

"Look, I've seen the gold, I've touched it with my own hands. These guys out there, they're dangerous, they've killed all my friends, they did this to me." Russell held his hooked hand up to his eye patch. "You need to get a message to her." Russell was insisting. "You have to."

"OK. Why don't you write down some names for me, I'll do some investigating."

"I don't have any names!" Russell shouted. "I just know that they are dangerous, very dangerous, and won't stop until they get what they want. They're pirates, modern day pirates, just as bad as ever, that's what they are." Russell's stomach was growling from lack of food and his head began aching for another drink. He was feeling more and more agitated by Mitch's ambivalence. He wanted to loop his brass ring around Mitch's neck and shake some sense into him. It looked like no one there was going to believe him.

"Well, I'll tell you what, Russell." Mitch was calm, he knew Terri, she would be OK. "Terri will be back here in less than a week, in six days, I'll talk to her and find out what's up."

Russell didn't like what he heard and drew Mitch closer, his one bloodshot eye looking right square into Mitch's, the smell of alcohol reeking through the large toothless gaps in his front teeth. Grabbing onto the front of Mitch's shirt, twisting it, he drew Mitch closer.

The old man's strength shocked Mitch. This old guy practically lifted Mitch up onto his tippy toes. Mitch hadn't considered what this guy was capable of.

"I lost everything to these guys. Let's hope you don't lose your Terri. If I were you, I'd go find her right away." Russell urged then let go of Mitch's shirt, dropping him back down on his heels, watching the now scared look on Mitch's face. *This guy Mitch, he's just an office worker*, Russell thought, *he probably can't even imagine what danger is*. With that thought, Russell shrugged and walked away, disgusted. He didn't think any of the people he had met that day would ever understand real danger. He was done, Terri wasn't anywhere to be seen, and he wasn't going to start looking for her on his own. And no one else seemed to care much.

<u>37</u>

Terri was perched at the tip of the bow on the inflatable, holding on as if it were a bucking bull, bouncing over the choppy seas. Looking out into the ocean for any familiar signs she might recognize, another day had passed and she hadn't even felt close. She was looking hard for the dark, deep, wide channel she remembered.

On the shallow side of the reef looking east, all visible landmarks—mountain peaks, the end points of an island—were behind her. There was nothing to lineup on. She was just looking out at empty vast blue ocean and light turquoise seas. It all looked the same, just water.

She lifted her right arm and pointed, with David turning the wheel to follow her signal. They slowly glided through the turquoise shallows, following along the shallow side of the reef, looking for the promise of a deep channel.

She hadn't seen Walter all day and didn't want to. She was scared of him and what he might do to her. All she wanted was to find this place and then to go back home to St. Todos.

****

Up ahead, she saw a promising sign, a strip of deep, dark blue. It had the look of a channel leading from the shallow water through the reef to the dark blue. *Could this be it? The channel we swam through?*

She let the boat glide past, then held up her arm closing her fist, signaling David to come to a stop. She had her short wetsuit on, ready to jump in and look. She rolled overboard, with Matt following. Terri swam away, leading the search.

This spot began to feel somewhat familiar. At first she couldn't really tell for sure, places on the reef were looking all the same, the same seascape, the same fish—like wallpaper repeated over and over again for fifteen square miles. Then a large colony of staghorn coral growing up from the bottom and branching out to the surface like a huge shade tree caught Terri's attention. *A familiar sight!* Her eyes widened as she began to remember seeing this beautiful untouched site. Now she turned to Matt with excitement. Her job was done! She gave him the thumbs-up hand signal with both hands.

Her breath started to labor as she swam faster, looking for the channel's entrance in the coral. She was this close to going home. A wave of relief took over as she swam up to the opening. *There it was*, the channel she had been looking for. Turning around, she motioned Matt to follow her in as she swam up to the area where she had found the plate and the money clip.

The channel itself was approximately forty-five feet deep. Matt motioned Terri to surface with him.

She was thrilled, her job was done. Sure, they were rough, sure, she was upset and pissed off, but she would let it all go and walk away with a good story once they anchored in the harbor and she could go home.

Rising to the surface, they looked down below at the whole reef from directly above. For the first time, Terri had a different perspective on the dive spot, unnoticeable from under the water.

Matt had his arm up and out of the water, motioning David to speed over in the dinghy. Looking down and to the left was part of a submerged boat lying on a layer of coral: it could only be recognized from a certain angle.

David was standing up in the dinghy, taking coordinates with his compass, signaling with his handheld radio to the ship to take their coordinates.

They had found what they were looking for.

Walter let out one long blow on the ship's horn. Matt and Terri swam over to the inflatable, and they all rushed back to the ship.

****

"Congratulations, Terri." Walter was at the back of the ship as the three arrived. He had on a full wetsuit. Mask and fins in hand, he wanted to witness the find himself.

Terri's mood darkened at the sight of him.

"Well, I found what you were looking for. My job is done." Terri was confidently looking up at Walter, trying to smile.

"Let's go take a look at this find so I can confirm for myself."

The inflatable rocked as Walter stepped down. It now felt crowded with the four of them as they pushed away and sped back to the dive spot. Matt had positioned a buoy so they could zip right back.

Terri was forced into the water with Walter and Matt to show them exactly where she had found things. Walter swam over the reef to get a closer look at the ship on the coral. There it was, the haunting back transom of the boat, the *Ol' Wife*, faded, weathered, rotted from the years. Underneath lay the treasure. They could anchor the ship on the deep side of the reef, the windward side, not too far away, and work from there with the smaller workboat.

They swam back to the inflatable, where Walter discussed his plans as if Terri didn't exist. They were going back to port.

She kept quiet and to herself. She just wanted to go home.

38

"Yes, absolutely, I'll call you as soon as I find out anything." Mitch was scribbling notes around a phone number he had written down while talking with Terri's mother who was saying that Terri had called and announced she needed a change. Terri had said she was done with tourism, so was going to quit her job and go work on an archaeological dig at sea. Terri's mother and father had tried to talk some sense into their daughter, but sense had fallen on deaf ears. Terri had told them she was ready for something new, and that she would call them again after her first two weeks on the job at sea. So now her parents were worried they hadn't heard from her at the two week point.

Her father had actually tried the number Terri had given them. They'd had the gumption to insist on having one. But Terri told them she would contact them as soon she came to shore, that this number was only in case they had an emergency of some sort. The phone number rang to an answering machine which played a short message: *"Archaeology Unlimited, leave a message."* Now, call after call, her parents had never reached a real person, just always the same message, and they had never gotten a call back. They were beginning to worry. So they had done the only other thing they knew to do, call Mitch.

Mitch dialed the number that Terri's parents gave him as soon as he hung up from their call. A man's voice, one with a slight English accent, gave a very brief announcement. *"Archaeology Unlimited, leave a message."* After that message, Mitch heard a beep and then a second announcement, *"There is no room to leave a message."*

Mitch tapped his pen on the desk. He hadn't heard from Terri at all. Neither had Melvin, nor had anyone else for that matter. Terri had said she would be back to see them all, to spend her week off after two weeks at sea. Yet, with Terri that sort of plan didn't mean much. And she was not really much of a communicator. So there was no telling where she was now.

Or, Mitch told himself, maybe he should take a trip over to Vandorn as Terri's mother had just suggested, to visit Archaeology Unlimited's base for himself, to see who those people were and what they were actually up to.

Mitch picked up the phone and dialed. "Just letting you know I won't be coming into work tomorrow." He hung up and continued to tap his pencil on the desk. He picked up the phone again and dialed. "Melvin, it's me, Mitch. I just hung up from a call from Terri's mom and dad. They're worried. I'm going to take a trip over to Vandorn, see if anyone knows about this Archaeology Unlimited. They must have an office there or something. I have this phone number for them Terri gave her parents...."

Mitch continued tapping the pen after he hung up. He looked back at the phone number and notes he had written down. "Terri, what have you gotten yourself into? Shit."

PART FOUR

BREAK FREE

VOLUME TWO: RAPTIS TRILOGY
****

<u>39</u>

The ship was anchored out in the middle of the harbor on the sleepy island of Vandorn, a truly beautiful site. Onlookers were stopping to examine the ship's beauty from afar, such ships rarely anchored in this port. The ship was capable of docking at the harbor's small dock, but stayed out, anchored away from the others.

Mitch had left early that morning, taking off by himself, in his own ride. With twin one-fifty horsepower outboards, his Whaler flew over the calm sea. On the water in his speedboat, fast, stealthy, Mitch was in his element. Coming around the south point, Mitch was surprised to see the big ship anchored out at the entrance to the harbor. It had been two weeks and the ship was sitting right here? So where was Terri?

Questions began to spin in Mitch's head as he thought about the two men, Matt and David, who Terri had taken off with to work on some sort of project. Then Mitch's imagination ran wild with jealously at the thought of David and Terri together, which everyone had been suggesting behind Mitch's back. But Mitch tried to control this jealousy boiling up inside as he slowed his speed way down at the harbor entrance. He motored over to the dock at the Rockside Marina and tied up for the morning.

******

He recognized the yellow inflatable tied up there as well. There wasn't anyone around the dock. A bartender who also doubled as the marina's morning manager was busy cleaning behind the counter. Mitch walked toward town, not sure what he was looking for, but to look around, to see if he could locate this Archeology Unlimited. Their place was apparently somewhere near town according to Terri's weak attempt to describe where it was located when Mitch had questioned her.

Walking around the two-block town, he couldn't find anything resembling the office Terry had vaguely described. He resisted asking anyone questions, not wanting to draw suspicion. He started to walk back toward the marina when he heard the whine of an outboard motor. Looking out, he could see the yellow inflatable gliding out of the marina with four men in the boat.

Mitch took a chance. He walked back to the marina and sat at the bar, directly in front of the bartender and marina manager, and ordered an orange juice. He was served a glass of fresh mixed Tang with one melting ice cube floating at the surface, with a small winged bug floating next to it.

"That'll be three dollars." Mitch didn't want to argue with that, he simply put the money down and even included a tip for the lukewarm orange water. Mitch wanted information.

"Sure is a beautiful ship out there, isn't she!" Mitch tried to make conversation.

The bartender simply nodded yes.

"Where do you think she's from? Looks so mysterious."

The bartender shrugged. It was apparent he wasn't interested in talking.

Mitch finished the orange-flavored lukewarm drink and quickly put this marina on his list of least favorite places to visit. Mitch walked away from the bar without a nod. In the background he heard the whine of the same outboard motor approaching the marina again.

He looked over and watched as the inflatable came back in. He slowed his pace and picked a destination to walk to so he could blend in and observe. This time it was two of the men with a third person, obviously not Terri. A tall, muscular black man was the first to exit the dinghy. Together they walked up the dock without talking, the tall black man two steps behind the other two. The two men in front walked up to the bar and sat down, totally ignoring the third man, who now just turned and walked away.

On a hunch, Mitch followed him.

****

It was a short walk from that bar to the town. As Mitch followed the man, it appeared he had an intended destination. Mitch was now sticking out like a sore thumb. There was no hiding in a two-block town.

Moses was aware he was being followed and smiled all the way, as he had nothing to hide.

Mitch meandered across the street into a small local art gallery, trying to be discreet in a town with no other visitors, just locals engaging in their daily business. It was not an easy task

He watched as Moses walked into the business office across the street. He was greeted by a female with a large frame and a happy-to-see-you hug. She stood back, her hands up on his shoulders while looking at him, then gave him another hug. *Too young to be his mother, too motherly to be a girlfriend. Aunt? Sister?* Mitch watched out the large window of the art gallery, trying not to be too obvious.

Mitch saw that this man never talked, just listened. Mitch saw him reach into his pocket, pull something out and hand it to the woman. She thanked him with yet another hug. Moses was smiling as he waved goodbye and left.

Mitch stepped out of the gallery right behind this man, Moses, who Mitch did know not was named Moses. Then they started to walk, with Mitch following.

Moses stopped abruptly right in the middle of the sidewalk, and watched as Mitch, caught by surprise, kept walking. Moses locked eyes with Mitch as he passed by. Moses let out a smile, somehow sensing that Mitch was a good guy.

Mitch continued to walk back toward the marina. Now the mouse was following the cat. Mitch took a chance and slowed down, letting Moses catch up.

"Couldn't help but notice the nice ship you work on," Mitch smiled as he looked right at Moses.

The man smiled back at Mitch, genuinely looking Mitch right in the eyes as if he were talking to him. But Moses was not saying a word.

"I've been looking for my friend, Terri," Mitch went on. "I was under the impression she worked on that ship."

The two continued walking as Mitch held this one-sided conversation. "We haven't heard from her, I'm sure she's just fine. But her mom is concerned. She told me she was supposed to be off work this week." Mitch let out a nervous laugh as he handed this man his business card.

The silence from the other man was uncomfortable. The man continued to listen as they started to walk.

"Well, if she is on board, Terri I mean, would you let her know to contact her mom? Her parents are worried."

Moses slowed down for a moment, his expression changing to concern with the mention of Terri's mom.

Mitch took it as a good sign that Moses was understanding what Mitch was saying.

Moses looked at his watch and continued walking.

Mitch fell back in his pace and watched Moses walk back to the marina.

The other men were still there at the bar, now laughing in unison. Moses walked up and stood on the periphery, making sure they saw he was there but careful not to patronize. The men he had come there with motioned for Moses to go and wait in the inflatable as they finished their drinks.

Moses complied.

VOLUME TWO: RAPTIS TRILOGY

****

<u>40</u>

Terri stayed in her bunk room all morning. She was packed and ready to leave. Although unable to look out any windows, she was confident the boat was anchored out in the harbor off Vandorn Island. The water felt calm and still, the area protected like a bay.

She could hear the engine on the inflatable. They were coming back from the second trip that day. Standing in front of the mirror, Terri watched herself as she practiced, "Melvin, I'm sorry. I'm sorry Melvin—Melvin, I blew it...."

****

Terri's confidence up now, she decided it was time to make her move. She grabbed her two bags, one in each hand and headed down the empty corridor. But the door connecting to the stairwell was locked. She put both bags down and tugged.

She looked up the stairwell through the round window in the door and could see tanned calves walking back and forth, some she didn't recognize. She grabbed the door handle and shook it hard again, hoping to get someone's attention.

It worked! Moses appeared out of nowhere on the other side, smiling at her, looking over his shoulders for anyone watching. He unlocked the door from the other side.

Terri looked him right in the eyes, smiled back, and whispered her thanks to her secret friend who never replied in words.

She grabbed her two bags and snuck up the gangway to the next level's landing. She looked to the back where the dinghy was attached. No one was paying attention or thinking of watching it. *This is going to be easy.* Terri thought of zipping away on that inflatable with no way for them to chase her. *Ha!*

******

Terri made it almost all the way there before her plan was foiled. David and another man walked over to the stern from the other side, and stood between her and the dinghy, just talking. Terri backed up and turned, trying to slink away without being seen. Coming up from behind was Matt and still another man she didn't recognize. All of them were surprised and not too happy to see her.

In a split second, that very moment, she made the decision to let go of her bags and bolt for the side of the boat. She was there before any one realized, held onto the rail, then catapulted her legs over, heading overboard. She let out a loud scream as she splashed into the water below, hoping someone other than her shipmates would notice her and come to help.

******

Mitch did hear a faint scream and splash in the background. The scream was so unusual, so random in the morning hours, he couldn't help but hear it. Mitch could recognize that scream anywhere. *Terri.* Looking toward the sound, he saw the inflatable dinghy take off from the back of the ship.

Terry swam as fast as she could, her heart racing. She was struggling: her clothes and shoes were pulling at her speed. She tried to stay focused and make every stroke count as she heard the dinghy's engine start and head toward her. She swam for the cover of painted fishing boats anchored out, attached to buoys. She ducked under and swam to the other side, hiding as she caught her breath and made a plan.

******

Mitch watched the inflatable circling the other boats. Rapidly he was able to determine exactly what was happening.

But the cat and mouse game ended as quickly as it started; the inflatable easily trapped Terri with nowhere else to go.

"Get in here, you stupid idiot," Matt demanded, grabbing at her as she tried to dodge his grip.

"Hey, look you guys, I just want to go home, OK? You get it, don't you, Matt? Come on, you got what you came for." Terri felt like she was pleading for her life.

"It just doesn't work that way, princess. I'm afraid you're coming back with us."

Two men picked Terri up to pull her in. She refused to help, letting her weight hang like a dead whale. But the more she resisted, the more they crammed her face into the side of the rubber boat. They picked her legs up and shoved her into the boat real hard. No one could see them surrounded by the empty, colorful boats.

"Not one more word out of you."

The boat sped off.

Terri lay helpless on the plywood floor. One of the new men in the group was holding her down with his large foot flat on her back. The rest of her body bounced and slammed against the plywood floor boards.

****

The men led her back to the cabin as she protested all the way. "Hey! Let me go! Just let me go now!" Terri was dripping wet as they pulled her down the hall.

"Shut up." One of the men shouted.

"I've gotten out of worse you know, you might as well just give up." Terri was kicking, pulling, and being completely defiant.

"I think I said shut up!"

"You know, I bet you don't even know why you're holding me. They don't even trust you with that. So that means you're a loser and you know what? I'm a winner and winners win." Terri's adrenaline was pumping so hard she couldn't feel a thing or keep her mouth shut.

"I said shut up." His fist came down on her like a head on collision: you see it coming, no time to react. As his fist came across Terri's face her jaw cracked to the left and she bit into her tongue, piercing the backside of it with her molars. Her mouth filled with blood. Her body catapulted across the length of the small cabin and slapped against the wall like a rag doll before she dropped to the floor. Blood ran from her mouth as she opened her eyes and looked up.

"You won? Looks like the beginning of a losing streak to me." The man smirked at Terri and walked out the door, slamming it behind him, leaving her on the floor. He took a rope and lashed it around the doorknob in the hallway outside, tying the other end on an opposite doorknob. She wouldn't be able to open that door.

41

Mitch felt uneasy. What he had just seen and heard from afar — well, something about it just didn't look right. He was convinced he had to go out to that ship, he had to see Terri, he had to take a look for himself. He had nothing to lose, he felt as if he had already lost her. He felt this was innocent enough; he had to find out if she was OK for her mom.

Mitch was greeted by two men as he pulled up to the back of the boat. He recognized them from the bar.

"Yes sir, so what can we do for you," they offered in a professional tone.

"I know this may seem odd, but, my friend, Terri…."

The two men glanced at each other and back to Mitch.

"… It's just that, well, when she left I didn't get to say goodbye. Is it possible…?" Mitch let his sentence drift off as he looked up, hoping they would invite him on board, or better yet maybe Terri would wander out to the back. Where was she?

"I'll ask her if she'd like to see you." One of the men stayed with Mitch while the other disappeared.

******

"Get up!" The door swung open without a knock. "You have company." Walter was pissed off again. "You have to make him go away, and now!" Walter was glaring at Terri now, inspecting the damage to her face that his henchman had inflicted. He left and came back with a wet washcloth, throwing it down at her. "Wipe your face clean, tend to that wound."

Terri did what she was told.

"Let me see you. Hmm." He saw the swelling in her jaw, it was going to bruise a lot. "You're going to be so convincing that he leaves, leaves us alone, and never comes back."

He? Who? Someone came for me? Terri felt a glimmer of hope. "Company, for me?" She spit out, praying it was Mitch.

"And if he's not off the ship within five minutes, we will move him off the ship permanently. Do you understand what I'm telling you? Either you make him go away or my men make him go away, and that won't be pretty." Walter watched Terri's eyebrows rise, and he knew he had her attention with that.

"In fact, just so I can be sure you do understand what 'permanently' means," he leaned closer, "I will make you watch my men make him go away." He put his fingers up to Terri's forehead, simulating pulling the trigger on a handgun. "Now, clean up your appearance, you're a mess."

She wiped her face.

"Now, follow me."

Terri followed Walter to the stern of the boat where Mitch was standing.

"Terri! What happened?" Mitch was shocked at her face, red, swollen, with blood dripping down her cheek from a slash wound.

"Mitch, what the hell! I can't believe you came out here to check on me. It's just like when you got jealous over John, get it? You need to get out of here, you're embarrassing me, just like with John!" Terri said this, trying to sound more convincing, while trying to give a clue.

"What did they do to you?" was all Mitch could get out.

David took a step closer toward Mitch, a gentle warning not to get any closer to Terri.

"Come on Mitch, you know what a klutz I am when a boat is rocking; I fell down the ladder trying to step down forward, stupid me." She was hoping Mitch would see right through her story with no other bruises elsewhere on her body and no limping to back it up.

Mitch was staring right at Terri. Walter was as well. Terri started up on Mitch again.

"Yeah, well my face doesn't feel so good. Kinda like someone checking up on me who has no right to, OK? I'm fine, go away." Terri did her best to look and be mean, hoping Mitch would get the clue through her anger. But it was a long shot, she knew this, still it was the best she could do.

Walter stepped in. "I think you've heard enough, you are interrupting our work schedule. She's just fine."

Mitch looked at Terri, her eyes swollen red. That cut on her face didn't look good, and just then it had reopened. And John? He wasn't jealous of John! What was that about? Before he knew it, David and Matt were on each side of him, blocking him.

"Would you like something to drink before you go?" David offered in an unconvincing way.

Mitch looked at Terri, she was moving her eyeballs back and forth. He took the clue.

"No." Mitch was cautious, looking at Terri again for another clue.

She raised her eyebrows high and smiled suggesting he said the right thing. "Don't come back here, Mitch, I mean it!" she yelled at Mitch.

He watched her as they escorted him back to his Whaler.

Terri looked at Mitch, staring. He knew that look, that was fear. She stayed behind next to Walter as he left.

As he started his engine, Mitch was sure. None of this felt right.

David tossed the bow line into the boat and used his foot to push Mitch off and away. Then David continued waving, smirking as Mitch put his boat in gear and motored off.

42

Russell was already half drunk, all alone at his bar in the heat of midday. In fact, Russell's head was now laying on the bar top.

The small Locket Key bar was vacant as Mitch motored up to the dock. Everything was quiet, even the lizards were napping, sheltering from the high noon heat. Mitch walked up to the bar from the dock and sat down next to Russell.

Russell opened his eye and tried to sober up.

"Weell, looky who's here," Russell managed to mutter as he reached across the bar for his drink.

"OK, it's time to be square with me, who are these people and what is going on out there? At first I thought they managed to turn Terri against me. But now, I was out there and well, I think, I don't know, but I think she was trying to tell me she was in trouble." Mitch was having a hard time spitting it out, telling this drunk bar guy, Russell, all this.

Russell peered at Mitch. "Yes well, didn't I tell you that was coming? I tried to let you know, I tried to tell you that they don't care about Terri. They're just using her, and when they're done, they will quickly dispose of her. Now they're anchored out at sea, way out at sea, I can't get out there."

"There are five big men total and a local guy, the cook or something, the only local guy it appears. I followed him into town, he wouldn't talk to me, not a word, but he smiled at me, looking me right in the eyes. I think he could be on our side."

"Local man, didn't speak? Handsome? Muscular man, should be in his mid-forties?"

"Yeah, that pretty much describes him."

"Well, I'll be damned, how'd he get to be on board that ship?" Russell half chuckled to himself.

"You know this guy?"

"Moses. If it weren't for him, none of this treasure would've been found to begin with. His father discovered it." Russell looked down at his brass ring. "If it weren't for Moses, I wouldn't be alive today. For years I cursed him for somehow finding me and saving me, I wanted to die. Well, look at me." Russell held up his hooked hand.

For the first time Mitch was looking past the faded eye patch, scars, and beyond Russell's tattered confidence. Now Mitch was connecting to the man behind the mask, and he could feel his pain.

****

"Those first ones, they came in like bloody pirates and took the treasure we so brilliantly found and salvaged, then they killed my friends, all of them. They did this to me in the end as they got away." Russell pointed to his hand and face. "They took what was mine. And then the universe took it away from them. We had a plan and it worked. We rigged the boat with explosives, down it went in an instant, no one saw where, no one has been able to find it after all these years." He shrugged and took a long drink, "Until you two came along...."

Mitch was trying to keep it all straight.

"Now, after all these years, thinking it was gone forever, lost at sea, it's found again. They are back to reclaim it. I don't know exactly who they are, but they're taking what was rightfully mine…again. And, taking what was, is, yours." Russell looked at Mitch with his one good eye.

"The question is, young man," Russell tapped Mitch hard with his rounded, hooked hand, "what are you going to do about it?" Russell continued looking Mitch in the eye. Then he shifted gears and insisted, "We have to move now!" He slammed his hook on the bar top to further make his point.

The hollow brass resonated with an eerie ring.

"We've got to get Terri out of there."

The wheels in Mitch's head began to turn, thinking he didn't want any trouble. He just wanted to get his friend Terri back.

Russell knew what they were up against. He rolled his brass prosthetic back and forth like a wheel on the bar top as he thought.

"I think I have a plan, get me a piece of paper." Mitch tapped his pencil on the table and then, when handed paper, he began to pencil his thoughts out.

VOLUME TWO: RAPTIS TRILOGY

****

<u>43</u>

Every morning on the ship started the same way. By the time Terri got up, everyone was already gone. They were out at the anchored workboat, underwater, digging. They didn't allow her out on the dig. Sometimes David or Matt would stay behind to help inventory the gold, but Walter was always there, every day, lurking around, most of the time hidden inside in his office. She was never allowed to eat with the other workers. Moses would slip her something light on the side when no one was looking.

Everyone treated Terri as if she didn't exist, except Moses. She followed him around whenever she could. One time Terri followed Moses to his secret getaway. She watched him go through the electrical room door and close it behind him. She waited for him to come out. After twenty minutes of impatience, she went ahead and walked in where she found Moses sitting there in his own little world, looking at some pictures that were posted on the wall. She thought these were of his family.

Terri never found out why Moses didn't talk, he couldn't tell her. Terri had so many questions about him. At first she had tried everything to get him to communicate with her. He would just sit and smile pleasantly at her, as she talked continually. She could tell he understood everything she was saying. She told Moses everything, including how she felt. Sometimes Terri would find Moses there in his little retreat late at night, perspiring in the heat, leaning against the wall. But he always appeared happy, although when he kept seeing Terri there so often, he started to wonder whether his cabin door shouldn't have a lock.

"I don't know, Moses, I froze, couldn't do it. I knew he was going to ask me to marry him, then this job came up. The next thing you know, I bolted...." Terri went on and on about Mitch and all while Moses just listened. She looked into his eyes. He smiled back into hers. She was sincerely grateful to have a friend, one who would listen. "But Mitch is probably one of the best guys you'll ever know or meet!"

****

The first time the plane approached, everyone on the ship watched with binoculars. It was unusual to see a small plane flying way out here. The plane circled around once, and then again, waving his wings back and forth before disappearing back into the afternoon clouds.

"Someone's trying to say hello." David was sheltering his eyes with his hand as he looked up. He was scribbling down the identification numbers as the plane disappeared.

Terri was sitting out on the front bow, always her favorite spot in the sun on any boat or ship, looking out at the horizon. She was grateful David and Matt had let her get some fresh air. She privately smiled now, as she could recognize that plane anywhere, she had even taken a few rides in it herself. That was Melvin's Cessna, his four-seater, and she was positive that was Mitch in the passenger seat. *They found me!*

The second day when the plane circled again, Terri boldly waved, wanting to let them know she saw them.

44

The small plane again appeared in the sky, just the way it had the days before. With all four compressors working steadily, the noise from the plane went unheard by most and ignored by the rest. Bored with the plane's daily antics of waving its wings and circling before leaving, they had stopped paying attention to it.

But Terri waited out on the bow, watching, waiting for it. This small plane had become the highlight of her day. This small plane let her know that her friends, her real friends, were there keeping an eye on her.

****

Melvin tipped his wings back and forth, saying hello to Terri one last time as his plane disappeared back into the clouds.

Mitch had seen Terri on the bow of the ship, and he had seen that everyone else there was busy working underwater, same as the days before. Mitch and Melvin had detected their pattern.

****

Walter didn't like seeing this small plane, this made four days in a row now. This time, Walter noticed through his binoculars that Terri's friend, Mitch, was not in the plane that day. Something about this sent up an instinctive red flag. He ordered David to his side. "Take Terri out to the workboat, I want her underwater working with the others," Walter ordered

David. Walter, who was already walking down the ladder toward Terri, now grabbed at her arm.

David looked at Walter sideways. They had all agreed not to have Terri out there, she was too much potential trouble.

"You're finally getting your wish come true, Miss Terri, you're going diving." Walter pulled her up from the ground where she was sitting and pushed her toward David like a ragdoll.

David grabbed her arm to take control, then led her to the back stern.

"David, take her out there, let her dive, and then you come back here to the ship so you can deal with any trouble."

"Trouble? There's no trouble. But I sure do want to go diving! I'm so fucking bored!" Terri said.

Terri tried to keep up with David's pace as he pushed her into the rubber dinghy and sped off.

Upon reaching the work station, David had Terri quickly suit up, don her wetsuit, and put a heavy weight belt on as he pulled on the long low-pressure hose attached to the hookah, bringing it toward him.

Two lines came off of each hookah compressor. The compressors floated on the water's surface, each inside an inflated ring, pumping air down to the regulator mouthpiece in each diver's mouth. Matt and David shared this first compressor rig, the other two men used another.

"Put this in your mouth. Go down and tap Matt on the shoulder, tell him to surface. Then you just do as he tells you, and only what he tells you."

Terri rolled off the side of the boat and submerged underwater, doing just as she had been told.

Matt, surprised to see Terri there underwater, surfaced.

"Watch her, Walter's got a bad feeling about that plane today. He wants her underwater, we're expecting trouble from that Mitch," David explained.

"Great, she's probably already got her pockets full of coins." Matt put the regulator back in his mouth and submerged, swimming down to Terri.

She was floating in neutral buoyancy, hovering between the surface and the bottom, watching the progress, seeing what they had done to that beautiful reef that was now decimated, torn apart. *How could they!* She saw the uncovered remains of an old boat being dismantled and placed into large bins that were anchored down. She could see the grid they had lined out. It was an actual dig.

****

Mitch and Melvin had been observing the ship's daily schedule and the progress below. They were getting pretty clear about who was where and when, noting when Terri was perched on the bow of the boat, watching the horizon. They could see the others at the work station. They could see the clouds of sandy silt from the airlifts, silt drifting out in a long pattern in the sea's currents, proof of the destroying of the reef. The whole thing was easy to follow.

****

David was already back at the ship with the dinghy tied up to the transom. He found Walter watching the white dot on the horizon coming closer as the Whaler sped toward them. But Walter was distracted.

Walter thought back to the time David and Matt had reported to him that Terri was being followed on St. Todos, and also of the day they said someone there almost ran her over. At the time, Walter had sort of suspected maybe this was his hateful brother, up to no good. Now, Walter found himself wondering about Rodney, and even waiting for his no good brother, Rodney, to suddenly appear out there. Walter wondered why he was thinking this. But he couldn't turn this tape in his mind off. Rodney too, like Walter, was after their brother's, Drake's, treasure.

Walter decided that he and his enterprise would not be taken by surprise, they would be ready for anything.

Walter was determined to recover what belonged to him. He had spent through a large chunk of the family fortune looking for it. Rodney had disagreed about the expenditures on the search after ten years of futile looking.

Together the three brothers had lived for the sea, the hunt. But Drake's death, his going down with the lost treasure, was a sign for Rodney that the treasure was never going to be found again. Rodney had insisted they should just let the other two medallions go, move on, that they had plenty of wealth already. So, Walter told himself, this was all his now. Walter was the one who had found it, it was his money and his wealth that had paid for his futile search for the last thirty years. Walter wasn't about to share it with anyone now, not even his brother.

Yes, they would be ready.

45

The pair knew people would be watching. Russell lay under cover, down on the floorboards of the Whaler. This way all they would see would be Mitch. He would appear to be naïvely alone.

The ride out that morning was rough. Each time they hit the ocean chop, Russell bounced up and down and landed on his side. Both he and Mitch were wet from ocean spray, but Russell was soaked.

Russell hadn't felt this alive in decades.

****

All but Walter and David were out at the support boat, one man standing guard while the others were underwater, filling basket after basket. Terri was underwater with them, down at the bottom, holding the airlift steady for Matt.

The guard was keeping the air compressors running, filling the thirsty motors with gasoline. He diligently watched the hoses in the water and the winds to make sure noxious gasses emitting from the air compressors stayed away from the air intake of each hookah. There was always a danger of a breeze shifting, causing the intake valve to suck in the fumes and send them unknowingly to the divers below.

****

Four days ago they had found the heart of the treasure. Now Terri was watching in amazement as they stacked the valuables into large baskets, all to be lifted into the big ship by that crane in the back. They were hoping to be done within twenty-four more hours of working round the clock.

The first day they had brought the gold coins up onto the ship, Walter had grabbed at them while laughing like a little kid. There had also been other treasures brought up and then laid out on the table for the men to ogle. Terri had tried to work her way into the crowd of men that first night as they poured the first treasures onto the table. There were some pieces of gold stuck together in clumps of oxidized ore, and handfuls of gold coins loose and shining for each to hold and observe.

Pushed back out of the way, Terri hadn't been allowed to see or join in. She wanted to kick them all in the shins but knew they would kick her back. That night and most of the time from then on, no one spoke to her. They just grunted, pushed, and glared which was enough to make her do whatever they wanted, especially move out of the way. She had already felt the blunt punishment of several stiff hands. That night she reached up to her face and rubbed her cheek, feeling the healing gash, and knew she didn't want to feel that again. So she stayed away from the treasures like they wanted her to.

That night, she had watched the treasure party from afar while looking out to sea, constantly updating her escape route in her head. Occasionally she would make eye contact with Moses who was busy serving the others. Moses would wink at her and she would wink back, her way of saying hello to the only friendly face she knew. She did not like having to go back to her small enclosed prison bunk, she wasn't ready to sleep *or suffocate.*

Now, she recalled their wild celebration that night. At first the men had been drinking champagne and toasting each other like gentlemen. Soon they were drunken animals, all of them. Terri imagined all of them as pigs in sunglasses, laughing with excitement, urinating over the side of the ship, and vomiting in excess against Walter's demands for civility.

****

David and Walter stood there, watching the dot in the distance grow into a white boat, speeding toward them. It was clear to them as they were looking through the binoculars that it wasn't Rodney at all, just Terri's friend, Mitch. All alone.

"What is he thinking?" Walter wondered out loud to David. "I'm going down to my office, you take care of this stupid guy."

David watched Mitch approach as he made his way to the back transom were Mitch would eventually be pulling up. This was going to be easy, David thought to himself, smiling. *This guy, really? Against me?*

David stood on the back of the ship with his arms crossed against his chest.

But Mitch sped by at a distance. He didn't even look over toward the ship, ignoring David who was standing there waiting for him. Mitch stayed close to the reef in the shallower water and headed for the anchored workstation, that vessel with the back transom opened wide, filled with air compressors and that large swinging arm with a pulley. There was a smaller, orange inflatable dinghy attached to the back.

David watched this. Surprised by Mitch's path, David walked over to the starboard side of the ship and watched Mitch pull up to the workstation and talk to the guard. David could see the two talking, but had left his binoculars somewhere at the top of the ship. He went back up to retrieve them.

VOLUME TWO: RAPTIS TRILOGY

****

46

The large man on the support boat watched in complete surprise as Mitch pulled up alongside. Mitch had posted an official-looking emblem on the sides of his boat. Mitch reached into his back pocket smiling, watching the large man as he reached for a bang stick hidden behind the wheel.

"Whoa, hey, just a minute," Mitch said, opening a small black leather case revealing a very shiny important looking badge. "I am from the Bureau of Tobacco and Firearms."

The man stood there with his mouth hanging half open in confusion. The sound of the compressors droning in the background made it hard to hear and understand, but he did understand important looking badges, they meant authority of some kind.

Mitch went on, "Please show me your vehicle registration, and your license for that bang stick. We have reason to believe you are out here digging on the reef illegally."

"I don't have any vehicle registration, not way out here, I'm working. You need to go to the large ship over there, they are the ones in charge." The man was dumbfounded that this was happening here, out in the middle of nowhere. But Mitch's badge looked so official, he felt obliged to comply.

Mitch kept the man busy and looking at him, while nudging Russell with his foot to let him know that the man wasn't looking, that it was safe for Russell to move. So Russell climbed out the back of the boat, slipped into the water like a snake so he wouldn't splash. There was a lot of strength in Russell's one remaining arm, which was so deceiving.

******

Russell maneuvered himself to the back ladder of the support boat. He adjusted his mask around his leather eye patch to keep water out and looked down below. Bubbles were rising in a constant stream, moving through the large cloud of silt suspended in the water. Layers and layers of sand were being sucked up through the two large tubes and then were showering out the end with a powerful blast of air from the compressors above.

The bubbles of compressed air were growing larger and larger as they forced their way to the surface. Fish were darting in and out of the silt, picking and eating their own recovered treasures.

Russell could see four people down below. He recognized the boxes they were moving and stacking into the baskets. They were old and rusting, falling apart as they were moved. Russell had filled those boxes himself what seemed like a lifetime ago.

Over to the left he could see the crumpled remains of the *Ol' Wife* being collected and stored in other baskets. They were preparing to take all the evidence with them. Russell realized quickly that all this evidence was everything that would validate Russell's life, his past story, everything that made him the man he was today. No one had ever really believed his stories about the treasure he had found and lost. Russell's head began to swell and pound with uncontrollable anger and revenge.

As usual, Mitch hadn't wanted any trouble, so he'd decided to handle David and the main ship. Russell hadn't been quite sure what that meant, but the old guy had a few tricks of his own. And now, once Russell laid his eye on the operations below and saw the remains of the gutted out *Ol' Wife*, Russell's own plan began to unfold. These men, this operation, he had to stop this and take back what was his. He knew he had nothing to lose except the painful memories of the past thirty years, memories he had been trying to wash away daily with alcohol and isolation.

Mitch had the man in the boat so manipulated, looking here and looking there, everywhere but toward the back, that the man never noticed Russell as he slipped out and away from everyone's view— and just in time. David found his binoculars and peered out to watch.

"Thank you for your trouble. I'll go ask at your mother ship, over there. Is there anyone there who could answer my questions?" Mitch tried his best to talk in a deep, formal, authoritative voice, anxious to get out of there before the guy asked him for a close look at his badge.

"I've been telling you mate, go to the ship, go to the ship!" The man was scratching his head as he was watching Mitch push away.

Mitch left, successfully leaving Russell behind, leaving Russell hanging on to the back of the workboat out of sight, as he and Russell had planned.

They'd planned that Russell would keep an eye on these guys, using the dinghy to get away if there was trouble of any sort. The workboat was soundly anchored down with the compressors running, and there would be no way those men could get that workboat moving anywhere quick enough to catch Russell in the dinghy, at least not without a lot of sweat and work.

Mitch had explained to Russell that this would give him, Mitch, time to talk with Walter and David, to get Terri off that main

VOLUME TWO: RAPTIS TRILOGY

****

ship one way or another. Of course, neither Mitch nor Russell knew that, on this day, Terri had been sent out to dive with the others.

Russell hung off the back of the workboat, watching the men below and keeping an eye on the man above. The man above was watching Mitch speed off. With the sun straight up overhead, the heat had become almost unbearable, so now the man peeled off his white tee shirt, looked over the side of the boat, and dove in.

Russell realized this man was going to have to climb up the ladder to get back into the boat. Russell was stealthy as he placed his satchel in the inflatable dinghy, careful not to make a splash, and drifted up to the bow of the workstation. He stayed hidden as he watched the man duck underwater to cool off, then climb up the ladder back onto the workboat.

47

Mitch pulled up to the back of the ship like he belonged there, his head held high with confidence. He knew just how to bring his baby in at full speed and stop on a dime, drifting sideways to the back transom with ease.

David was impatiently watching all this, smirking as he was thinking just what he could do to Mitch.

"What are you up to?" David demanded as he put his foot on the wet bow of Mitch's boat, suggesting he was going to push it away at any moment.

"Look, David is it? Like I said before, I just want to talk, I just want to see Terri. You understand, right? I don't want any trouble."

"How did you find us out here?" David demanded again.

Mitch tied off his stern line securing the boat, listening to David.

"David, let me say it one more time, I don't want trouble, I just want to see Terri." The secret of a magician is to keep talking, keep your audience's attention, as you perform your magic trick. Mitch confidently stepped up from his boat onto the back deck.

David stood there, shocked that Mitch would actually have the nerve to step up onto his ship. He watched Mitch walk toward the three steps of the wide teak ladder leading up to the galley.

David really didn't have a plan, not past intimidating the hell out of Mitch anyway. David had never really hurt anyone intentionally, but now, he was going to have to get rough, scare Mitch. He reached for Mitch's shoulder; Mitch turned with a fast punch to the gut that sent David backward.

Losing his balance, David fell back onto the side of Mitch's Whaler and then a humiliating slip sent David splashing into the sea.

Mitch was already standing in the main galley looking around as David came up from behind him. He was soaking wet, humiliated, and now ready to destroy Mitch. He grabbed Mitch by his right shoulder and swung him around as he cocked his muscular right arm back. Before David could let it go, Mitch had already ducked and swung his left knee up, kicking David hard in the groin.

Mitch watched David crumble with surprise. Mitch quickly had David's right arm twisted around, with David dropping to his knees, wincing in pain within two moves.

"Was this what you were going to do?" Mitch pulled David's arm up backward while David tried to pull away. "I told you I didn't want trouble."

David looked up and Mitch pulled harder.

In his much younger years, Mitch had been a devoted student of martial arts, his skills at a master level. There was never a martial arts community on the island for Mitch to be part of, so he had developed new interests, and no one ever knew about the great skill Mitch had. "Where's Terri?"

David sucked up the pain. Grimacing, his arm was being yanked up out of the socket, but he wasn't about to give it up to this guy. David had been through worse.

Mitch pulled David's arm back and upward again. "Where's Terri?"

David still refused to speak.

Mitch had arrived ready for anything. Now he pulled a short rope out of his back pocket, putting a small noose around one of David's wrists, tightening it until he could see David close his eyes with pain. Mitch then looped the other end of the rope once around David's neck and back down to his other wrist, tying it off. If David tried to pull out, he would choke himself.

"When I get out of here, you'd better run, I'm going to kill you!" David was so humiliated, praying no one would see him like this.

Taking the sweaty wet kerchief from around his neck, Mitch shoved it into David's mouth to shut him up as he protested. Mitch, satisfied with his work, patted David on the head as David sat there stewing over how he was going to get out.

"Let's hope it doesn't come to that, OK, David?"

Mitch began to search the ship for Terri.

But with Walter in his office and Mitch's dramatic arrival, what they'd all failed to see was the other speedboat in the distance, quickly drawing closer.

VOLUME TWO: RAPTIS TRILOGY

****

<u>48</u>

Back at the workboat, Russell had his own agenda and was busy carrying it out, mainly by silently taping small amounts of plastic explosives around the hull. Watching the men down below him, he worked quickly, not knowing when and whether anyone else was going to surface. When he was done, Russell put his long thick dive knife in his mouth, then lifted himself onto the back transom.

This rocked the boat, drawing the attention of the man on guard.

He turned and saw the stranger's back with long, gray tangles of wet hair, sitting faced out to sea. The guard was completely puzzled as to who he was and how he'd got there.

"Hey!" the stranger shouted at Russell and walked toward him.

Russell stood up with his back to the large man, focusing on the sound of his footsteps.

"Hey, I'm talkin' to you!" The man stepped right up to Russell's back as he spoke.

Russell turned around quickly. With one swift motion and unexpected force, Russell put the thick dive knife in up behind the man's rib cage, jamming it into his chest cavity, twisting as he pushed.

The man's eyes opened wide in shock as he realized what was happening to him. His mouth gaped open. He drooled strands of deep red foaming blood before he could get a word out. His heart was severed. He reached out with his arm in a fighting reflex as Russell's one eye looked into his.

Russell was smiling as he watched the life drain out of the stranger.

The man fell to his knees, then forward, knocking his forehead on the back transom as he went down. Russell let the knife remain in him for now. He had more work to do. Russell purposely stepped on the man's back while climbing into the back of the boat.

The blood pooled around the dead man on the white deck.

****

Russell reached into the satchel he kept around his neck and pulled out two long pieces of one-inch diameter tubing, each with a small plastic funnel haplessly attached with duct tape at one end. He positioned a funnel around each of the exhaust tubes on the two compressors. Walking over to the side, he gently pulled on the leashes attached to the floating hookah rigs supplying air to the men below. He leaned over and taped the other end of the tube next to the air intake valves of the hookahs. The noxious fumes descended into their breathing air below.

Russell looked over to the mother ship. He could see Mitch's boat tied to the back transom, no signs of trouble. He grabbed the one handgun he could find on the workboat, checked to see if it was loaded, and put it in his satchel.

The men underwater were working hard, hammering at the precious coral. They were moving broken off pieces of the coral away with the streams of sand the large tubes were sucking up. They were destroying the reef step by step, to get to the treasure there. And non-stop, they were furiously filling so

****

many caged baskets with the heavy gold and platinum they were harvesting.

****

At first, no one paid much attention to the foul taste of the air. They had gotten used to the trade winds shifting and occasionally sending a taste of exhaust down the hose. With no tanks to bind them, they continued to move freely, breathing hard, sucking as much air as they pleased. At this depth their bottom time was almost unlimited.

Their movements began to slow and become more labored.

The smallest of the men was the first to succumb to the poisonous gases, the air too heavy to inhale. His head pounded as he looked down the reef for his dive mates. His head swirled in confusion. The black circle around his vision grew larger. With no oxygen left in his body, he slumped forward onto the jagged coral. His mask caught on a large piece of the sharp coral at the neoprene mask strap.

His heavy head fell further, scraping his face down the front as he continued to slump forward with his dead weight. His teeth clenched tight around the mouthpiece delivering the poison. Streams of green oozed out of the wounds on his deeply scraped face. Reef fish began investigating, darting through the green stream downward to the source.

Even Terri, who'd been standing fairly still at Matt's air intake, felt her head start to pound and she began to feel nauseated. Her vision started to close in, but she saw the man next to her slump over. She pulled him back and saw the whites of his eyes begin to burst, engorged with blood.

Terri's deepest instincts kicked in: something was wrong. She dropped her weight belt, spit the regulator out of her mouth, and swam to the surface, carefully exhaling all the way up. She sprawled out on her back when she saw the light of the surface through the black in her vision. She passed out as her body rose to the surface, still floating on her back.

Russell was busy rifling through everything, confiscating what he wanted or felt was useful as the compressors droned on, emptying its exhaust into the mouths of the men below. He placed a timer for the explosives in a drawer, then heard a splash erupt not far from the boat.

Russell saw the body float up on its back. He saw the long blond hair and recognized Terri. Shocked, Russell immediately dove in, reaching for her neck and checking her pulse. She wasn't breathing. He kicked up above her and came down, his mouth attached to hers right away as he held her head back and blew hard: her lungs expanded. He took another deep breath, kicked up and again came down with his mouth attaching to Terri's, blowing his air into her lungs.

She gurgled phlegm and began to cough out the saltwater that had entered her lungs. Russell wrapped his arm around her and swam toward the back of the boat, lifting her onto the back transom, checking her pulse and breath. He rolled her up and into the rubber dinghy attached to the back, she was breathing but still passed out.

******

Down below, Matt had been busy lifting sand away with his head in a downward position. His head had begun to pound into a migraine headache. He backed out and righted himself, thinking too much blood was flowing to his head upside down. His veins were filling with poison as his body used up the oxygen in his body. The taste in his mouth didn't register until he looked over and saw his limp dive mates. But no Terri.

Matt saw that the small man was slumped forward, his mask dangling on the coral. And the other man was fifty feet away, floating motionless in a standing position. Matt swam over and turned him around to see that the vessels in his eyes too were bulging, gorged with blood to the point of exploding, while white frothy bubbles were forming around teeth clenched tight around the mouthpiece. Now this man began to twitch and gyrate in unnatural convulsions. His eyes suddenly opened wide in terror and burst as he succumbed to the poisonous gasses.

Matt spit out his regulator mouthpiece and swam for the surface as stars began to form in his vision. Constantly exhaling to avoid an embolism as he rose to the surface, the stars shooting across his eyes were giving way to blackness. He instinctively sprawled his body backward as he could see the light of the surface ten feet away. Floating on his back, his body lifted to the surface.

****

Russell hadn't noticed that the one hookah rig had drifted and that the warm clear hose delivering the exhaust to the intake valve had developed a kink, preventing all the gasses from being sucked into the air intake.

Matt was strong, his lungs and heart overdeveloped from so much athletic prowess. It didn't take long for him to regain consciousness; he woke up looking over at the boat.

Russell saw Matt and reached down into his front pocket, feeling and patting his trusted smaller knife. What a surprise, it was right there. Russell adjusted his satchel around his chest for ease of reach and patted his loaded gun. He thought best not to reveal his knife. His knife would be the bigger surprise, and his gun the back up.

Matt swam hard, charging to the back of the boat, and then hoisting himself onto the back transom. Matt's full thick wetsuit and the vest wrapped around him didn't slow him down.

Full wetsuit, shit, didn't think about that, will this knife go through and fast enough? In a split second, Russell scanned Matt's body for weapons. Matt was underwater, how could he have a weapon? Russell quickly changed to Plan B as Matt slowed to catch his breath.

Looking Russell in his eye, Matt climbed in, now just three steps away.

Russell reached into his satchel and grasped his gun.

Simultaneously, Matt reached around to his right side and released the thirty-eight caliber bang stick attached to his vest, holding it in his hand.

Russell was the first to let off a shot, hitting Matt square in the intestines. Russell had been aiming higher, and this should have been all over right then.

Matt reached down, clenching his stomach. Blood quickly flowed past his fingers and dripped onto the deck, mixing in with the other man's blood, now a darker thicker mass in contrast to the fresh oxygenated blood pumping out. The two streams swirled together as the boat rocked sideways.

Matt looked at Russell as shock began to set in.

Charging forward, Russell was able to dodge sideways, but not before the bang stick was pressed into his left thigh where it exploded on impact. The impact propelled Russell backward into the side of the cabin, with his gun twirling away out of reach and falling into the cabin. It was his good old reflexes that had his good side stop him from falling and let him quickly stabilize himself. Then Russell used his weight to prop himself up against the railing to keep steady.

As he steadied himself, Russell leaned forward just as Matt charged him. Russell could see Matt was holding onto his oozing gut. As Matt came forward, Russell quickly pulled his knife out and inserted it up into Matt's chest cavity, pushing, twisting back and forth, using the momentum of Matt's weight as Matt fell forward into him.

Together, they slid down the side onto the deck.

A determined Matt reached for Russell's neck, grabbed it and squeezed as Russell tried to push him off.

Matt's eyes slowly rolled back into his head while his blood began to drip out of the sides of his mouth. Matt gurgled his last frothy breath while staring into Russell's eye.

Russell lay there in pain, bleeding, with Matt's two hundred and fifty pounds sprawled on top of him. The boat rocked. Russell leaned forward in intense pain and vomited. Pulling his kerchief from around his neck, he let out a painful groan as he began to tie a tourniquet around his upper leg. He could hear Terri moaning from the small inflatable as she began to wake up.

"I'm gonna be sick...." was all she could get out as she threw up on the floorboards. She didn't know what had happened or how she had gotten there.

VOLUME TWO: RAPTIS TRILOGY

****

<u>49</u>

The other boat was closing in.

Mitch left David tied up and gagged in the main galley. He snuck down the port side of the ship, searching for any signs of Terri. All of the doors were shut; he looked and listened before walking down the hall, not knowing what was behind each door. He put his ear up to the first one, listened for any sound, and gently tried the knob. It was locked.

Mitch could hear David trying to shout through his gag to alert Walter.

Mitch found each doorknob was locked as he worked his way down six locked doors. He turned left to loop around to the starboard side and found an ornate teak door in the center. He could hear someone in there. He pressed his ear against the shiny wooden door and heard footsteps, one set.

Mitch tried to think of a plan as he snuck back down the hallway to check on David.

David screamed at Mitch, red faced, making muffled sounds of frustration through the gag, struggling against Mitch's nautical knot expertise: David had finally seen the next boats coming their way.

But Mitch heard two gunshots. He ran to the back stern and looked out to the workboat. He didn't see anyone out there. Russell was slumped down on the floor trying to gather strength. The bright yellow dinghy was still attached, floating from the back. Mitch scoured the waters around the boat for any signs of Russell. Nothing.

But then Mitch noticed a two-foot cylindrical rod with an orange handle wedged on a shelf by his feet. He picked it up and read the red and yellow sign on the side: *Caution*. It was a bang stick. He pulled on the back part of the stick the way the picture on it suggested. The chamber opened up, revealing a thirty-eight caliber bullet. He closed it, moving the orange safety switch to the on position. He lifted his pant leg and slid the eighteen-inch hollow rod into his sock.

Mitch then walked back to David and told him, "You're coming with me." He loosened the knot and tied David to the railing. Mitch jerked upward on the tope which then tightened the loop around David's neck, nearly chocking David as well as twisting his arm back and up all in one motion. David's muffled reluctance continued as Mitch pulled him up.

Too late, the sound of an approaching speedboat caught Mitch's attention. He looked at David. "Who's that?"

David struggled to communicate.

Mitch pulled the kerchief out of his mouth.

"I don't know, pirates," David spoke in a nervous tone.

Mitch turned and watched the boat in the distance, then shoved the kerchief back into David's protesting mouth.

******

Terri sat up and looked around. She saw Russell slumped against the wall, his eye halfway open. Terri's head ached as she crawled toward the transom and onto the boat. Nausea took over. Her head was pounding as she leaned and vomited overboard.

Russell saw her and smiled, he was so glad to see her alive.

She couldn't avoid the large pools of blood on the back deck as she stepped in them, making her way over to Russell. He had tied a bandage of some sort onto his leg and was in serious pain. In the background, they both heard an approaching vessel and wondered who it could be. They couldn't see it.

"Can you move?" Terri was at Russell's side, trying to lift him.

"Someone's coming, we need to get out of here, and get help to Mitch."

"Mitch? Mitch, he's out there?"

"Yep." Russell moaned as Terri helped him stand up and maneuver to the rubber dinghy. He rolled in with a painful grunt, relieved to get off the workboat.

****

Mitch shoved David forward toward the teak door, his large, muscular frame being manipulated easily with Mitch's grip on the rope.

David tried not to panic, his mouth gagged. *Can't warn Walter.*

Mitch could sense David's urgency.

VOLUME TWO: RAPTIS TRILOGY

****

<u>50</u>

Walter checked the chamber of his pistol. Three bullets left; the other three had gone into the bang sticks.

Walter had heard gunshots ring out, but didn't know what was going on or who else was on the ship. There in the inside cabin, Walter was still unaware of the approaching speedboat.

David struggled, kicking at the door.

Mitch responded by pulling the ropes hard.

"I have a gun and I'm going to come out now," Walter announced, opening the revolver chamber, spinning it and snapping it closed, making sure the sound was identifiable to all. The first of the three bullets was lined up in the chamber.

The door opened and Walter stepped out with his gun pointed at David and Mitch.

All three heard the engine of the speedboat shift into neutral as it pulled up to the transom.

"Walter!" the voice shouted out, "I know you're here. Come on now brother, let's talk...." The voice was low and had a vague accent similar to Walter's.

And now this voice was coming toward them. Mitch stood with his back against the wall, using David as a shield.

Walter smiled. He wasn't surprised by this arrival, he'd been waiting.

"Walter? Let's talk." The voice was coming around the corner, closer.

Walter spoke. "Rodney? No need for guns. There's plenty to share." Walter knew his brother, he wouldn't be alone. Walter leveled his pistol toward Mitch's forehead and whispered, "Let him go."

Mitch released his grip on the ropes. David pulled the rope off his neck, punching Mitch in the gut hard with his elbow. Mitch let out a painful grunt and doubled over just as Rodney turned the corner.

Walter shot first. An expert marksman, Walter was surprised to miss and just hit Rodney's arm.

Mitch, already doubled over, dropped to his hands and knees, crawling. The next moment, Mitch was running to the back. On his way, Mitch saw Moses' head peek out the galley window from below. *Moses!*

David ran after Mitch and tackled him. David again was no match for Mitch, who quickly had David held tight. Mitch was twisting David's arms back, tying them together with the rope still in David's hands. Mitch crammed the kerchief back into David's mouth.

Five more shots rang out.

Rodney shot back at Walter, just trying to scare him, to stop him. Rodney really didn't want to kill Walter, as Walter was his blood brother. But Walter killed Rodney in Rodney's moment of hesitation. Walter used his last bullet on his brother.

Walter walked over and picked up Rodney's gun with no sadness, no regret. His brother had been dead to him for years. He walked to the back of the boat.

Mitch stood there, looking out to the workboat for signs of life, holding onto David who was trying to squirm loose.

Walter walked over to Mitch, pointing the barrel directly at his forehead. "Don't make me."

Mitch slowly released his grip on David.

"You heard me." Walter was pointing with the gun barrel. His back to the transom, he could hear a small engine approaching.

Mitch went as slowly as he possibly could, he didn't want David's gag to come out.

David could see Russell in the back of the dinghy. So David started to complain loudly through the gag.

The small engine turned off and the dinghy drifted up to the side, out of view.

David heard a loud painful grunt come from the back of the ship where the dinghy tied up.

Then there was silence.

Walter turned around to see what or who had made that grunting noise. No one was there. "Hurry up, damn it! Release him!" Walter demanded, positive Matt was coming in from the dinghy to help. Walter could see the tip of his own gun barrel quiver with the tension in his hand. Walter also was well aware that his knuckles had turned white and his palms sweaty. His thumb cocked the trigger back.

"And I'm telling you to put the gun down."

Everyone turned around to see Russell propped up against the wide wooden ladder at the back transom. Russell had his revolver pointed at Walter.

Walter shook his head with surprise to see old Russell so beaten up. "So there you are. Russell, look at you. Swooping in to be the big hero? One eye, one hand, and now it looks like, yes, one leg. What a streak of bad luck." Walter was almost laughing at the pathetic sight, momentarily letting his guard down.

"Why you damn thief!" Russell's elbow, the one elbow that had been propping him up, slipped forward and he lost his balance. The gun in Russell's good hand that had been pointed at Walter accidently discharged, missing Walter and grazing Mitch's left arm.

Mitch's body flung around. He felt a hot burning sensation above his elbow. He looked down and saw the open wound quickly well with blood. He grabbed it to try and stop the bleeding.

Walter smiled and shot back, hitting Russell and sending him down onto his back on the slippery wooden platform.

****

Terri saw Russell slipping toward the sea.

Russell couldn't help but cry out in pain as he caught his rounded hook on a cleat to keep himself from rolling overboard. With his other shoulder shot, this hook was all he had left to keep him holding on.

Russell could see Terri still hiding against the dinghy wall in fear. Now, as he pulled himself up, his hollow round metal hook began to straighten. He watched it and began to see the possibilities. He opted to use the leverage of his body weight to straighten it further.

****

Moses appeared from the galley and ran to Mitch's side.

"Get away from him," Walter shouted.

Ignoring Walter's demands, Moses grabbed a clean cloth from a table top and wrapped it tightly around Mitch's wound before Walter could yell at him again.

This time Walter walked over and put the gun to Moses's head. "Moses, I asked you to get away from him."

Moses moved away, giving Mitch a reassuring look as he backed up.

As he fell back, Mitch let go of the ropes tied around David. But David was still bound as if he were in a strait jacket and couldn't move.

Walter was furious. He pointed the gun back at Mitch. "Get up and start untying those knots, right now."

Terri couldn't stand it anymore. She could hear all the yelling and knew Mitch was hurt. She managed to work her way out of the dinghy onto the back transom, quietly checking on Russell. His pulse was weak and breath shallow. He was dying, she'd seen it before.

Walter stepped closer to Mitch, keeping the gun on him.

Mitch began loosening the knots until David's hands became free.

David pulled the gag out of his mouth and cocked his arm back again, swinging right at Mitch.

In one short move, again Mitch had David's strong hand, holding it backward with pressure until David stopped struggling because of the pain.

"Well, well. What do we have here? Karate hero, impressive." Walter cocked the trigger back on the revolver, pointing at Mitch's temple.

Terri let out a yell as she ran up the short three steps with a bang stick in her hand. She ran toward Walter crying out, "Stop!!!"

Walter pointed the gun at her as he laughed at the fight in her.

Terri hated it when people laughed at her. She lunged toward Walter with the bang stick which Walter easily grabbed away from her as she stumbled forward.

Walter grabbed her arm and jerked it around her back. Pulling Terri upward, he put painful pressure on her, causing her to either stand up or tear her rotator cuff.

"Ow! Ow! My arm!"

Walter put the gun to her head. He wanted to pull the trigger right then.

"Untie the rest of him now," Walter shouted to Mitch. As Walter shouted, his angry dry spit landed on Terri's face.

Terri tried to wipe her face off on her shoulder.

Mitch complied with Walter's demand, he didn't want Terri hurt.

David resisted the urge to slam his fist down on Mitch's face because Walter was ordering him to tie Mitch up.

Mitch reluctantly let David tie him up as he watched the barrel of the gun against Terri's head.

"Now take that linen shirt there and wrap a gag around her so I don't have to listen to that anymore," Walter ordered David.

David gladly wound the shirt up into a long rope and wrapped it around Terri's neck like a bridle.

"Don't hurt her," Mitch said, "take me."

"Take you, that's so sweet! I'm taking both of you." Walter pointed the gun back at Mitch. "You, get in the boat, now, or I'll shoot her right here, in front of you. Down the ladder." Walter pointed at the ladder with his gun.

Obediently, Mitch turned and backed down the three steps. He could see some blood on the wooden planks. The rest had washed away as Russell lay dead, on his back, his eye wide open.

Mitch couldn't help but look at his friend Russell as he passed by him to get to the boat. Mitch's hand was tied in front of him, so it looked natural when he leaned over to cover Russell's open eye and try to close it. As he did, Mitch felt a wink on his palm. The eye wanted to stay open....*ah*. He left it open.

David was coming down the stairs, watching Mitch as he climbed in the boat.

At the top, Walter stood with the barrel directly on Terri's temple.

She watched as Mitch let David attach his roped hands to the side of the Whaler and then tie his feet together at his ankles. He purposely leaned against Mitch's bad arm, making him wince.

"Now, any stupid moves and she gets it, right here, quick and simple." Walter tapped the barrel on her head, "and you probably know just how much I would love to pull the trigger."

Mitch could see the fear in Terri's eyes as they opened wider; she rocked back and forth between her two feet, watching him comply.

"We are all going to get into the Whaler now and go for a little ride." Walter began to shove Terri toward the three steps down. Mitch had left the keys in the ignition.

David started the engine, revving and then waiting with the gears in neutral.

Walter turned Terri around, pointing the gun at her forehead. "You're going to slowly climb backward down those three steps." He looked Terri in the eyes and put the gun barrel between them. With her hands tied, she held onto the teak hand railing and stepped down backward. She could see the floor of the boat, blood was everywhere.

Russell lay dead, close to the ladder on the wooden platform directly below. With her back to Mitch, she closed her eyes and took a long gulp. Somehow things were going to be OK, she told herself. But when her eyes opened, she could still see Russell's dead body. It was looking right at her with that eye, and the blood was still everywhere.

She continued down the ladder, slowly, with Walter right behind her. She looked down at Russell. In that moment, Terri felt guilt about his death. The thought that she had caused all this exploded in her head as she dropped to her knees, sobbing next to the dead man. At that moment, she didn't care if Walter was going to shoot her. *Maybe it would be best*, she thought. *How can I live with this?*

****

It was everything Russell could muster to keep playing dead as Terri was leaning her head against his leg. He had wrapped his leg tight to the point of cutting off circulation to stop the

TREASURE HUNT

****

bleeding and pain, and now he wanted to kick her off as she lightly tapped her head against it!

"Get up." Walter was behind her, pulling her body up with her hands behind her back.

At first Terri played it with dead weight but soon the pain of her arms being pulled backward was too much. She was forced to stand up. But while her head had just been resting on Russell's stomach, she had been able to hook her gag on Russell's belt buckle. Now, as she was being yanked into standing position, her gag caught and pulled off her face. Her mouth was free! "Let me go!" she shouted, "You killer! Let me go!" She struggled against Walter's grip and against the pain in her rotator cuffs as he yanked on her.

Walter put the barrel back up to her temple, reminding her to behave. He turned her back toward the boat and pushed her forward. David was waiting at the side of the boat for her to step in. He grabbed at her and pulled her in, not minding her foot placing. She stumbled sideways as David yanked her back with delight.

"Come on David, I thought we were friends, really? What are you going to do? Kill us? Then what? Your whole life a fugitive, just because you think you're going to be so rich you can hide well? You think this guy's not gonna kill you?"

David shoved her down next to Mitch. "Shut up!" he yelled right at her. "I've had enough of your mouth!" David cocked his arm back. He was trying to scare her silent, his fist ready and face contorted, red with anger.

"Oh yeah big man, hit the little girl." Terri was taunting him, looking him in the eyes.

David looked back at her, his arm quivering with tension.

"I hate you! I hate you! I hate you!" was all Terri could get out. She tried to spit on him but her mouth was too dry from the gag and dehydration.

Mitch was looking over at her and trying to make eye contact; she finally looked over at him. He used his eyebrows and his head, looking at her and then down at his shoe. *His shoe?*

She looked hard, not making a connection.

Mitch did it again; she looked, and didn't get it. Mitch rolled his eyes back.

She got careless with her frustration. "What?" she cried.

Everyone looked over at her.

Mitch rolled his eyes again.

"David!" Walter shouted, "tie her to that seat, now." Walter was still on the back wooden platform.

"Yes, immediately. Can I put her gag back on?" David pushed her down onto the bench next to Mitch.

She looked over to Mitch. He was leaning forward. *What the hell?* Looking down his leg, she saw the bulge coming upward out of his sock. He lifted his eyebrows just enough that Terri could see.

Walter looked down at Russell. Terri's gag was still attached to Russell's belt buckle.

Russell wanted to close his eye as he said a quick *Thank you Lord* in his head. He knew he would only have one chance.

51

Walter was looking down at Russell's dead body, noticing a large gold piece around his neck. "Sorry old chap, you should have turned your head the other way, not gotten involved." Walter almost had a sincere tone in his voice as he talked to dead Russell. He reached down for the twisted linen gag Terri left snagged to Russell's buckle.

Walter then reached further over for the medallion Russell had placed around his neck in hopes of luring Walter in with pure greed. With all the life and strength Russell could pull together, one last time, he reached up with his eleven inch pointed brass arm and in one motion he caught Walter by total surprise.

Walter was unable to react.

Russell sat up as he shoved the brass dagger he had formed earlier by straightening out the circle with the boat cleat. He pushed harder up into Walter's chest cavity, pushing, pulling back, then pushing harder as Walter fell further into him.

Russell pulled back and pushed once more until two inches of the pointed bloody brass tip broke past Walter's large strong bones and through Walter's back. Now, with his heart pierced through, the blood pulsed out his back, turning his crisp white linen shirt bright red. As his heart pumped its last beats, Walter groaned and his gun dropped out of his hand onto the platform.

****

Terri screamed in horror, standing up.

David watched in shock. It had all happened so rapidly. David's first instinct was to jump out of the boat to Walter's aid. He scrambled to Walter's side and rolled him off Russell's dagger. Then he grabbed the gun up off the platform and shot at Russell. As David's feet were slippery with the blood, David only hit Russell's shoulder again.

Russell moaned in pain.

Terri was at the stern line, unlatching the boat from the ship. The engine was on, it was in neutral and the current was moving the boat away.

David was still back on the ship platform, confused. Several times now, he reached over to the boat with his long arms in attempts to reach the boat and pull it back. With each attempt the boat floated further out of his reach.

Mitch and Terri looked at each other. Both had their hands tied, and Mitch's feet as well.

"Terri, you can do this." Mitch got her attention, "Put it in gear, take us away."

"But Mitch! Russell! And what about Moses! We can't leave them behind!"

David checked the chamber of the pistol he took from Walter, one bullet left.

"Get us out of here!" Mitch yelled at Terri.

She stood and did just that. She reached with her hands, which were still tied behind her, and shoved the boat's chrome handle into forward. Then she pulled on it, sending the Whaler off with a fast jerking speed going into the small choppy wake. She toppled forward but held on and steered. She couldn't see where she was going, as her body was turned backward with her hands behind her.

Terri drove blind as Mitch guided her.

"Left! Left!" he shouted.

"Yours or mine?"

"Damn it, Terri." Mitch stood up with the boat rocking. Now that they were far enough away from David and his loaded gun, Mitch was able to get himself out of his ropes within seconds. He rushed to grab the wheel and turned the boat, sending Terri sideways crashing onto the soft bench seat.

"You coulda said your left." Her face was smushed against the vinyl.

"And listen to you argue with me one more time?" Mitch slowed the boat to a standstill and released Terri from the ropes around her wrists.

She flung her arms around him and they hugged.

Together they looked over as the sound of the inflatable's engine whirred on. They saw that David was heading over to the work station in the inflatable. Mitch made a wide turn and headed back for the ship. He pulled the bang stick out from his sock.

Terri grabbed it. "Nice move. Bang stick in the sock."

"You finally noticed." Mitch was in pain, trying to focus. "It was on the ship. Now's our chance to go back and get Moses and Russell, but we have to move fast, real fast. David'll be back as soon as he sees us and he has a gun.

"Yes, yes," Terri said, smiling as she stroked the long black cylindrical tube, "and we have a bang stick."

"Surprise Terri, keep it a surprise, and put it down before you hurt yourself."

They rushed back to the boat for Russell and Moses.

✱✱✱✱✱✱✱

The adrenaline rushing through Terri's body kept her from focusing on the fear. She tied the boat off and rushed to Russell's side. "I'm right here, buddy." She stroked the side of his face, untangling his wet bloody hair that was stuck in his mouth. His eye was still open. Blood trickled from the side of his mouth down his cheek.

A tear from Terri's face ran down and dropped onto Russell's cheek.

He looked up at her, trying to talk. "Thhhh…ee…bo…." he slurred.

"Yeah, yeah, the boat." Terri stood up and looked out at the boat. Then she went and examined Walter's large dead body lying next to Russell. She rummaged through Walter's pockets until she found it: the gold medallion on the money clip. She held it up briefly to admire it before she stuck it in her pocket, along with Walter's wallet. She couldn't help but put her foot on Walter, something about it felt good, and when she pushed, that felt better. She kicked Walter hard and smiled. His body let out a pocket of gaseous exhale. Grossed out, she moved back to Russell's side.

Mitch had left the engine running on the Whaler and stepped past her, walking up the stairs. He wanted to find Moses.

"Don't you worry, were gonna have you to the doctor, and you'll be feeling better in no time." She was doing her best to comfort Russell, stroking his side as he tried to tell her something.

"Thhee…boo…aat, the boooat!" he got out, coughing up blood as he struggled for a breath. "The boat!"

"Yes, the boat, it's OK, a short boat ride and you'll be safe." She didn't know what the hell Russell was talking about.

She moved his arm, hoping to make him more comfortable as his eye grew wide with fear.

"Oh my God, I'm so sorry, really so sorry, did that hurt? I won't move it again." She was so busy talking to Russell that she never noticed the inflatable had already made it back.

VOLUME TWO: RAPTIS TRILOGY

****

<u>52</u>

Suddenly David was climbing through Mitch's boat and was stepping onto the ship platform. Coming up from behind Terri, he picked her up with the back of her shirt, pulling her off of Russell.

Terri let out a scream for help.

"Mitch!" she cried.

****

Mitch was down in the ship calling for Moses to come out of hiding, telling him it was OK. He heard Terri scream in the background and turned around, shouting out for Moses while making his way to the back end of the ship.

There he found that David was holding Terri against himself with the gun to her head. Mitch came through the swinging hallway door and approached slowly, stopping when David told him to.

"You know, I've always hated this bitch." David looked at Terri then at Mitch.

"You asshole," Terri couldn't resist.

David was shaking and bleeding heavily, his wound had opened further.

"But I really learned to hate you too." Shaking, he pointed the gun at Mitch. "Question is, which one of you first?"

"It doesn't have to be either of us, David, I understand how you feel." Mitch took a half step forward.

"Stop! Stop right there!" David wagged the gun at Mitch, trying to make him stop. David was beginning to act desperate. "Do you? Do you know how I feel?" He shouted back at Mitch. "Everyone's dead out there, my buddy, my brother Matt, and now Matt's uncle, he's dead."

Mitch thought he was going to be thrown a break; it looked like David was going to lose it, break down in front of him. Then Mitch could make his move.

David lifted his head up, looking right back at Mitch. "And now, it looks like all this will be mine."

"What the fuck, are you kidding?" Terri was pissed, she was reading it like Mitch, she thought the guy was going to bowl over crying any minute now.

David tightened his grip around her chest, squeezing her injured arm.

"Ow! You asshole!" She stomped her foot trying to smash his toes, anything. He chuckled at her and cocked the hammer back on the handgun, looking at Mitch. "Aren't you tired of listening to that?" David questioned Mitch.

Mitch stared back, not moving.

Behind David, out of view, Mitch could see the whites of Moses' eyes peeking through the window on the galley door. Moses was watching the gun being held to Terri's head and listening in.

Mitch stared hard through David, trying to make eye contact with Moses.

Mitch watched as the door slowly, quietly, opened. Moses tiptoed out from behind the door, looking at Mitch.

"Say good bye to Terri, Mitch," David laughed.

There was a sudden blood curdling scream, so loud, so desperate, everyone turned. "Aaahhh!" Moses screamed at the top of his lungs.

When David turned his attention, Terri wrestled herself loose and ran away.

David recklessly shot at her and missed as she ran. David's shot hit the railing. The hard wood split with a loud crack as Terri quickly climbed down the back ladder, almost stepping on Russell. She noticed his eye was shut, but she kept moving.

Mitch stepped forward, swinging with his arm, then his leg, sending the gun flying out of David's hand to the ground. David fell backward.

Moses stood paralyzed in fear.

David jumped up, pumped with adrenaline. Now that he knew what to expect from Mitch, he was ready.

Mitch was already swinging.

David hopped up and they sparred, kick for kick, punch for punch, in what appeared to be an even match.

Terri climbed back up the back stairs, running and screaming.

"I've got the bang stick, I've got the bang stick!" She was holding it up in her hands when she stopped, watching the two fight.

"Damn Mitch, I didn't know you could fight like that." Terri was amazed.

David took advantage of Mitch's split second loss of focus and kicked him square in the chest, sending Mitch's body across the room and against the wall.

"Hey! Totally not fair!" Terri smacked the bang stick on her hand like a tennis racket, waiting for Mitch to get up. He was laid out on the floor, not moving.

David circled around the chair, moving toward Terri. He was more than an arm's distance away, moving sideways and looking her directly in the eye as he took a step closer. David reached down with his right hand and picked up the gun.

Mitch was still unconscious.

"How easy is this?" David said, pointing the gun at an unconscious Mitch.

Terri was infuriated now. Two steps away, she charged at David, pointing the bang stick at his chest.

David turned square to her, pointing the gun at her and pulling the trigger: click.

Terri pressed the tip of the bang stick hard into David's chest, retracting the trigger. But on contact, the trigger hit the primer, igniting the bullet. It blasted right through David. She heard a second click as David instinctively tried to shoot off another round from his handgun as he was falling back and down, dead.

Moses ran to Terri and put his arm around her. Terri stood there looking at what she had just done.

She'd shot David.

53

Mitch opened his eyes and saw Terri and Moses standing there. He began to get up, moaning a little as he did.

David was lying dead on the ground with a large bloody hole in his chest.

Mitch managed to stand up and walk over to David. He pried the gun out of David's hand, and put it on a table.

Next Mitch went to Terri and hugged her.

Terri was shaking, her eyes fixed on Moses. She had heard it, and knew Moses had as well: that click, click. David had shot twice, but there had been no ammunition in the chamber. And Moses had been unarmed. Terri's knees were about to give out just as Mitch sat her down.

Moses left and returned with cold drinks.

Terri cracked open the first can she grabbed and gulped. "I think Russell, Russell's dead," was all she could get out. She remembered Russell lying on the back transom with his eye shut. "His last words were 'the boat.' He was trying to save me from David, can you believe it? He was trying to save my life." She put her face in her hands and started to cry.

Both Moses and Mitch put hands on her back and patted her, hoping to calm her.

It wasn't long before she was done crying and was wanting to sit next to Russell, so he wouldn't be alone.

The three of them walked to the back and down the steps. As they did so, Terri explained how David had been coming from behind her, and Russell had been gasping, warning her, he kept saying the words, "the boat."

Now Terri knelt down, looking at Russell. She stroked his cheek.

Russell's eye slowly opened.

"Russell! Russell! You're alive! I thought you were dead!" Terri was so happy, tears streamed down her cheeks again.

Frothy blood came out as he opened his mouth and tried to whisper, "Th...ee...boa...." He gasped, coughing up more blood.

"Yes, it's OK Russell, I didn't see the boat, but it's all over now." Terri stroked his hair as she spoke to him. "Moses? Can you please get Russell some water?"

Moses quickly left.

Mitch knelt down at Russell's other side. "Russell, hang in there buddy, you saved Terri's life, we're going to save yours."

Russell shivered in the heat as he attempted a half smile with one corner of his mouth.

Terri wiped away the dripping blood.

Russell tried to whisper again, "The...boat...." He finally got it out: boat.

Mitch looked over at Terri, who shrugged.

"He's probably delirious, Mitch," Terri looked back at Russell, "We'll cool you down, Russell."

****

Moses returned with a cold glass of water. Terri tried to get Russell to drink. When he wouldn't, she dipped her hand in the cool water and wiped his face, cleaning and cooling him off.

"Boooaaaatttttttt, boat," Russell kept murmuring.

An explosion erupted.

The huge sound coming from some distance away rocked them and the large ship they were on. It sent a fireball straight up into the sky. Gasoline cans and filled gas tanks exploded with the heat, adding extra fireworks. Burning debris rained down out of the sky.

Mitch, Terri, and Moses turned in horror as they watched the workstation boat obliterated into shreds before their eyes.

Russell turned his head out toward the sea. His eye began to smile, Terri could tell. The smile in his eye spread to his mouth as they all watched the flames burn. Russell's good hand brushed past Terri, pointing out toward the sea.

****

Russell's mind rushed back to memories.... "Russell! Russell!" Robert cried out. "Come on! It's here! Right here!" Robert was young and wearing his usual worn out, cut off khaki pants with a white tee shirt.

They were right there, all aboard the glistening *Ol' Wife*.

"Yeah buddy! Come on!" Eugene agreed as his young body motioned wildly for Russell to swim over. Brent popped his head out of the cabin. "Don't make me come get you! Swim! Swim!" His goofy buddy was shouting at Russell like this was just yesterday, and he was motioning with his arms for Russell to dive in and swim over.

VOLUME TWO: RAPTIS TRILOGY

****

Russell stood up, looking out to sea toward his friends. Then he dove into the glistening turquoise sea, swimming effortlessly and without pain until he reached them. He climbed up the back of the old boat, the *Ol' Wife*, into the arms of his friends who were all happy to see him, cheering, clapping, such a big deal they made of it.

They each took turns hugging Russell and rejoicing that the gang was all together again. Russell looked down, his hand was whole again, he reached up, his face whole again. His leg, his arm, he was his young self again. He laughed with his friends; he hadn't felt this great in decades!

And right there before them all, right there within their reach, was the same treasure that they had been seeking! Now here it was....

****

Terri was stroking Russell's face as Mitch announced the man had taken his last breath. Mitch reached over and shut Russell's eye. Moses knelt down next to Russell and crossed himself, closing his own eyes. Terri noticed Moses moving his lips like he was saying a prayer.

The muscles in Russell's face were relaxed, some of the wrinkles seemed to have disappeared.

"I think he's found peace," Terri said, looking at Russell.

They leaned forward and looked together. It was easy to agree, something about Russell's face, he looked at peace.

<u>54</u>

First on the list of priorities, they took Russell's body and did him proud, a burial at sea. They carefully wrapped his body and drove far out into the deep blue sea. Mitch said a few words about the heroic man who had saved Terri's life.

With his deep concern for others, Moses crossed himself.

Terri wept, holding onto the white sheet wrapped around Russell. She had brushed Russell's hair and removed the eye patch. She thought he looked like Jesus lying there. The scarred cheek and the socket where his eye once was, well these didn't look so bad, he wasn't scary at all. Terri sang a verse of *Amazing Grace* the best she could, then let out her best bosun's whistle imitation, "Ohh-eee-ohh," as they carefully rolled him into the sea.

All three were teary eyed as Mitch and Terri instinctively broke out in song to commemorate the feeling of the moment. It was their theme song, their favorite song, they both knew the words. Well, Terri knew at least some of them: "Lean on me ... when you're not strong ... I'll be your friend ... I'll help you carry on ...."

Then they silently motored the Whaler back to the big ship.

******

When they got back, Mitch did the first thing he knew to do. He found the ship's radio and dialed in to channel twenty-two, calling out to his friends in the coast guard auxiliary. He was going to need help with this ship. With everyone gone, he was laying salvage rights to the large vessel as well as to the treasure find.

Terri was already snooping around the ship and found herself in Walter's office, opening and looking in all the drawers. She opened the humidor and sniffed. Moving to the large cabinet, she found small crafted boxes filled with fine gold coins in one of the bottom drawers, coins which she started to count into obsessive stacks. She reached down into her pocket to feel the money clip one more time and smiled.

Moses stood next to Mitch, following him, waiting for orders. He could hear Mitch asking for help with no one answering back. Moses walked over to the console and turned a few knobs; the engines rumbled on. Moses grabbed the wheel, looking over at Mitch.

"Are you trying to tell me you can captain this ship?" Mitch had never put much thought into who'd captained this ship. Until then he had sort of assumed it was Walter. "Well how about that!" Mitch smiled, patting Moses enthusiastically on the back.

Moses was on the verge of laughing out loud, nodding his head yes. His eyes were half closed with joy, his mouth smiling so widely.

Mitch pressed the handle on the radio and announced to his friends that they did not need anything, repeat, they did not need anything after all, because: *The captain has now appeared.* "Beautiful, Moses, I love you!" Mitch patted him on the back. "Let's go ahead and turn it off for now as we make a game plan."

Terri and Mitch got into the Whaler and sped off to the workboat ruins as Moses stayed behind and waved. Terri and Mitch circled the debris field of the exploded workboat, there wasn't anything left. They could see that what was left of the boat had sunk down below, immediately.

Terri and Mitch donned their masks and fins and rolled in. They looked below and saw the stacks and stacks of baskets of treasures. Terri took a deep breath and dove down. She couldn't make it, her arms stung and she was exhausted, she came back up. She watched as Mitch effortlessly swam around the deep bottom, shot arm and all, he was her hero.

Terri saw the two dead men floating lifeless in the water, the lead on their weight belts keeping them suspended in neutral buoyancy. She didn't see any signs of Matt anywhere; his body had exploded into a thousand tiny pieces and was feeding the fish now. She tried to count the baskets of gold that had been collected off on one side.

Terri and Mitch were back to the main ship within two hours. Moses had already had time to fix snacks and clean David's blood-splattered mess. Terri insisted they eat up at the bow of the boat, that anything else would just bring back a bad memory. They agreed and sat down with her. There was a long, long silence as they all relaxed and just breathed, looking into the sunlit sea, sipping on cold tropical drinks, dipping endless cooked shrimp tails in cocktail sauce.

Of course Terri was the first to break the silence as it all began to settle in. She looked toward the others and held her drink up to salute. "Gentlemen, we are going to be rich beyond our dreams!"

The three of them clinked their glasses and began to laugh in exhaustion. It was all over, and it was all theirs!

THE END

VOLUME TWO: RAPTIS TRILOGY
****

Basic Scuba Diver Gear Diagram

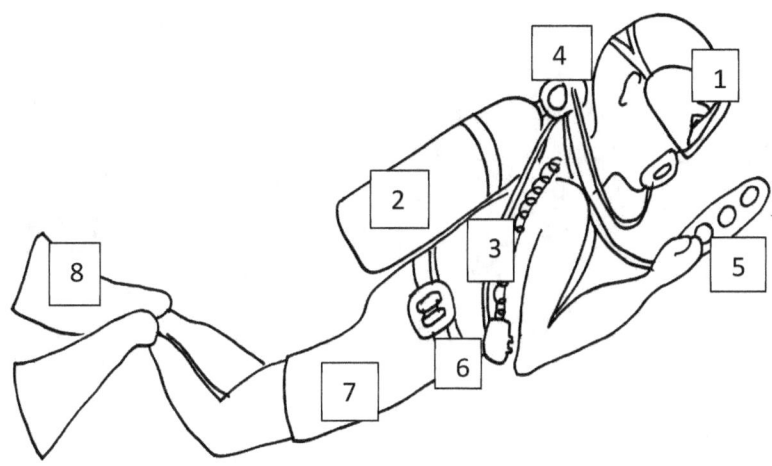

DIVERS:

(1) Our **DIVE MASK** provides a space of air to see through.

(2) Our **TANK** of air is attached to our backs.

(3) Our **BOUYANCY COMPENSATOR** is worn like a vest. It fills with   air from our tank.

(4) The **REGULATOR** comes in two STAGES. The 1ˢᵗ STAGE attaches to the tank's valve and breaks down the immediate pressure from the tank. You also attach all your gauges to the 1ˢᵗ STAGE as well. The 2ⁿᵈ STAGE goes in your mouth: you inhale and exhale through the 2ⁿᵈ STAGE.

(5) Our **PRESSURE GAUGE** is attached to the 1ˢᵗ STAGE of the regulator. It tells us in PSI, pounds per square inch, how much air we have.

(6) Our **WEIGHT BELT** offsets the buoyancy of our body fat and wetsuit.

(7) We lose body heat in even the warmest of oceans. The layer of water between us and our **WETSUIT** keeps us warm.

(8) Our **FINS** propel us through the water.

See the following pages for other
Diving and Boating Terms
used in this book...

VOLUME TWO: RAPTIS TRILOGY
****

Scuba Diving and Boating Terms
Used in This Book

ANCHOR LINE: The ANCHOR is attached to the bow of the boat with a long nautical rope, the ANCHOR LINE. Dropped down into the water, it sinks to the bottom and holds the boat in place.

BANG STICK: This is a long cylindrical "stick" with a handle on one end. The other end holds a bullet. When the stick is pushed into an object, the bullet is triggered and released into that object. Some divers use the bang stick for safety (for example, as a shark deterrent).

BOUY: This is a round bright marker floating on the ocean's surface, usually left to mark an area for certain use (such as an underwater fish or lobster trap, or a place a boat can tie up to).

BOUYANCY COMPENSATOR: This is a vest the diver wears, attaching it to the TANK. This COMPENSATOR VEST controls the diver's BUOYANCY on/above and below the water's surface. A hose is attached to the 1ˢ STAGE of the REGULATOR to fill the vest with air from the tank or with air by mouth (when simply blowing the air in). As the diver descends deeper into the water, compressing and becoming heavier, adding air to the vest helps achieve a NEUTRAL BOUYANCY, a suspended floating.

BOW: The front of the boat.

CLEAT: This is attached to the top side of a boat, used to fashion rope around to hold it, or to attach different objects.

CONTROLLED BREATHING: Because the diver is breathing air that is compressed, and is further compressing when DESCENDing, the diver must be aware of breathing at all times. The diver CONTROLs breathing to conserve air. The diver also CONTROLs breathing when ASCENDing. While ASCENDing, the COMPRESSED AIR in the diver's lungs expands so the diver must consciously exhale slowly.

DINGHY: A small boat used to maneuver to shallower areas larger vessels cannot reach.

HOOKAH RIG: Instead of wearing a TANK, the diver can have another air source, an AIR COMPRESSOR, floating on the surface. To this compressor, long hoses are attached and on the other end is the diver's mouth. A single AIR COMPRESSOR on the surface can serve more than one diver at a time.

PORT: Looking forward toward the BOW, the PORT side of the vessel is to the LEFT.

PRESSURE GAUGE: This gauge is attached to the 1st STAGE of the REGULATOR. This gauge informs the diver of the amount of air in the tank, by PSI.

PSI: POUNDS per SQUARE INCH is the pressure of the air the diver puts into the tank. Tanks are designed to hold between 2250 PSI to 3000 PSI of air.

REGULATOR: The 1st STAGE of the REGULATOR attaches to the tank's VALVE and controls the air pressure in the tank. The 2nd STAGE of the REGULATOR is attached with a low pressure hose to the 1st STAGE. The diver puts the 2nd STAGE in the mouth to inhale air.

SAFE BOTTOM TIME: Because the diver is breathing compressed air, there is only so much time the diver can stay underwater without having a NITROGEN build up in the diver's body. The NAVY SUBMARINERS developed tables for divers that tell them the safe time limits for remaining down at certain depths. Too much NITROGEN will make the diver sick.

SCUBA: This is the general acronym for SELF-CONTAINED UNDERWATER BREATHING APPARATUS.

STARBORD: Looking forward toward the BOW, the STARBOARD side of the vessel is to the RIGHT.

TANK: The diver brings air down underwater compressed into a tank which is worn on the back. On top of the tank is a VALVE with a handle. When the diver attaches the REGULATOR, then the VALVE can be turned on to release the air to the 1st STAGE of the REGULATOR.

TRANSOM: This is the rear outside of the boat. A platform with a ladder can be attached to the TRANSOM for divers to use to climb up onto the boat.

VISIBILITY: This is how far the diver can see underwater. Mud, silt, and sand in the currents all effect visibility. In ZERO VISIBILITY, the diver sees only 6 inches in front of the mask.

WEIGHT BELT: The diver wears a belt with lead in it to help offset the POSITIVE BUOYANCY of the body fat and of the wetsuit if wearing one. This belt has a quick release to ditch the lead in an emergency.

WETSUIT: Even the warmest ocean waters are below the diver's body temperature and eventually the diver gets cold. The diver uses different thicknesses of neoprene, worn as different WETSUITS. It is the layer of water there between the suit and the body that helps keep the diver warm.

RAPTIS TRILOGY
Volume One: DIVE TOUR • Volume Two: TREASURE HUNT • Volume Three: REDEMPTION

Raptis Trilogy
Afterword

This keen, sharp, edgy sense, this suspended from real life sensation, this journey into a terribly thrilling, frightening, disturbing, even evil situation, this is the thriller reader's experience. A great thriller writer is an artist. And we turn to this art to not only distract us from life, but to let us live out our worst fears in the world of fiction, to allow our imaginations to do this in fiction and then when done, simply close the book. We love the suspense, we even crave it. We may hate the fear, but we can't turn away. Instead we turn the page for more.

So what is a thriller? Well, if you've been on the edge of your seat, or at least feeling on edge while reading these books by Tracee Raptis, you know the thriller reader experience. And indeed, Tracee Raptis knows how to bring out in we readers a strange suspended curiosity, a sort of must-know what next, almost a temporary addiction or at least compulsion to read on and on, to want to know what the bad guys are doing, to want to know whether and how our heroines and heroes survive, to want someone to survive.

Suspense, fear, hate, love, perseverance, twisted brilliance, the odd, the strange, the evil, the good, the hero and anti-hero, are all involved. (Of course here in these Raptis Trilogy tales, our greatest hero is a heroine named Terri who may, we hope, survive all three of these Raptis Trilogy tales.) Author Tracee Raptis knows these emotions, she knows how to bring these out in readers, even in her characters. Her wisdom screams into our minds that this story is, or at least could be, real real real, really real and this is all the more unnerving. Fasten your seat belts, readers. Something's lurking in the shadows....

Dr. Angela Browne-Miller
Editor-in-Chief, Metaterra® Publications
www.Metaterra.com

TRACEE RAPTIS

THRILLERS

I'd like to thank my editor, Dr. Angela Browne-Miller, for believing in me and showing me the way. And a special thank you to my family and friends for their encouragement and support.

TREASURE HUNT

****

About the Author
Tracee Raptis

Adventurer, painter, sculptor, diver, author Tracee Raptis was born and raised in the Coachella Valley, in Indio, California. She fell in love with the ocean as a child and spent as much time as possible with her family in the Corona Del Mar coastal area, in Orange County, California. Tracee became a certified scuba diver at the age of fifteen. At the age of 19, she followed her dreams, left her life in the U.S., and headed off to the Caribbean islands where she taught scuba diving and led scuba tours for many years. There her life was filled with adventure, romance, and a great love of the underwater world. One of Tracee's most exciting adventures in the Caribbean was working with an underwater archeological expedition company, discovering how much mysterious and intriguing history is down there under water, and searching for treasures lost in time. "There is a whole wild and mysterious world down there, one that reveals its beauty, secrets, and dangers as it wishes to. You have to really live in it, be with that world for a long time, to start to see what it is all about," Tracee says. Tracee now lives in California where she is writing several books and book series.

About the pre-quel and sequel…

YOU HAVE JUST COMPLETED

Raptis Trilogy, Volume Two:
TREASURE HUNT

NOW YOU CAN READ THE
PRE-QUEL AND THE
SEQUEL TO
TREASURE HUNT:

Raptis Trilogy, Volume One:
DIVE TOUR

AND

**Raptis Trilogy, Volume
Three:**
REDEMPTION

***

Brought to you by
Metaterra® Publications

Stay tuned for more from
Author Tracee Raptis….

Find these and other books by
Tracee Raptis on
Amazon.com

Watch for announcements on

TraceeRaptis.com
and
Metaterra.com